SEA SALT *and* COFFEE BEANS

Grace Santamaria

Distributed by Simon & Schuster

ISBN: 978-1-998672-04-2
Ebook: 978-1-998672-05-9

FIC134000 FICTION / Immigration
FIC056110 FICTION / Hispanic & Latino / Women

#SeaSaltandCoffeeBeans

Follow Rising Action on our socials!
Twitter: @RAPubCollective
Instagram: @risingactionpublishingco
Tiktok: @risingactionpublishingco

To Annie and Mami

And to the women taking risks to follow their dreams

SEA SALT *and* COFFEE BEANS

Chapter One

There's something about U.S. immigration officers. It doesn't matter how kind they are, how good-looking, or whether their last name is Johnson or Gomez, my reaction will always be the same: the answers I practiced over and over mysteriously vanish from my mind, and I will act as if I am smuggling a guanabana in my carry-on. That was my reaction the last time I showed up in front of one, after holding my pee in the non-U.S. Citizens area for over an hour. The stop-and-go of the queue did little to calm my nerves because with each tiny step, I was getting closer to the officers behind the thick sheets of glass, a delayed torture of sorts. Tired of feeling alone in a room full of people, the only thing left was over-analyzing the officers. The experience would be less traumatizing if I knew what to expect from each.

I noticed some passengers were purposely lingering in front of the line, avoiding one of the officers. As I got closer, I realized I would do anything to prevent him myself. This officer's accent was thick and fast, and I could hardly make out his questions to the people who landed at his booth. My English was decent—none of that *me defiendo* excuse I get from people who can barely string a three-word sentence, but I didn't stand a chance with him.

There was another one who wanted travelers out of his face in less than a minute, gradually raising his volume to the point where he practically yelled. On two occasions, he ordered the people he was questioning to step into one of the side rooms. *El cuartico*—that mysterious windowless room where some unfortunate travelers are taken for interrogation, and saying the wrong answer can land them right back in Colombia.

I made a silent prayer that I wouldn't get him.

Not all of them were terrifying. There was an older officer who greeted every passenger with a smile, didn't fret when he had to switch to Spanish, and returned stamped blue passports with a charming, "Welcome Home." I stared at him with longing eyes, calculating the odds that life might give me a little break and allow me to be interrogated by him.

Then there was the hot one—the one I had spotted the minute I walked into the immigration hall. He was tall, with very dark hair and crystal blue eyes—eyes that would automatically turn him into the hottest guy on the block where I am from; eyes that only appear in American movies and are usually accompanied by American accents. He also had a chin dimple—those are nonexistent in Bogotá. Out of the eight available candidates, he was the one to yell "Next!" when I was first in line, and I didn't know if that made me the luckiest or the unluckiest person there.

With Dad's old carry-on positioned a few inches ahead of me, I slid my burgundy passport through the hole in the glass and waited. I had savored the moment in my mind so many times, how I would feel when I finally crossed the threshold. I was almost jealous of my luggage, practically on the other side, while I waited to be grilled with questions. Officer Handsome flipped through the pages of my passport—bored by the lack of stamps, marks, or any indication that I was a national security threat—until he landed on my visa page.

"Sofia Rodriguez," he muttered to himself, not even trying to roll the R. "How long are you planning to stay?" He didn't look up from the screen, which was probably laying out all the reasons why I wasn't fit to pass. I stared back in horror as if he had just asked me to name ten U.S. senators. When no words came out of my mouth, he looked up, locking those gorgeous blue eyes with mine.

"English?" He arched an eyebrow in a way that could've been flirty, but not on this occasion. He was most definitely annoyed.

"Yes," I spat out, softening the sound of the *y* and the *s* as I had trained myself to. Not only did he have the eyes, but he also had the squarest jaw I'd ever seen. It was hypnotizing. Of all the times I had replayed the immigration scene in my head, I did not consider it would be with someone like him.

"What's the purpose of your visit?" he tried again, a little slower this time. I sensed the forced politeness and immediately knew that he didn't find me as mesmerizing as I saw him.

I'd been taught to believe that U.S. immigration officers could sense a lie before we hopeless immigrants even opened our mouths. But just how much of the truth could I spill out? Somehow, *I'm here because my family is out of cash, and I'm the only one who wants to work, but I'm out of a job* didn't quite cut it. Also, *my brother has a problem with alcohol and my mother stopped caring*, or *I'm here 'cause I needed to escape and also send them some money so they don't starve*, didn't seem like the right answer either.

"Student," came the reply after a long pause, the flimsy handle of the carry-on becoming a cane, the only barrier against collapse in front of the hundreds of travelers queued behind. He let out an unsurprised puff, like he had already reached his quota of students for the day, then did some more flipping before he stamped, closed, and slipped the passport back to me.

Behind me, I heard Officer Nice giving away another one of his highly coveted "welcome" to a man wearing a jersey of the Colombian national fútbol team. The man smiled as he returned a curt "gracias" to the officer.

Meanwhile, Officer Handsome yelled, "Next!" and I knew that was my cue to enter a new life filled with opportunities and dreams.

I had nothing to declare, no checked bags to claim, not even someone to call to let them know I'd landed safely in Miami. My sole companion was the old carry-on. In it, I was dragging the combined weight of the dreams Dad and I shared—years of plans, conversations, and hopes of a better tomorrow squeezed into the same piece of luggage he had used. My entire life fit into that carry-on. Not that there was much to pack: two pairs of jeans, two pairs of shoes, sweaters I didn't know I'd never wear in Miami, a temporary student visa, and the two thousand dollars I had left from my part of Dad's inheritance.

It was the first time I traveled alone and my second time at that airport, but somehow, I knew where to go. The flow of passengers guided the way past the maze of conveyor belts, beyond customs officers sipping coladitas from La Carreta strategically positioned at the arrivals gate, then through metal doors marked with an ominous *No Re-Entry* sign. There was no looking back, not even a moment spared to find a bathroom. This was the final stretch of a marathon begun two years earlier.

I cut through clusters of families clutching red, white, and blue foil balloons, past boyfriends armed with overpriced flower arrangements, and repeated "permiso" at least twenty times, until I finally crossed the clear double doors—that sudden threshold between the freezing airport A/C and the scorching heat outside.

Taking a deep breath, recycled air gave way to the heavier atmosphere of Miami International Airport's cave-like arrivals area. I became just another figure in the crowd of travelers, enveloped in the shared cloud of noise and exhaust fumes. A traffic officer in a bright orange vest waved at cars blocking the throughway. Loud conversations erupted from all directions, carrying more Spanish accents than I knew existed. The weight of the decision to move to Miami descended suddenly, but despite the fatigue and lingering doubt, a smile formed. I had made it and knew this was Miami's way of whispering, *Welcome home.*

Three years later

Waving at departing airplanes was part of my morning ritual. I didn't make a big show of it, just a wiggle of my fingers from the steering wheel when the planes lifted off. Usually, there was enough time to wave at three airplanes. Sometimes four. It all depended on the mood of the thousands of drivers who forced their way onto the expressways during morning rush hour. It was eerily quiet here. In Bogotá, traffic noise was intense, with honking and the screech of bus brakes and motorcycles coming so close to the cars they're practically rubbing. I never complained about the traffic as it was part of the Miami package, and I was determined to fit in just like everyone else did.

A ray of sun hit my face; its heat intensified because I drove with all the windows down. The A/C was broken, and it would be another couple of weeks before I could save the money to fix it. At first, it produced a slightly cool breeze, but after a week, it had given up. Now it was just sucking the heat from the outside, churning it in its entrails to raise it a few degrees, and then spitting it out into my face. So, I opted for the windows-down option. It was so much easier to enjoy the landscape this way. Beyond the car bumpers and red lights, the scenery looked like one of those Miami postcards displayed at tourist shops—a row of palm tree crowns over a background of deep blue sky.

As a fourth airplane prepared to depart, my cell phone vibrated. I scanned the screen, then sent the call to voicemail when I saw it was Mom. There were only two things I could be doing at that moment—be on my way to work and stuck in traffic, or early at the office and drowning in deadlines—and Mom wouldn't care either way. She was probably getting out of bed thousands of miles away and had just checked her account balance on the bank app, the way I had taught her. She would keep calling until the amount changed.

The streets leading to the office were even worse than the expressway, but at least they allowed me to finish what I hadn't accomplished at home. Two lights away from the building, I began layering as much makeup as necessary to conceal everything my employer didn't deem to be utter perfection. At the first light, I squeezed the light brown matte foundation out of sample packets and spread it with my fingers. At Sunset Cosmetics, my freckles were a sign of sun damage, not the result of generations of ancestors claiming their stake on my skin. On the next light, I applied lip color. The shade was *golden rush*, which seemed appropriate for the morning mayhem. Some days I just wanted to skip the makeup session, but I couldn't show up at a cosmetics company covered in sunspots and flaunting undereye circles and pale lips. Not when the corridor leading to my cubicle felt like a runway, with discerning eyes ready to scrutinize me from every angle. If looking like a beauty blogger was a requirement to keep my job, then so be it. I'd apply as many layers as necessary to trick them into thinking I was still the Colombian beauty they had hired two years before.

By the time I crossed the last traffic light, I was decent enough to show up at the office but still not up to Sunset standards. I hovered the mascara wand as I approached the gray office building, but gave up when I almost poked my eye. I always felt a little guilty when I covered my eyes with makeup. They were the facial features I was most proud of, the ones I had undoubtedly inherited from Dad. My hair texture was the other one—thick, dark, and an unruly mix between wavy and straight. I had twisted it into a low bun earlier that morning, still wet from the shower, hoping to achieve some version of those loose beach waves I saw everywhere in my Instagram feed. But my mane had other plans. The second I yanked the scrunchie loose, it met with the humid Miami air and expanded to its natural form. So much for the beauty blogger look.

After some debate with the mirror, I decided that arriving on time mattered more than looking like I was ready for a photo shoot. The thought of losing my job made my heart race like I had chugged three cups of black coffee.

I folded the small overhead mirror just in time to notice I was inches from the car in front of me. I dipped my foot onto the brake, feeling the entrails of my rusty, twice pre-owned car squeal. It finally stopped just as it tapped the other car's bumper, long enough for nearby drivers to register the scene and leave a tattoo of my tires on the pavement. I would probably be featured in ten different lobby stories about an idiotic driver who caused a traffic jam that made everyone late.

I'm sure all the makeup I applied wasn't enough to cover the color disappearing from my face. I waited for the other driver to burst out of the car and make a scene in the middle of the street. To my surprise, the other car kept moving. I let out a sharp breath of relief. Maybe they were late to work, too.

My heart still raced when I squeezed my car into the last available parking space and jumped out. I couldn't risk being noticed by the HR micromanagers for being late, as my job was the one thing making my Miami postcard life possible.

As I ran across the parking lot wearing my old *Havaianas*, I checked every car I passed. My stomach roiled when I saw Rafael's Mercedes. Was it possible that the one day of the week he arrived on time always coincided with the day I arrived a minute after nine a.m.?

I swapped the flip-flops for pumps during the elevator ride, then stormed out to press my badge against the entry pad that recorded my arrival time. It made a sharp beep, and I rushed in, the metal caps in my heels making a clickety-clack noise on the white tiles. Twenty pairs of eyes peeked from the edges of cubicles as I paraded down the hall, mumbling a few polite buenos días to whoever I made eye contact with, then deposited my lunchbox, bag, and flip-flops in my gray box right at the center of the floor.

I had been sitting at the same old cubicle since the first day I walked into Sunset Cosmetics, watching from afar as my colleagues rose to the levels of managers or even directors, snatching one of the highly coveted window-adjacent cubicles. Others had left the company for better positions elsewhere, but not me. I spent my days putting together briefs, creating media plans, analyzing beauty trends, and predicting the next big hit in cosmetics. Some days, I felt I was running the marketing department on my own. I was sure someone had to be watching. Someone had to notice I was the last to leave the office every day, how I never missed a deadline, how nice I was to everyone, even the jerks from finance. That someone would soon offer me the promotion I deserved. And who knew? Maybe I'd get my very own window cubicle washed by natural sunlight.

The number of unread e-mails loaded and multiplied in front of my eyes—an overwhelming amount of work—but I was distracted by my phone going off again. The word MAMI flashed in big, angry letters.

"¿Mamá? Ahora no puedo hablar," I whispered into my cell phone as I ducked my head under the desk and pretended to shuffle around some brochures. HR had an unofficial rule about taking personal calls during office hours, and I had one of them sitting in the closest cubicle island. "Ya estoy en la oficina."

"Sofia, yo sé que ya está trabajando, pero ya arrancó el mes y estamos atrasados en todos los pagos aquí." Her rustic Spanish had its own melody, and it was still familiar to my ears despite the years that had passed since I had heard her voice in person. That morning, she called to tell me that it was already the third of the month and all the bills were due, but I didn't need her reminder—it was my constant preoccupation every day of the month.

"El viernes me pagan. ¿Pueden esperar un par de días más?" I asked them if they could wait until Friday, as if they didn't know exactly when my paychecks came in. Then I remembered I had promised my best friend Nina I would start pushing back at their constant demands for money, so I added firmly, "Acuérdate que yo también necesito pagar mi renta." I couldn't send what little I had left if I didn't pay my rent first.

She kept talking like she hadn't even heard the last part. "¿No tiene algo para mandarnos hoy? El resto lo envía el viernes." She asked me to send them whatever I had. They could wait until Friday for the rest.

I crawled further under the desk, trying to create an additional sound shield. About eighty percent of the office was fluent in Spanish. The remaining twenty percent didn't speak it but could understand every word, and I didn't want my cubicle neighbors to learn about my family's circumstances and how much they depended on me, the lowly marketing assistant on a work visa. My meager checking account balance flashed in my mind, followed by all the expenses I needed to cover. "Solo me quedan $200 en la cuenta. Y todavía necesito poner gasolina, comprar comida—"

"Pero todo eso lo puede pagar con la tarjeta de crédito, Sofia." There it was: the change in her tone when I said my account balance. It was an automatic switch that went off when the solution to her immediate problems appeared like a low-hanging fruit—send them all the cash I had and use my credit card to cover everything else. "Usted sabe cómo están las cosas de difíciles por acá." *You know that things are difficult here.* That was her signature phrase when the conversation reached its one-minute mark. It filled me with remorse to be reminded that I had found a way out and how much my life had changed ever since, while Mom and Santiago were still exactly where I had left them, like a fading photograph I had managed to escape from.

The sound of steps approaching startled me. I didn't feel like getting a warning from HR over Mom's insistence on money.

"Ya tengo que colgar." I needed to hang up.

"¡Sofia, mándeme un mensaje apenas envíe el dinero!"

I let out a quiet grunt. Of course, her last words would be *message me as soon as you send the money*. "Okay, Mami. Chao."

When I hung up, the steps had stopped, and a shadow hovered over my cubicle. Crawling from under the desk, then snaking up toward the chair, I swiveled it back in front of the computer, only to nearly collide with Evelyn from sales.

"Eve!" I gasped, clutching my chest with my hand. "You scared me!"

"Sorry." Evelyn leaned closer. "Did you come in late today?"

"I did." I felt my face go paper white, my skin absorbing all the makeup that almost caused me to crash earlier. "I didn't think anyone noticed."

"You don't know what happened this morning?" Her voice had dropped to a whisper, and she was practically trying to hide inside the cubicle with me.

A hushed chit-chat echoed in the office. Down the long hall, Marta, who managed trade marketing, was being ushered to the restrooms—or the central gossip station, as I liked to call it—by another two colleagues. Smudges of black mascara surrounded her eyes.

I snapped back to Evelyn. "¿Qué pasó?"

"They let Marta go."

"Marta? They fired her just like that?"

"I know." Her mouth twitched. "And I don't want to worry you, but I heard HR approved a bunch of marketing positions in the Mexico office."

My eyes went wide with dismay. Of course, I had to worry. The Mexico office had been expanding for the past few months, absorbing all the operations from the Latin American region. It was only a matter of time until they came after the Miami positions. And if Marta, bright and sweet Marta, who had trained the entire marketing team, who was practically an oracle of wisdom at the office, who was liked even by the jerks from finance, was let go, the odds of my position surviving were slim to nonexistent.

"Oh, shit," I mumbled.

"I know. No te vayas a paniquear ahora. I'll let you know if I hear anything else." She offered a small, sad smile and disappeared into the cubicle maze.

I returned to the list of unread e-mails, which seemed to have duplicated in the past five minutes, and stared at the laptop with my fingers frozen on the keyboard. The monthly media plan was due end-of-day, but it was impossible to focus when someone from another corner of the world was actively recruiting to fill the position I had. And maybe I was being a bit dramatic, but I always got antsy the first days of the month, when the due dates rolled in, and the cash flow dried out.

My budget, the list where I checked off my monthly expenses as they were paid off, lay on my desk. Not a checkmark on it. Rent, money for my family, electric bill, cell phone, car insurance, international student loan payment, food, and gas. In that specific order. My stomach tightened. There wasn't much I could cut. The first paycheck of the month was devoted to rent, and the second was meant to cover everything else. If I lost my job and didn't receive an income for two weeks, I'd fall behind on everything.

The clack of heels on the floor echoed in the office. I knew the sound well; it meant more work was coming. I closed my eyes for a moment, hoping the avalanche of incoming assignments would disappear. When I opened them, Giselle looked down at me from outside the cubicle.

Even after two years working together, my breath still caught every time she appeared, and I couldn't help a pang of self-consciousness from kicking in. It was easy to see why: long, sultry brunette waves framed big hazel eyes and a swollen upper lip. Giselle always met her sales quota, nailed new-client pitches, and had several shades of Sunset bronzers expertly contouring her caramel-colored skin. She had absolute domain of the break room during lunch on Mondays because she always had an interesting story about her weekend, her workout, and her general awesomeness.

But she was not here to talk about her weekend. That much I was sure of.

"That lip color is nice," she said with a forced smile. I noticed she didn't add *on you*. I smiled back but didn't answer. Her compliments had lost all meaning since I figured they were just a hook for the next part of the conversation.

"Sofia, hun, do you have a few minutes to spare today?" Her tone was lazy and sweet, and I wondered if that was part of her secret plan to have all the men in the office swoon after her.

"Um, I have to turn in the August media plan by end of day." I glanced over at the number of emails on my screen—97 unread—and wished those would disappear, along with Giselle.

"Oh, this would only take a moment of your time. You are so good with PowerPoint. My client is coming tomorrow, and if you could review my slides to make sure I don't have any typos and make it look pretty. You know—like you always do." She flashed her perfect smile while the rest of her face remained intact. Women like her seemed to possess some mysterious immunity to the telltale wrinkles that time etched around everyone else's eyes.

"I don't know, Giselle. I have so much work today."

"I'd really appreciate it." She tilted her head just the slightest bit. "I'll let Rafael know you worked on it."

I thought about it for a moment. It would be good to have Giselle on my side. She could vouch for me in case of a downsize. I could work on her deck in the morning and tackle the media plan in the afternoon.

"Alright, send it over. I'll look at it."

"Thank you so much, hun. I'll send it right over." She sounded relieved. That is, until her phone beeped, and her eyes went automatically to it. A grin spread across her face. Her attention seemed to float away, the conversation between us suspended in mid-air. "Oh, and it'd be great if you could have it ready by four p.m., please? I have Pilates at six and would like to review it before I head out."

I turned back to the screen, already regretting what I had agreed to. Her request loomed larger by the second, the cursor blinking accusingly against the white background. The sound of Giselle's heels faded in the distance, and I was left alone with enough work to entertain me for a decade.

An hour later, an email containing Giselle's deck popped up in the lower corner of my screen. I held my breath as twenty-seven slides of crap loaded. Before me, the shittiest business plan was waiting to be deleted and built from scratch. Lunch would be cold lentil soup at my desk while I worked on it.

A low chirp came from my cell phone.

> **Mami:** Sofia aquí estoy pendiente para ir a buscar la plata apenas me avise.

The image of Mom materialized—perched at the weathered kitchen table, eyes fixed on the phone screen—waiting for my confirmation that

I had sent the cash. The stress from being financially responsible for my small family only intensified.

Here's the thing: my plan was to have life figured out by the time I was twenty-three, but I was already two years behind schedule and barely making ends meet. By now, I should've been paying the rent on time, living debt-free, driving with a full tank of gas, and sending my family the money they so desperately needed. Perhaps a night out here and there would be nice. But dreams had transformed into distant possibilities, and getting my ass to Miami was only the first part. I was still trying to figure out the rest.

Some days, it felt like those things were not meant for people like me. Maybe those luxuries were reserved for people like Giselle. Maybe it didn't matter how much I tried; I was destined to eat lunch at my desk and jump from one deadline to the next, all for a paycheck that disappeared before I even had a chance to see it in my bank balance.

The sharp, confident clack of Giselle's heels echoed through the office. I looked up from my computer long enough to see her crossing the glass double doors with two colleagues. Their conversation traveled across the open space. One of them was on the phone making a lunch reservation. My gaze followed them until Giselle's ivory suit faded in the hallway, and my stomach twisted slightly.

Then my phone rang—not my cell phone, but the landline of the cubicle. The caller ID announced *Navarro, Rafael,* through the smoky screen. I stared at the grimy phone that remained an unappealing dirty beige color no matter how many times I scrubbed its surface. That's how it was at Sunset: the money was spent on the reception—the glossy façade for others to see, to lure young women to click the bait, leaving nothing to spare on decent telephones.

Rafael was probably the only person to use the archaic system still, and I knew what the call meant. After a morning of unofficial chitchat about the expansion of the Mexico office and the Miami staff cuts, the caller ID could've said You're Fired. I stared at it while I gulped a spoonful of soup, knowing I was living through the last few seconds of life as I knew it, naïvely wondering if I could avoid what was coming by ignoring the call altogether. I answered on the last ring before it went to voicemail, my voice still thick from swallowing too fast. "Hello?"

There was laughter, the voice of at least one more man, the faint sound of a TV, and finally, a door closing.

"¿Aló?" I repeated.

"Sofia," Rafael said, surprised to hear me, like he had forgotten that he had called me. "Come to my office, please."

"I'll be there in—" He hung up before I could finish the sentence.

Gazing at the lentil soup with yearning, I sealed the Tupperware with a definitive click and began the short journey to his office with heavy steps. Holding a folder in front of my chest, I used my other hand to pull up the scoop neck of my top without making a show of it. It wasn't a deep cut or anything, but Rafael's eyes liked to linger on my breasts longer than necessary, especially when I was alone with him.

I stretched the top to its maximum coverage before I knocked on his door and walked in. Rafael was seated at his desk. Behind him, a glorious view of the bay and the airport filled the floor-to-ceiling window. The traffic on the expressway had cleared up, but the airplanes were still departing one after the other, disappearing into the blue Miami sky. A light gray wall on one side of the office had a sleek shelf holding plaques and awards he had received throughout the years. The opposite wall held a mega flatscreen set on a news channel with the volume too high to be able to get any work done. His desk was covered with the makeup samples I had brought the previous night, and the notebook where he kept a to-do list of his tasks rested on top. One of the lines didn't have a checkmark on it.

As the door shut behind me, he looked up from his cell phone, not precisely radiating that he was pleased to see me, but still allowing his eyes to scan my body swiftly. He let out an annoyed little huff, then tried to soften it with a shadow of a smile.

"Have a seat," he commanded, pointing the remote at the TV to mute it. The intensity of his gaze made me uneasy. I shrank into the first chair before his eyes could venture any lower than my chin. "I don't have good news for you."

That was the first thing he said. Not, how are you today? Not, did you hear about Marta?

My heart crumpled.

It was only noon, but I could already feel how Rafael was about to take my postcard life and shit all over it.

Chapter Two

I was exposed.

Rafael's office was in what was known as *the Sunset VIP area*—steps away from the kitchen, on the way to the restrooms, and close to the exit. I could hear the foot traffic increasing by the second and could sense other employees decreasing their speed as they walked past the window panel, their gazes digging into my neck—nothing like a second serving of fresh office gossip on the same morning. By the time I walked in, whatever news Rafael had for me was as good as public.

"I just got off a call with HR."

My fingernails dug deeper into the cushion of the chair.

"There's no easy way to say this, so I'll get to it, and then I'll answer any questions you may have." His eyes kept bouncing from his cell phone to his laptop screen, and I immediately knew he had no intention of answering any questions. "They are downsizing the office. They plan to move half of the headcount to Mexico by December."

There was something detached about how he said it, like he was informing me the kitchen had run out of coffee. Or like he had some sort of intel that his position was untouchable, and the downsize would stop before it reached him. That made my heart break a little more.

I knew it was coming, but I didn't think it would happen so soon.

"I think you are an asset to the marketing department, Sofia, but this is out of my hands. They are determined to reduce expenses, and U.S. salaries are eating up our margins." He paused for an instant, confident he didn't need to add anything else for me to understand.

"So my position—" I began.

"They already started the search for your replacement." He pushed the words out with little grief.

Behind Rafael, an airplane was departing, and another was positioning itself to do the same. Twin jet skis jumped on the small waves of the bay. The palm trees lining the expressway swayed in the wind. A few seconds of bad news shook my life, while the rest of the world remained untouched.

"Sofia?"

"Huh? Right. Yes. I understand." My mind was foggy, a mashup of balances, resumes, and unpaid bills. "Um, so what happens now? When is my last day?"

"There is no official date yet. Actually ..." He leaned closer, locking his eyes with mine for the first time, then letting them travel down my neck. His coffee breath hit me, making me sink into the chair even more. "It's still confidential, but I wanted you to hear it from me first."

"Do you have an idea?" I was determined to get as much information as possible before I ran away from his office.

He sighed, a short and snappy exhale, his eyes drifting up at the clock on the wall behind me.

"A month at most ... maybe two." His hand drifted back to the mouse next to his laptop, and he gave a nervous tap with his index finger. "HR also mentioned your visa sponsorship."

The room seemed to spin in slow, nauseating circles. Once. Twice. Until reality collapsed into a single question: Was I losing both my employment and legal status in the country during this meeting?

"I warned you to look for another job months ago—you've been job hunting, right?"

Ah, the job hunt ... my least favorite but completely mandatory weekend activity. Yes, I had been job hunting. No, it wasn't going very well.

"I have." A lump appeared in my throat. It was equal parts painful and stubborn.

"You knew you were running a risk by accepting this position ... of becoming unemployed and losing your visa." There was the slightest hint of compassion in his eyes. It could've been pity, but it was hard to tell. His parents had migrated to Miami from Cuba in the sixties, part of the mass exile escaping the regime and looking for a brighter future for their family. The blood in his veins was as unfamiliar to this country as mine. But the moment evaporated quickly. After all, I was one more case lost in the sea of immigrants trying to make it in Miami.

"Is there anything you can do?"

"You know this decision comes from above." He leaned back in his chair, and his eyes briefly met the picture of his kids on his desk. "My hands are tied."

I remember when the picture included Rafael's now ex-wife. It was one of those studio portraits where they were all flashing perfect smiles at the photographer. The image had been replaced by one of his two kids playing in the sand simultaneously as the news of his divorce spread in the office. Then came the rumors of an affair, and lawyers, and impossible alimony payments. Rafael's hands were as tied as mine. He wouldn't risk his only income source over me.

"I know this is a lot. You should take the rest of the day off. Have lunch, then go home and follow up on your open applications, polish up your LinkedIn profile ..."

Giselle's sales pitch echoed through memory. The task suddenly took a new, ominous significance.

"Our only deadline is the August media plan, but you've been working on it, right? Is it ready?" he asked, turning back to the laptop.

"Um, the media plan, yes. It's almost done."

"Send it over when you are ready. Then go home." He offered a limp, condescending smile. "You are gonna be fine, Sofia. You're a good worker and—" he was about to say something else when his eyes widened at something on the screen. "Oh shit, I forgot to join this call."

That was my cue to get up and leave. I uncurled my nails from the chair's cushion and stood up, already feeling the pressure of the news weighing down on me.

As my hand reached the doorknob, Rafael cleared his throat. I turned around and found him lightly tapping his coffee mug against the desk, staring at me with pleading eyes, like he was apologizing for something he hadn't yet said.

"Can you please get me a refill? I'm so late, and I don't know if I can go for the next hour without coffee."

It wasn't the first time he asked me to play barista for him. I had rehearsed the replies before. There were so many to choose from, ranging from *I can't, I'm really busy* to *That's not my job, so get your ass off the chair and get your own coffee*. Perhaps adding a curse word before coffee for emphasis. The comebacks popped into my mind, but nothing came out when I opened my mouth. Instead, I found myself slowly walking back to his desk. He handed me the mug, turned back to the small camera over his laptop, and flashed a winning smile while he greeted his colleagues.

The remainder of the afternoon dissolved into a blur of activity—fingers flying across the keyboard to perfect Giselle's presentation, systematically ignoring the growing stack of messages from Mom, and trying to forget the mortifying image of parading around clutching Rafael's coffee mug. I sent Giselle a polished pitch deck minutes before the deadline to allow her to review it and make it to class on time. I was still working after the office emptied and Rafael departed with a casual wave, long after the fluorescent lights automatically flickered to life and the office was filled with silence. After submitting the media plan, I gathered my things and dragged my feet to the exit. The soft hum of the A/C escorted me to the door, so imperceptible I could hear my heartbeat thumping furiously in my ears.

I had missed the opportunity to go home early. I had forced my body to hold the urge to pee for four hours. I had wasted my afternoon on a project I wouldn't receive any credit for.

But instead of feeling sorry for myself, I looked back at the empty office and turned off the lights, nostalgia consuming what little energy I had left in me. After all, I didn't know how many more nights I would have the privilege of being the last one to leave.

Only one more stop before going home. Togo was beating the door with such force that I could hear him from the elevator. I found Catalina's key at the bottom of my bag and opened the apartment door. Out came my neighbor's sixty-pound chocolate lab, all hair and muscle, already holding the leash in his mouth. He wagged his tail so hard that I was afraid it would fall off, and I briefly wondered if he had the same reaction when his owner arrived instead of me.

Outside, at the doggie park that overlooked the bay, I spent forty minutes watching Togo run with a freedom and carelessness I craved. Rafael's words were fresh in my head, a constant reminder that I was supposed to be job searching, not walking in the park with someone else's dog. And sweet Togo, completely oblivious to the task ahead of me, wasn't interested in wrapping up his sunset walk. He didn't care that I had spent the entire ride home arguing with Mom about money, or that my main source of income was being assigned to someone in Mexico. Oh no. All Togo wanted was to jump in the puddles, socialize with the other dogs, wag his tail every time he saw me, and take the largest dump the park had ever witnessed for me to pick up.

It took me another ten minutes to stop Togo from sniffing every bush, cross the hallway, and push him back inside Catalina's apartment. The last thing I saw before I closed the door were his eyes—large and black and droopy—like he already knew it would be hours before he'd have the joy of greeting another human being. I turned quickly before I could simmer any ideas of bringing him over to my apartment, a mere twenty-second walk away.

My building was the tallest one on a trendy Midtown block, in what Miamians called an 'up-and-coming' area, which was a fancy way of saying that if you went a little too far, you'd end up in the wrong side of town. Low couches and floor-to-ceiling mirrors flanked a sprawling white lobby. Young valets were usually seen meandering in the hallways, scurrying out of the mail room surrounded by a cloud of smoke, and perfecting TikTok challenges while a car queue formed around the block. I'd dreamt about living in that building for months. I'd seen women strutting down the lobby on Friday nights with their golden tans, expertly applied makeup, and boobs bursting out of sequined mini-dresses, the muscles in their mile-long legs flexing when they slid into cars that were as sparkly as they were. While emulating that look was never my priority, there was something inexplicably tempting about that glam lifestyle. They must have been doing something right if they could afford the recklessness of a new pair of shoes every weekend.

When a unit became available, I jumped at the opportunity. It was vacant for less than a week before the real estate agent—a twenty-something who arrived in a BMW blasting reggaeton—showed it to me in two minutes and urged me not to overthink it. He had three more showings lined up for that same afternoon, and two of them had just moved from Buenos Aires and were ready to beat any offer. I asked if he thought it was overpriced, and he scoffed like it was the most ridiculous question he'd ever heard and then replied with the same tagline prominently displayed in the rental listing: *Nothing beats this location*. So, I ignored the hefty figure next to the required deposit line and signed the paperwork, thinking the apartment would come first and all the other good things would immediately follow.

My apartment was like all the other ones around it—a toned-down version of the opulent models developers love showing off. None of the "luxury" finishes that were proudly mentioned in the rental ad were present, such as the small window with a wall view of the adjacent tower, which had been conveniently staged as a "city view." A week into living in the rental, I realized what makes an apartment luxurious isn't the apartment itself but the upgrades and the furniture and the lifestyle my money could create. However, with the largest chunk of my salary going towards rent, and most of the rest going to my family, there was little I could do regarding lifestyle improvement. Once the contract was signed, I settled for the overpriced rent and below-average amenities, like my assigned parking space on the eighth floor of the parking garage.

My front door let out a ghastly squeak as I walked in and switched on the lights. The faint scent of clean laundry and Clorox welcomed me home. It didn't look anything like the upscale homes of the rich and famous, or the rooms featured in the copies of *City Furniture* I got in the mail, but it was my little corner of Miami, and for the past ten months, I'd been squeezing the juice out of my lemon of an apartment.

I had stopped drawing the blinds on the only small window when I realized no one could look at me from a concrete wall, and I had nothing to look at either. The walls were an appalling chalk white, and the floors—apart from the kitchenette and the one bathroom—were covered with a questionable, pale brown carpet. I had devoted several hours to scrubbing the stains on it, a task that did more to tone my arms than clean the carpet. The "modern and sleek kitchen" consisted of a gray Formica countertop and a floor area so reduced that it could hardly fit two people.

The first thing I did every day when I got home was arrange a cushion over the cigarette burn on the couch. I didn't smoke, and the mark was a reminder that the couch was secondhand, like most of the things I owned. I'd grown up squeezing several lives out of every physical asset we owned. The textbooks I'd used were preserved and passed on to my brother Santiago two years later. The hems on my pants were dropped before we even considered getting a new pair. Empty glass containers once filled with jelly were thoroughly washed with boiling water and then added to the glassware collection. When I first arrived in Miami, I was surprised to see how quick people were to discard goods that still had a few lives ahead of them. Ice maker stopped making ice? Time for a new fridge. Car engine leaving oil stains in the driveway? Right on time to switch the car lease. Shoes worn down to the metal caps of the heels? Time to dump them at the nearest Goodwill drop-off. This is where I found most of the pieces that made up my home. I was determined to make it look like my dream space and ignore the small inconveniences that started popping up soon after I had moved in.

A cardboard box in the corner was full of stuff I'd collected to send to Mom and Santiago. For three weeks, I also used it as an auxiliary table to place my bag and keys when I walked in. A pair of blue jeans and a receipt rested on top. I needed to exchange them for a larger size because Santiago had grown one full size on his waist and had forgotten to tell me. There were four tubes of toothpaste that I estimated would last them until I could send them the next box and two pairs of soccer cleats Santiago had requested—though I suspected he was planning to sell at least one of them. Santiago had also asked for a new cell phone. A cell phone! And he emphasized *new*. That day, I tried to be clear with him that electronics were cheaper here than in Bogotá, but they weren't free, and I would gladly send him my phone when I switched to a new one. He'd grunted and said he'd had too many years of my hand-me-downs already.

My eyes fixed on the half-empty box of basic necessities that would soon travel to Mom and Santiago. The inventory looked inadequate against the magnitude of their needs. Failure wasn't an option—not for them, not for Dad, whose absence had created this burden, not for the promises I had made to myself about being the one who would make things right.

Since I'd already wasted enough time walking Togo and catering to Rafael and Giselle, I skipped dinner altogether. With unemployment and deportation breathing down my neck, how could I think about food? I set the laptop on the kitchen counter and took a deep breath.

This was it. All this time, I'd been job searching out of sheer curiosity, but now it was a necessity. I'd taken a massive leap from student visa to work visa, and the conditions of my temporary stay in the U.S. were clear: If my employment at Sunset ended, I would have a sixty-day grace period to leave the country.

Despite so many companies shifting headcounts to Latin America, there was always a fair amount of local recruiting. Open positions loaded onto the screen. Most of them were Junior levels—an assistant to an assistant, a six-month assignment, an unpaid internship. In a city like Miami, there will always be someone willing to do the same job for less money. I would've taken any of them if only they had the benefit I was looking for: *Work visa sponsorship available for the right candidate.* Even the senior roles, those I contemplated with lusty eyes, with their triple-digit salaries and the promise of growth opportunities, wanted individuals with permanent work permits. Hope and energy fled my soul with every single posting.

Two hours of failed job searching later, I had not submitted one new application and exhaustion had settled in. My head wobbled to the side, a yawn stretching every muscle in my face, but I persisted.

The bills would continue rolling in, Mom and Santiago would continue depending on me, and the country would kick me out.

Five more minutes and I'd call it a night.

I glued my eyes to the screen's glare, filtering, searching, hoping.

Just ...

One ...

More ...

And then I saw it.

WorldMedia, a massive media agency, was hiring. I scrolled down to the bottom of the page until my eyes met with that magic ingredient: *Willing to sponsor H-1B visa.*

I blinked a few times, so exhausted I thought I was imagining the entire thing. This post was legit, only a day old. The position was not exactly my area of expertise. After all, I had never worked at an agency, much less managed an account. But there it was—fate's twisted way to hint my time in the U.S. wasn't over in the form of a job opening that was too good to pass up, with a fifty percent increase from the salary I was about to lose, at a marketing firm less than fifteen minutes from my apartment.

I scrolled back up to the section listing the dreaded requirements and measured my own skills against the bullet points. My initial excitement lost its momentum as my eyes scanned the list. I met about half of them. I had the business degree and the background in beauty industry marketing, but I was missing the five years of experience and the "leadership skills" they wanted.

I wouldn't get it.

My resume would get lost under a pile of hopefuls who were better qualified and more experienced than me, and my submission would be nothing more than a waste of energy and the last ounce of hope I had left. I checked the Excel spreadsheet where I logged in every job application. This would be entry forty-seven.

When I started job searching many months earlier, I fantasized about every application. I'd search for the office address in Google Maps to find out how many miles I'd have to commute every morning. I'd visit the company's corporate website and memorize all those trivial details no one remembers after getting hired (no one ever asks who the company's founder was during an interview, anyway). I'd get my hopes up the same way some people romanticize about what they'll do with their winnings after buying one lottery ticket.

I had stopped fantasizing after entry twenty-nine.

Slowly, I typed my personal information in the form and waited for my resume to upload while I took one more look at the requirement list.

Forget it. Why apply? I wasn't going to get it. This would just be one more rejection, the same as the forty-six that came before.

Maybe it was the desperation kicking in, or the exhaustion. Still, I left the laptop on the kitchen counter and walked to the other side of the living room, determined to put as much space as possible between me and a decision that wouldn't amount to anything.

Then I took in my little apartment—the second-hand couch, the small window, the cardboard box, the almost empty cupboards in the kitchen, the pile of bills neatly stacked on a corner of the counter. It was not the Miami I had dreamt of, but it was *my* Miami, and I was not ready to give it up.

I remembered Rafael calling me a good worker earlier that day. His voice and eyes were full of disbelief, and a mush of emotions stirred in me.

There was no need to overthink it.

I had nothing to lose.

So, I rushed back to the laptop before the form timed me out and hit submit.

Chapter Three

"I have something to tell you," I announced to Nina while we waited to cross the street, barely able to contain my smile.

"Please don't tell me you are talking again with that idiot who ghosted you. What was his name? Felipe? Fernando?" Nina said while she twisted her curls into a top bun. The four people waiting to cross the street pretended not to hear, but I saw their shoulders tense.

"No," I said between gritted teeth. "No, that's not it." Why was this light taking so long? I had chosen the worst possible moment to break my news to her.

"Okay, but he's still an asshole." Her words rose above the noise of the afternoon rush. Sometimes I forgot she could only speak in three volumes: loud, louder, and loudest. She was using her loud mode, still high enough for the entire Brickell Avenue population to learn about my failed romantic life.

If that wasn't enough to call attention, the rest of her was—from her full hips to the way they swayed. We had been walking her dog for ten minutes, and already, she had caught the eye of the exact same number of men, but she didn't even notice. Ninety percent of her focus was devoted to Dante, her two-year-old Maltipoo, and the remaining ten percent was split between the scarcity of men in Miami and my story.

If she would just listen to my story.

"Men in this city are shit. I tell you," she announced while I furiously pressed the pedestrian light button. "I'm here because my job wants me here, and the real estate market is good. But dating? Not so much."

A man looked up from his phone at us and rolled his eyes.

"Right, the job market. That's what I have to talk to you about." I tried and failed miserably to get her on track.

"Like, I don't even know why you're still on Bumble when nothing good has come out of that."

The pedestrian light finally changed, so I picked up Dante from the sidewalk to cross the street. While walking, I gave Nina one of my *would you just shut up and let me talk* looks, and she gave me an apologetic smile.

"Sorry, girl—got carried away." We reached the other side, and I set Dante on the sidewalk. "Alright, the job market. Tell me everything. Did Rafael say anything today?"

"Nada. It's so freaking awkward," I exclaimed. "I know. He knows. I bet over half the office knows, but no one talks about it."

"Not to your face ..."

"Right." The weight of despair settled in my heart. "Rafael wants me to keep it all confidential, making it that much harder to ask for recommendations and stuff."

"Don't waste time, Sofi. It's easier to switch jobs while you are still employed."

"I know, I know. That's what I wanted to talk to you about."

I waited for Nina to pick up a pile of dog poop from the sidewalk. I needed her undivided attention to tell her my news, so I let the seconds stretch until she turned to face me.

"What is it? Tell me!"

"I got a call from WorldMedia." I tried to suppress the giggles, but I couldn't. It was the first time I was telling someone, and I had already known for an entire day. Saying the phrase out loud made it much more *real*.

"Ohmigod, Sofia! Congratulations." A huge smile broke out on her face, the kind of genuine grin that reminded me why she was the only person I would confide my news to. "Did you check about the visa thing?"

I nodded my head in an almost imperceptible way, a sheepish smile taking over. "It's just a first interview, and I know I'm not gonna get it, but I think—"

"Hold on!" She cut me off mid-sentence, looking as if someone had slapped her in the face. "How do you know you're not gonna get it?!"

"For one, I don't meet the requirements for the position."

"What's the title?" She lifted her chin with such confidence that anyone would think she was an HR expert.

"Senior Account Manager." I lowered my eyes as I said it, embarrassed as if I were a teenager applying to become the company's CEO. I had never expected a WorldMedia recruiter to call for an initial screening and to recite the available time slots for an in-person interview.

I took the call as a sign. If WorldMedia could consider me a candidate, surely other smaller companies had to be interested. It was the slight push I needed to resume the job hunt with more force than ever before.

"And why would you not meet the requirements? You pretty much run the marketing department at Sunset." Nina's loud*er* volume was back.

"They are looking for someone with five years of experience who has done people management. Frankly, I don't know why they called, but I'm going to the interview. To practice, at least," I said.

"They chose to call you. Let them choose whether you are fit for the position."

"I don't want to get my hopes up." I pushed the words through clenched teeth.

"You need to walk into that interview like the job's already yours. You hear me?"

"But it isn't mine." I shook my head. "They'll ask about my background and think it isn't enough."

"Employers don't make hiring decisions based on your background. They make them based on your *potential*." She rolled her eyes as she spoke, as if she were reciting the best-known truth in the history of HR.

"Well, silly me!" I said in a playful voice, trying to soften a conversation I had hoped would be celebratory but ended up as a training session. "I've gotten it wrong my whole life, then!"

"I'm serious, Sofia."

I took a deep breath, letting the idea sink in. There was no way it could be so easy.

"What if they don't?" I refuted.

"What if you stop expecting the worst and focus on the interview?" she snapped.

I fell silent for a moment, the pressure of Nina's wisdom spiking my anxiety.

"Regardless of my expectations, there's a good chance I won't get it," I concluded.

"Then it wouldn't be the right company for you. But still, you walk into that office like you own it, okay?"

We walked silently for a moment, her words lingering in the humid afternoon air. Nina should know, as she had been through this a while back. She already had the three-figure salary, the ocean-view apartment, and a lease on a car that got switched into a new model every two years. And we were less than a year apart.

"Alright. I guess I still have two days to convince myself that the position is already mine."

"Good." She finally looked pleased. "What are you planning to wear?"

"I was thinking black slacks and a white collared shirt, maybe."

She turned to face me. "Please don't go to the interview looking like a waitress."

I laughed, hard. "Okay. What would *you* have me wear?"

"Wear the dress I gave you."

Ah, the teal dress. The piece I had only worn once before, to the office. That day, Mark from finance asked me if I wanted anything from Starbucks, and Giselle didn't show up at my cubicle, asking me to do her job. Nina had gifted me the dress on Christmas, with a note that read *Power dresses for power bitches*.

Maybe Nina was right, and I was meant to be a power bitch. Whatever that meant.

"I'll wear the dress, then."

The afternoon turned amber and then violet, the air slightly cooler in the shade but still scorching hot where the last rays of sun hit. The traffic got worse before it finally ebbed into the batch of drivers who were the last to leave the office or the first ones at happy hour.

We spent the next hour discussing everything I could—and could not—say during the interview until I was mildly convinced that the job was already mine.

Everything was good until Dante started whimpering, and the image of Catalina's dog appeared in my mind.

"*Miercoles*. I forgot about Togo!"

"Togo? You still haven't talked to your neighbor about the dog walking?" Nina's eyes went wide with dismay.

I shook my head, embarrassed.

"Don't tell me you have to leave."

"I promised her I'd walk him tonight." I fumbled through my bag for my car keys. I still had to run a few blocks to get to my car.

"But it's Friday night!"

"She texted me earlier today that she's working late. I completely forgot." The key to Catalina's apartment was at the bottom of my bag. My fingers clutched it. Then I gave a quick wave to Nina. I didn't dare look her in the eyes for fear of triggering what she was probably holding back, but she voiced her thoughts anyway.

"Sofia! She's not paying you. You're doing her a favor, but even favors have limits."

"We are down to three times a week," I said, then I bit my tongue at how pathetic it sounded. When Nina made a face, I added, "She works at BanLatam, and she'll let me know if there's an opening." I knew how naïve those words sounded, the blind optimism behind them. I'd been walking Catalina's dog for four months, and never, not once, had she asked for my resume, suggested I apply to work at her company, or even asked how things were going at my job.

Heck, I don't think she even knew my last name.

"And you believe her?" Nina's hand gestures were back in full force. "If she is taking time away from you to drape this entire city with resumes, then she needs to find some other idiot to pick up after her dog."

The last part drowned in the music blasting from a car, but I heard her. And I knew she was right. I had agreed to do it all those months ago because I honestly thought I could be friends with my neighbor. But there was no space in my life for someone like her.

Or maybe it was the other way around.

Sweet Togo knew walk time was over the minute he finished doing his business, so he had developed a talent to hold it in for as long as possible. After I deposited him back in his apartment, I bumped into Catalina in the hallway.

The smell of booze and the smudged mascara were enough to reveal she was *not* working late. It was Friday night, and happy hour had started early. The sight of me was not enough to sober her up, but it made me feel like the biggest fool in the building. I wanted to toss her key back and tell her to pick up after her dog like every other dog owner did.

But the words didn't come.

Instead, I muttered a foolish, "Hi, Togo is waiting for you inside," and kept walking, my eyes fixed on my apartment door, thinking how maybe—just maybe—nothing good would come out of the dog walking. Perhaps it was time I stopped it, because as Nina said, even favors have limits.

Later that night, my phone chirped. I ran to it, half expecting World-Media to say they had made a mistake and were canceling the interview. But it was Nina.

Nina: I thought we were having dinner together :-/

Me: Sorry. I'll make it up to you. Promise.

Nina: Are you doing the shopaholic's house tomorrow?

Me: Yup. Cleaning duty awaits.

Nina: Just promise me you'll be ready for the interview on Monday.

Me: I won't let you down XO

Nina: You better, bitch.

I settled on the counter while I made a brief stop in the Bumble app, because there's no better way to waste time than scrolling through Bumble profiles. I had heard of other cities where the profile list ended. Stories of places like Milwaukee, where users kept getting the same faces every day. That didn't happen here, in Miami—land of the flashy and the shirtless—where there were always new dudes sharing their profiles and competing for right swipes. Bumble had turned into my guilty pleasure in lieu of having an actual boyfriend. I wished job applications were as easy as Bumble. I swipe right, the company swipes right. And *poof*! I get a job offer with a permanent residency, 401K plan, two weeks of paid vacation, and retirement benefits. Sadly, all Bumble had to offer was men.

The ones who caught my eye were usually the ones with dogs. I had wished for my own dog for years, since I was a girl living in Bogotá. It was the other dream I shared with Dad—a sunny beach in Miami, throwing a ball into the shallow waves for my dog to fetch. But I could barely afford to maintain myself and my family, let alone a dog. The next best thing was to walk the neighbor's dog or to find a boyfriend with a canine companion, like the men in the profile pictures. But even a dog wouldn't guarantee I'd land a date with someone who wasn't an asshole, or, God forbid, someone as broke as me.

Four minutes of senseless swiping later, Mom's name popped up on the screen. The vibration made me jump. It was as if she was scolding me, telling me to *stop wasting time and get to job hunting*. I picked up—because heaven knew she wouldn't stop calling until I did.

"Hola, Mami."

"Sofia, ¿qué pasó que ayer no nos llamó? ¿Está bien?" I'm not even sure why she asked if I was fine. We both knew she was not calling to check on me.

"Todo bien, Mami." I looked at the rejection column in the file with the job application entries. "Me estoy alistando para ir a dormir."

"Que bueno. ¿Y ya pudo juntar el dinerito del mes?" Yup, she wanted to know about the money. The predictability made me sad.

"Yo no *junto* el dinero, Mami. Yo trabajo por el dinero." I rolled my eyes, frustrated that I had to explain that I worked for every dollar I sent them, and felt my stomach turn at the conversation. "Apenas esta mañana me hicieron el depósito de la quincena. Tengo que revisar que pagos tengo pendientes, y les paso la plata." I had gotten a paycheck deposit that same morning, and despite her insistence on money, I needed to cover my expenses. I couldn't take care of them if I didn't take care of myself first.

She gasped and muttered something I didn't catch. There was someone with her.

"Pero niña, si usted sabe la falta que nos hace esa platica. Dele la prioridad a su casa."

Those words made me freeze.

Darle la prioridad a mi casa. She was asking me to prioritize my home.

Where was home? I had not returned to that house since I had left three years earlier. With every passing day, another memory seemed to fade away. Like the small room I had to share with my brother, where I had to put up with his snoring when he got home wasted at four a.m., or the pile of bills on the worn-out wicker basket by the dining room table. I never understood how a new dress and aguardiente for my cousin's quinces could be more important than the electricity bill. Mom seemed to apply the same inexplicable rationale to every decision she made because the house was slowly falling apart, paint was peeling on the exterior, and the floor tiles were cracked inside. But the answer was always the same when I questioned her about it. *No hay plata para eso*. There's no money for *that*.

"I'll send you what I have now, Mom."

That night, my bank account hit a zero balance.

Also, Bumble ran out of faces to show me.

The first time I met Mrs. Garcia, the woman whose house I cleaned, she didn't ask me to call her by another name. In Colombia, we use "doña" or "señora," always followed by the first name. Calling this woman in her forties by her last name was downright comical to me, another reminder of the huge divide between us.

Every other Saturday, I cleaned her house for extra cash. I developed a system to ensure I didn't skip any corner of the house, and I moved through it like I was checking boxes off a list.

Vacuum entire house—check!

Kitchen sink, pantry, stove, cabinets—check!

Living room rugs, accent cushions, baseboards, picture frames—check!

And so on until I had gone through every nook, and the place was sparkling clean.

Cleaning for Mrs. Garcia was a curiously intimate thing. After spending so many hours tinkering in every corner of a house—sorting someone else's dirty laundry, getting rid of food that has gone bad in the fridge, or trying to ignore the colorful phone conversations she had while I was scrubbing the floors yards away—I was bound to find out things about her that I wasn't supposed to.

For example, I learned that Garcia wasn't her maiden name. She had kept it after divorcing Mr. Garcia, a man I had never met. He had been caught with another woman and didn't have any objections to his wife's alimony demands. He threw money at the problem, Mrs. Garcia, and moved on with his life. In Colombia, when a marriage ends, so does the cash flow, or at least there's some fight over it. I didn't know if Mr. Garcia was the exception or the rule, but I knew that's where my pay came from. I also knew Mrs. Garcia didn't have to work and could spend her days booking vacations, arranging private trainers, and shopping. So. Much. Shopping.

The first time I walked into her closet, it took me a full minute to adjust everything I knew about closets. First, I wasn't used to walk-ins. Back home, a closet was just an opening on the wall flanked by accordion doors or a curtain. Mrs. Garcia's "closet" had enough space for a center table, a small couch, and a window. The walls were covered with built-in shelves and drawers with lights that seemed to shine from within. Glossy shopping bags were squashed together on the couch, their contents spilling onto the floor; unused coats hung on the walls with barely any space between them; shoe boxes were stacked so high over the closet furniture that they reached the ceiling. A word with no direct Spanish translation popped into my mind—*hoarder*. I didn't know the term existed before I came to the U.S. because there was no occasion to use it back home. But her closet was the only area of the house that looked like this, which disqualified her as a hoarder. The word that replaced it in my mind was *shopaholic*—another unfamiliar concept where I come from.

Mrs. Garcia gave me detailed instructions on how to navigate the maze of bags, explained where each garment needed to hang, and how she wanted her shoes arranged by color and heel height. Then she gave the closet a satisfied look and left quickly, as if she had suddenly remembered there was something else she needed to buy.

Once alone, I couldn't help checking some untouched sales tags. My eyes widened with disbelief—$800 for a pair of jeans? $1,200 for stilettos? $3,200 for a cocktail dress? How could one dress cost more than what I made in a month?

After a few cleaning sessions, Mrs. Garcia stopped following me around the house or showing up unannounced to check in on me. She'd also stopped giving casual instructions over my shoulder.

That's not the detergent I told you to use on the bathroom floor.

Please take care of that brown spot to the right.

Can you please prepare lunch today? I just got my manicure done.

Let me be clear, I was thankful I had the gig. I had heard horror stories about maids who had to deal with bug infestations, flirtatious husbands, or clients who refused to pay because, at the end of the day, they felt the house wasn't "clean enough."

A few times, I wondered how nice it would be to swim in the immaculate pool, take a minute to sit on the couch to rest my feet, or eat one of her artisan nut bars when my stomach rumbled in hunger. More than once, I'd held one of the new dresses, felt the weight of the fabric, the intricate lace details, the quality I'd never find in my closet, then gingerly checked the untouched price tag. Would she even notice if one of those dresses disappeared? Could Mom sell it in Bogotá? Could I show up at Saks and exchange it for store credit? But I had gotten good at crushing all those temptations quickly. I imagined Mrs. Garcia spotting the dress in my bag on my way out, calling the cops to report it, and my getting kicked in the ass so hard I'd land right back in Bogotá. The thought alone made me clean better and faster. After all, I needed the extra income, and Mrs. Garcia always paid on time. All cash (obviously) because, although I wasn't undocumented, it eliminated all the fuss and paperwork that came with hiring help. I knew if I did my job well, every two weeks, I'd be rewarded with six crisp twenty-dollar bills tucked in an envelope with my name on it.

Whenever I had to deal with a stubborn clump of hair plugging the drain hole, or Mrs. Garcia asked for help changing the A/C filter or replacing light bulbs around the house, I'd remind myself of the phrase I used so many times when people asked me what I was planning to do for a living in Miami, "Yo hago lo que sea." I'll do anything.

I also thought of asking Mrs. Garcia to donate her used clothes so I could send them to Bogotá. Surely Mom could offer them to some neighbors and take some of the monetary pressure off my back. Mrs. Garcia must have had piles of unwanted clothes if she was bringing home a bagload of them every week. But the opportunity never came. She moved quickly from room to room, usually on the phone, ignoring me most of the time. I didn't know how to bring it up. The clothes reselling venture went from dream to ashes in a matter of weeks.

That Saturday morning, I parked in the usual spot facing the house, grabbed my cleaning supplies, and waited. There was a big reason I couldn't get out of my car. From behind the wheel, I could see Giselle's white convertible BMW parked in the driveway two doors down from Mrs. Garcia's. Yes, *that* Giselle. She usually left at fifteen minutes to the hour because her Pilates class began at 9 a.m., but it was already 9:05 a.m. and her car was still there.

Dread stirred in me at the thought of bumping into her in the driveway while carrying my yellow gloves and wearing Clorox-stained gym pants. When I first took the cleaning gig, I decided I wouldn't discuss it with anyone at work. I wasn't comfortable with the idea of my colleagues knowing I was the cleaning lady of Giselle's neighbor, and I wasn't ready to ask Giselle to keep a secret.

I waited a full five minutes with the engine off so I wouldn't waste gas and lowered my window so I wouldn't suffocate.

I wondered if she had given up on Pilates. My fingers fidgeted with the car keys, my eyes glued to her front door. And just as I was calculating the odds of crossing paths with her in the twenty seconds it took me to reach Mrs. Garcia's front door, she walked out.

She looked stunning even with a clean face and wearing nothing but gym pants, a sports top, and sneakers. I ducked behind the wheel, mortified, and prayed to the stars that Mrs. Garcia wouldn't walk out right then. Thick drops of sweat formed on my forehead and slid down my cheeks.

She hadn't stepped out more than two steps when a muscular arm pulled her back in. She giggled as the arm twisted her around, making her come face-to-face with a grinning man wearing only boxers. He gave her a long kiss, one hand pulling her from her lower back, the other one squeezing her ass. I swear I could hear her giggle from my car, a laugh that was sultry and coy at the same time.

After a minute or so of playing the ridiculous game of *I have to go,* and *no, you don't*, she freed herself from his embrace and turned back to her car. And then something disconcerting happened, something so out of place in Giselle's rosy world that I was tempted to break cover and poke my head above the steering wheel. Even with the obstructed visibility, I saw Giselle's eyes *roll*. Not a subtle roll. A full-on, annoyed, discontented roll. Then I realized the cause of the eye roll was *him*—the man who couldn't bear to see her go—and all she wanted was to get to her car as fast as possible.

She hopped in her convertible and drove off, not turning to look back once, even as the man waved from the threshold.

It might not have been much, but the knowledge that even Giselle's perfect life had its flaws, that even she could be stuck in a less-than-ideal situation, or worse, stuck in an unwanted relationship, was the encouragement I needed to get out of my car to clean Mrs. Garcia's house like I never had before.

With Giselle's car disappearing in the distance, I jogged to Mrs. Garcia's front door—I was already ten minutes late—as I mentally noted what I would tackle first. I rang the doorbell and wiped the sweat off my face, then I stood straighter and took a deep breath.

After all, I still had a whole house to clean.

Chapter Four

I was running late for the interview. How crazy to think that after waiting for the opportunity for so long, I'd find myself rushing down the lobby in my building. I caught a glimpse of myself in the vast lobby mirror and mouthed a secret *thank you* to Nina. My teal dress was knee-length, capped-sleeve perfection. I looked beautiful and confident, like I was ready to take on the world, but the *power bitch* version of me did not match the turmoil that was going on inside.

Like a mantra, I kept repeating to myself that this was just practice. Other chances would come, and I should consider myself lucky to have made it this far. Meeting with WorldMedia could give me the boost for other, more realistic opportunities. I didn't deserve the position. Heck, I didn't even deserve the interview. Then the flicker of hope would appear again.

WorldMedia was fifteen minutes away, in an upscale office building located in the fancy Brickell Key area. Still, I wasn't the least bit interested in enjoying the skyline and the glimmering buildings. That morning, traffic was hell, and the rising bridge sign began flashing when I was about to cross it. Little beads of sweat appeared on my forehead, threatening to wipe off my makeup.

I decreased speed and searched for the address while my phone's GPS gave directions to me. It was tricky. The office building came into view on my left, but a boulevard was dividing the street. I had to wait until the next roundabout.

Banging my hands against the steering wheel, I watched the World-Media building vanish in the rearview mirror. As disheartening as it was, my only choice was to keep going and make a turn at the following roundabout. I pushed the gas pedal, screeching the tires against the pavement on a turn with a ten-mile per hour speed limit. The noise reached every corner of the quiet road. I didn't care. I decided then and there that rejection would come from failing the interview, not because I hadn't shown up. As I made the final turn, I gripped the steering wheel tighter and scanned desperately for the parking lot entrance. I could still make it if I didn't make any more mistakes.

My eyes shifted from the GPS to the time as it changed from 8:58 a.m. to 8:59 a.m.

Of course, I missed the gray sedan cruising in front of me.

My head bounced forward as I hit the brakes, but it was too late. The two cars collided with a quick thud, like the muted crunch of metal giving way.

Every inch of my body started shaking, and the heat started slowly leaving me. If I had unglued my hands from the steering wheel, I would have collapsed on the chair.

In my years living in Miami, I had kept a spotless record. Some colleagues warned me that if someday I applied for a green card, every single past mistake would come up because nothing was ever deleted in *el sistema*. Afraid to ruin my chances, I maintained a low profile. Not one speeding ticket, not one glass of wine during happy hour, not one late credit card payment—even if I only sent the twenty-dollar minimum. Nothing that could call any type of attention. I was a model citizen without being an actual citizen.

So, there I was—the young woman whose right to live in Miami was hanging on a thread—facing my worst fear: a traffic accident.

And it was my fault.

And I was late to my interview.

A man exited the car. His shirt was hanging outside of his pants with only one button fastened. He stumbled towards me, holding on to the top edge of the car door. At first, I thought he was injured and needed to hold on to something to keep his balance. Then I noticed the sweaty sheen over his face, the tangles in his overgrown brown hair, and his glassy, red eyes. Terrified as I was, the sight of that stranger approaching sent a chill through my entire body. He managed to reach the back of his car and rub his hand against the dent on the bumper. It didn't look too bad from where I was, but I waited for his reaction as I stepped out of my car without making a sound. After a few failed attempts to focus on the dent, he turned to face me with the same groggy movements.

His eyes widened a little, then traveled down, stopping at the edge of my dress as a grunt escaped his mouth. My body entered panic mode. I could feel my kneecaps shaking. I struggled momentarily to find my voice but managed to push the words out.

"I'm so sorry. Are you okay?"

Another visceral sound came from his throat.

"Do you want to call the police?" My voice was shaking. I knew calling the police was the right thing to do, but the last thing I wanted. I did not need to open a case now—not when I was about to lose my visa.

"The police?" His bloodshot eyes widened, a hint of panic in them. "No. No. I don't need to deal with the police today."

He turned around and zigzagged his way back to his car. My heart quickened. "So, you don't want to file a report?"

"Ehhh ... not for these two pieces of crap. Not worth the trouble."

"Oh." I liked every word of that phrase, even the part when he said my car was crap. I liked it if it meant he wouldn't call the police, and I could go on my way.

He reached the driver's seat and barely made it in without hitting his head. Then he closed his door and drove away, leaving me in my lucky dress next to my crappy car with a busted front bumper.

As he drove off, I felt the drum of my heartbeat, the heat slowly leaving my face. Any hopes of making a good impression at the interview faded away and were replaced by absolute fatigue. My breaths were still shallow and uneven when I turned back to my car, still shaking, and silently praising heaven because it was a miracle the man had decided to drive away without even asking my name.

I was about to get inside the car when a male voice called, "Are you okay?"

"I'm fine," I replied without lifting my face to check who had asked. "He said it was nothing."

I didn't even bother to check my car for scratches. It probably had a new dent in it, but my car already looked like it had been to a wild night at the Monster Jam, so it was just another bruise to add to the collection.

"Yeah ... I don't think he knew what was happening," the man said. He had moved closer, clearly spiked by a curiosity that the other passersby didn't have. "You are not hurt, right?" His voice was deep with the tropical intonation of the islands and an accent that revealed it could switch from English to perfectly fluent Spanish in a blink. I liked it. I wanted to hear more of it. It didn't give me the creeps like the drunk whose car had faded as fast as it had appeared.

That's when I decided to look up. This guy's immaculate white shirt was neatly tucked into his pants. A laptop bag hung from his shoulder. He had full, dark eyebrows that were frowning under the morning sun. Perhaps it was the shock of having just smelled the other man's stench, but this one radiated a freshly washed scent that threw me off.

"I'm not. I hope I don't feel it later today." I pushed the hair away from my forehead; it was damp with sweat. Then I remembered the interview. "Oh shit, I had to be somewhere fifteen minutes ago."

"Glad to see you're okay." He dipped his chin in acknowledgment, and then he turned back to the sidewalk. His shoulders hunched slightly as he resumed his path, each step creating distance between us.

Something kicked in the second he turned away from me. A sudden thrill, like when I swiped right on Bumble. Only this man was right in front of me. I didn't have to wait for a blind date to find out he was more handsome in person.

I blurted out the first thing that came to my mind. "Wait! How do I get into the parking garage?"

He stopped and turned back around. "You mean for this building?" He pointed at the dark gray office building behind him. "Go up the ramp ahead and you'll see the sign on your right."

"Thank you. I'm so late. I was looking for the parking garage before I ... well, the accident."

"Never mind that. He drove away; you are safe." His lips curved in an almost imperceptible smile. "Go on to wherever you were headed before ... you know."

"Before I crashed. I know." I smiled. There was nothing funny about the accident or being late to the interview. But I couldn't help smiling. "What's your name, again?"

"Esteban," he said while looking for something in his wallet. "And you are?"

"Sofia."

"Nice to meet you, Sofia." He handed me a business card, and a giggle escaped me. It struck me as an awkward way to introduce himself. Also, who still uses business cards? He must have sensed it because before I had a chance to ask, he said, "I never know when I'm going to meet a potential client."

"Oh." He had a job, which was one of my top three requirements to date someone. I glanced at the card in my hand—a navy-blue heavy cardstock with the company name ALTAMIRA in silver font and the name *Esteban Rivera* right under it. "Do I look like a potential client?"

He smiled and the expression bloomed across his features—wide and uninhibited, revealing perfectly aligned white teeth. The kind that makes your entire face brighten up, altering the entire atmosphere around him. A smile just like his was another requirement on my list.

"I don't know." He chuckled and tilted his face a little. "Maybe." I could tell he wanted the conversation to go on, but I was late as it was, and I couldn't risk being a no-show.

"I have to go. It was nice meeting you."

To my delight, he looked somewhat deflated at my brush-off. "Let me know if anything hurts later today."

"I will."

"And I hope it goes well ... whatever you had to do fifteen minutes ago."

"More like thirty minutes. Thank you, Esteban," I said as I climbed back into my car, trying to suppress a smile by biting my lower lip.

We waved goodbye, and as I started driving, his broad shoulders disappeared too fast from my rearview mirror. I didn't catch where he was heading—work, most likely. I flipped over his business card, which I was still clutching onto like a talisman, and found an address that was not in Brickell Key. He was probably visiting a client and bumped into me by some divine chance.

Despite the whirlwind of the past thirty minutes, I could barely control my grin as I walked into WorldMedia's office.

And then it was showtime.

Two women sat at a long table in a glass office. A stack of papers rested in front of them. My resume was on top. When I walked in, I didn't know if I should apologize for being late or mention I had just had a car accident. The women smiled and asked me to have a seat, so I kept my mouth shut. One of them, who looked like a porcelain doll with blue eyes and black hair, complimented my dress. The other had beautiful, round features and big, brown eyes in a chubby face framed by curls of brown hair. She kept pushing her cuticles so much that little raw spots had appeared. She was either tired or nervous, and it was only 9:26 a.m. I tried to unglue my eyes from her nails as she slid my resume in front of the porcelain doll.

"Thank you for coming in, Sofia. I am Dianelys Gonzalez, client services director at WorldMedia. And this is Linda Prentice, Marketing

Director at Lamballe Cosmetics. I asked Linda to be here because the position you're applying for will manage Linda's account."

"Well, not *my* account." The porcelain doll chuckled. "WorldMedia is looking for an account executive to manage Lamballe, and they thought it was good for me to be here."

I tried to hide how intimidated I felt because I was about to be interviewed by two people—a possible future boss and a possible future client.

"Are you familiar with Lamballe?" Dianelys asked.

Was I familiar? I had idolized Lamballe since the day I received a free lip color sample at a department store shortly after arriving in Miami. I fantasized about buying their bronzer every time I got paid. I knew of every product launch and had seen every ad. And I secretly thought they were *way* better than Sunset Cosmetics.

"I am. I've been in the beauty industry for the past three years. In my current position, I analyze market insights, and we use Lamballe's performance as an industry benchmark." I heard the words coming out of my mouth like they were not mine, like I was possessed by someone else. Someone wittier, more intelligent, and absolutely more confident than me. Nina would be so proud.

Linda flashed a quick smile at Dianelys. She liked me. I could sense it. But it wasn't her I was meant to impress. If I landed this job, Dianelys would be my boss.

"It's great that you mentioned your marketing background. I'd love to have someone with more than just media experience for this position," Linda said.

"I manage the media budget and all media plans for our department, from planning to execution," I replied.

"The ideal candidate for this position needs to have at least five years of media management experience," Dianelys added.

My stomach plummeted so fast I almost felt it hit the floor. I wasn't going to lie, so I followed Nina's advice and answered their questions as best as possible: downplaying the skills I didn't have and enhancing the ones I did very well. For the next twenty minutes, they grilled me with speculative cases and issues they were having at both companies, and I tried my best to prove I was the right person to solve all their problems. Every few minutes, a nagging voice would show up and whisper the meanest things.

You're not that *good.*

Wait 'til they ask if you have any direct reports.

Anyone can do that.

Tell them you don't have a permanent work permit.

Are you sure you can handle the job?

It wasn't easy to think, nod, and formulate the correct answers while my inner voice tried to sabotage me, but somehow, I survived the interview. Linda had a smile on her face, and even Dianelys had stopped fumbling with her nails. The air in the office had gone from calm and cautious to friendly and chatty. My back was no longer rigid with tension. I knew I was extra comfortable when I accepted Linda's offer for a coffee from their Nespresso machine.

I pictured Nina clapping and cheering me on.

Then, of course, life had to take a dump on the moment.

"One more question, Sofia. You seem to be in a good position at Sunset Cosmetics, and I can tell you are very passionate about your job." Linda clasped her hands in front of her and leaned forward. "Why do you want to leave?"

Why hadn't some HR deity created a ban against that question? I placed the coffee cup back on the table, trying to make some time to recall the exact answer I had practiced with Nina.

"I've been with Sunset for over two years—and it has been wonderful. But they are not offering many opportunities for advancement, and at this point in my career, I'm ready to take on a challenge."

It wasn't technically a lie, and it wasn't the whole truth, but it was a good chunk of it. Linda grinned, Dianelys nodded, and my inner voice finally gave up, defeated. I felt the smile forming on my lips; the solution to all my problems lay in vibrant colors right in front of me.

I nailed that freaking interview.

Atta girl, you did it, my inner voice finally admitted.

I know, I answered back.

"Thank you so much for your time," Dianelys said as she handed me her business card. I never thought I could love business cards so much until that day.

When I shook hands with Linda, she said, "Thank you, Sofia. We'll be in touch with you very soon."

I practically floated out of that conference room.

I floated while I thanked the receptionist and entered the elevator. I floated as I crossed the lobby, wondering what it would be like to come to work at such a beautiful place every day. I floated when I saw from the building entrance the spot of the accident, the same spot where I had met Esteban less than an hour ago. Even though I might never see him again, my stomach dipped a little.

I stopped floating when I reached my car and saw my squashed bumper. I didn't have the money to repair it; frankly, it wasn't worth it. I was snapped out of my daydreams when my phone rang, and I saw it was

Mom, asking for money, again. Then my soul collapsed to the ground when I saw a parking ticket waiting for me on the dashboard.

Chapter Five

Rafael's gaze traveled from his laptop to my chest every few seconds. I had already pushed my seat as far back as possible without making the situation even more awkward, discreetly pulling the neckline up and the hem down to cover as much skin as my lucky teal dress allowed. I felt a warning bell go off every time he glanced my way, an uncomfortable chill creeping up my skin. We had reached that point in our meetings when I started wrapping up the conversation so I could leave.

We had spent the morning brainstorming ideas for an influencer campaign to launch a new mascara called *Miles of Eyelashes*. That had kept my mind occupied and away from replaying every event that had occurred during and before the WorldMedia interview. Rafael hadn't mentioned anything about the downsize since our meeting almost a week earlier. In fact, during the past few days, he had been determined to delegate every possible PowerPoint deck and report analysis to me, with deadlines too close to be reasonable. Anxiety wanted to take over, but I was close, *so close*, to getting the WorldMedia position and leaving Sunset, that I just agreed. I nodded with mechanical consent to the compliments, agreed to the impossible tasks, and surrendered to any other circumstance thrown my way.

When the meeting was finally over, I stood up and raced towards the door. I could feel his eyes glued to my ass when he said, "You look nice today." I didn't stop moving. God, he could be creepy—this man who could be my father, with his alternating, flirtatious, condescending personalities. That morning, I had received polite compliments from two colleagues, one security guard, and even from Giselle—though I suspected she only did it because she would ask me for a favor later. But the words felt inappropriate coming from Rafael, the same as they had for months.

As my hand reached the doorknob, when I was one step away from leaving that dreaded space, he rushed another order. "Sofia, can you close the door and stay another minute? There's something I need to tell you."

The five seconds it took me to walk back to the chair felt like I was crossing a gateway to another dimension—scary and dark—but I was desperate to see what was on the other side. I sat back on the chair but didn't even bother leaning back. I had a feeling this conversation wouldn't take long.

"Technically, I'm not supposed to tell you this—" He let the words hang between us like the preface of the most succulent *chisme*. I stared at him, munching the inside of my cheek, not trying in the very least to hide my impatience.

When his cell phone beeped, his eyes drifted to the screen, and my gut flipped.

"Rafael?" I pleaded. I was way past formalities with this soon-to-be ex-manager.

He let out an annoyed puff. "I received a call from HR this morning. They found someone to replace your position in Mexico." I saw a glimpse of a smirk on his face. "They are finalizing the hiring paperwork. I'm afraid it's a matter of days until they hand you your notice."

The news flew out of his mouth and crashed into my chest.

"But ... but you thought it would take at least another month?"

"The team down there moves a lot faster than we do. The reality is corporate wants to move all operational roles to Mexico and leave only management here in Miami."

The blood drained from my face until I was sure I was as white as the stack of papers on Rafael's desk. I was barely listening. For some odd reason, I kept thinking about the parking ticket I had received that morning and how I had maxed out my credit card and scraped the bottom of my bank account. How I had failed to see this coming. How unprepared I was. How much I needed Dianelys to call me with a job offer.

"Sofia?" Rafael's voice snapped me back.

"Huh?"

"I wish I could tell you to take the afternoon off, but I need you to wrap up the sales pitch for the mascara." As he said it, his eyes drifted to the door, and I knew the conversation was over. "I'll let you know if I hear anything else."

I made a beeline straight to my gray cubicle. I didn't want to talk with anyone. My vision was cloudy, and the last thing I wanted was pity from my employed and economically stable colleagues. I ducked under the table and pretended to shuffle around a brochure box. A heavy lump settled in my throat. Why was life yanking me out of my dream?

I had refreshed my email at least twenty times since the interview, furiously checking the spam, expecting to hear from WorldMedia, or any other companies I had applied to. But there was no new mail.

I slouched in my seat when my phone chirped. It was Nina.

Nina: So?! How did the interview go? Did they hire you on the spot?!

Sofia: Hey. It went well.

Nina: And???

Sofia: Idk . . . Still debating whether your dress is lucky or not.

Nina: Don't lose hope. Something will turn out.

: I really hope so.

Nina: It will. Don't forget I love you and I'm here for you.

I didn't have the guts to tell her I was about to be unemployed, for real.

If they fired me that same day, I didn't even have money to cover next month's rent. Heck, I didn't even have enough to pay for that stupid parking ticket. I depended on those bi-weekly Sunset paychecks even for the most trivial things.

I pulled my budget list and did the math for the rest of the month, desperation bubbling up in me. There was nothing to cut, and there were few options to produce extra income, either. I already devoted two Saturdays a month to Mrs. Garcia's townhome in Coral Gables. Finding another client to offer my cleaning services was always an option, but honestly, I wasn't crazy about discovering the secrets that lurked in yet another stranger's toilet.

I could do nothing about the rental payments, a fixed expense that took over half of my monthly salary. That amount alone was eating me up. The thought occurred to me to find a roomie to split the rent, but it was a tiny one-one, and where would I find someone willing to move into the living room and share a bathroom, knowing that I could be out of the country in a few months?

I could also file for student loan forgiveness or reduction, or stop paying for the thing altogether. But I couldn't fathom the idea of defaulting on that loan. My student status had been my entrance ticket to the country, and one of the things I had to get right to have a good credit score, which I had learned was a requirement for basically everything in the U.S.

The credit card balance would remain intact while I continued sending the $20 minimum payments until I had sorted out my life.

Then there was the Colombia money.

Mom and Santiago had to give me a break. It's not that I didn't want to help; I couldn't risk sending them money next month. They had to understand.

Would they?

I looked at my assets.

Well, *assets* may not be the word a financially sound person would use. In my case, they were more like *leftovers*. I could sell my car, but heaven knew it was impossible to survive in Miami without one, let alone hunt for a job. Plus, I wouldn't get more than 1K for that old piece of metal (subtract another 200 for the busted bumper). I had one-quarter tank of gas left, which had to last until the next cleaning duty, but that was almost two weeks away. My kitchen was nearly depleted of groceries, but I could survive on rice, beans, and arepas for days.

I could sell some old clothes and shoes on a thrift app, but it wouldn't help much. My laptop was another asset I needed for job hunting. I contemplated the desolate list. It was so short, embarrassing even. My net worth was zero.

When I dumped the cell phone back in my bag, I saw the two business cards I had received that morning. Those were assets, too.

I could follow up with Dianelys, but it was too soon, and I did not want to appear desperate.

And then there was Esteban's card.

Under normal circumstances, I wouldn't reach out so soon. I would've waited the mandatory two days Nina forced me to observe. But I needed something to cheer me up, and there weren't a lot of options available.

Sofia: Hey! This is Sofia.

I wrote *the girl you met on the street*, but it looked so trashy that I deleted it.

I put the phone to the side and turned to my overflowing inbox, the *Miles of Eyelashes* pitch draft, the marketing calendar that was due. Two whole minutes passed, and he didn't reply.

Well, there goes my asset.

Then my phone chirped.

I hoped it wasn't a message from Mom or Nina.

My eyes lit up when I saw it was him.

Esteban: Hey! How are you feeling? Any pain?

I had a massive backache, but it was hard to tell if it was the crash or the imminent poverty breathing down the back of my neck.

Sofia: Nothing unusual.

Esteban: Good.

Esteban: I'm glad you reached out.

I stared at my phone and realized I had nothing to say back. He was still a stranger I'd met on the street. He could be married, or a father of four. Texting him was a stupid idea, and I had more important things to do.

But he kept on writing.

Esteban: Did you make it on time to your appointment?

Sofia: I did! And no one seemed to notice I was late.

Esteban: Good. Things always work out in the end

Did they?

Sofia: I was really stressed out this morning. Sorry if I was rude to you.

Esteban: Not at all. You handled the whole thing very well.

Sofia: Did you see what happened?

Esteban: Yeah

Sofia: And?

This pause was longer than the others. I stared at the three dots in the message bubble, biting my lip with remorse.

Esteban: You weren't paying attention.

My stomach churned.

Sofia: Do you think he's gonna look for me?

Esteban: No

Esteban: The dude was so wasted he probably thinks he backed up into a tree and got away with it.

I chuckled, then remembered I had to keep my volume low, so I ducked under the table like I was looking for something.

Esteban: Do you want to grab a coffee later today?

I didn't know those nine words had the power to turn my anxiety into absolute bliss. I wanted to reply with a big fat YES, but it was Monday. I walked Togo on Mondays.

Sofia: Can't make it today.

I looked at the message and felt somewhat proud that I had something else to do.

Esteban: No worries. How about tomorrow?

Sofia: Tomorrow works.

Nina's teal dress was lucky after all.

I heard shuffling, so I looked up. Giselle was standing on the edge of the cubicle, looking down at me like an evil stepsister staring at Cinderella.

"Are you busy down there?" She lifted one eyebrow in that elegant way that I've never been able to master.

I tossed my phone in my bag and emerged from underneath the table, Giselle following every movement. She waited until I was seated to ask for the marketing calendars, which she needed in two hours, tops. She didn't care that Rafael had given me a different assignment for the afternoon.

She was another reason I couldn't wait to fly to WorldMedia.

I glanced one last time at the Miles of Eyelashes mascara launch plan, the one I had started working on with Rafael that morning. After spending most of the afternoon polishing the sales pitch, revising every number and graphic, and creating a small marketing plan masterpiece, I allowed myself to smile and stretch on the chair. The plan was good. It was so good that Rafael even replied, "Nice job," when I handed it over. I refused to bask in his compliments, but after the interview, I took every piece of reinforcement as a sign that I deserved the WorldMedia position. I mean, if I could come up with a launch plan from scratch, including a two-year sales projection and media recommendation, and put it into a deck so engaging, so convincing, that even Rafael had to admit I had done a good job, then surely I was ready for anything my future boss could throw at me. All I needed was the opportunity, and it was so close I could practically taste it. I could feel someone in WorldMedia was drafting an acceptance e-mail that very moment.

When I received a last-minute Zoom invite to go over the deck, I practically levitated out of my chair. I was usually left out of director-level calls, but the sales director himself had requested my presence to go over the sales pitch. I joined the call a minute early and took the time to imagine all the questions they could come up with and what my replies would be. When José—the sales director—joined, I was so excited that I couldn't contain my smile.

I waited as the screen gradually filled with testosterone. Three directors appeared in separate digital windows from the comfort of their homes, but Rafael was missing. I remained unnoticed as they resumed a passionate debate about a futbol match that might as well have occurred on another planet. None of them acknowledged me in my silent corner of the screen, so I continued to wait.

When it was evident that time was ticking without Rafael joining, José announced, "I have to jump off the call in fifteen minutes, but I had a chance to review the deck earlier today. This pitch looks fantastic. And the sales projections," He blew air out of his mouth, raising both eyebrows, as if he could almost hear the money chiming in. "It's golden. This could be the launch that makes our year, Sofia."

My heart started beating to the sound of a happy tune.

"Was the *Mile High* tagline your idea? Or was that the creative agency?" he asked.

"It was mine," I heard myself saying, my voice proud. "I think we can use it to run some ads for traveling clients, like at airports and Duty Free."

"I love it; this is great. I wouldn't change any of it before we pitch to retailers. What'd you guys think?"

His eyes drifted momentarily across the screen. The other two directors nodded. One of them was about to say something when Rafael joined the call.

"Hey guys, sorry I'm late." He puffed. His eyes quickly scanned the screen until they landed on a single point, and I knew he had just spotted me.

"Um ... hi, Sofia." His tone was ten times less cheerful than it had been seconds earlier, and that's when I realized he was not expecting to see my happy face at the meeting.

"Hi, Rafael," I said. "We were just starting to talk about the plans."

"Okay ... thank you." He cleared his throat. "Sofia, I'd hate to have you waste your time on this call since I already have all the information the team needs. I can take the guys through the plan."

My eyes darted to my reflection on the screen, making sure my expression remained undeterred.

"I'll stay for the meeting, if that's okay. In case anyone has questions about the benchmarks and the pitch—"

"You know, I just remembered we have a due date for the post-campaign analysis for skincare. Those usually take you a while. Why don't you take this time to work on it?"

I hated the indifference of his tone, as if we were in the office kitchen and he suggested that I try a different coffee flavor. I studied his face, trying to find a glimpse of humor, something to tell me he was joking, but ignoring the tightness around his mouth was impossible. Even José, who had been so enthusiastic about my ideas only a minute earlier, had turned into a frozen image. One of the other guys looked uncomfortable for a second, then turned off his camera.

My reflection was still cool, but it didn't reflect the turmoil bubbling up in me. I pulled myself up, determined to prove I belonged there as much as he did. "Oh, that's practically done. I started on it last week."

"Sofia, you don't have to be in this call," he said.

"I understand, but I can—"

"That won't be necessary. Thanks, Sofia."

In the seconds that followed, I hoped for any of the other men in the call to say something along the lines of "Come on, man, she can stay." But they didn't. No one vouched for me, not even José, despite knowing my name was plastered all over that deck. I think I nodded, or maybe I didn't. I sank into my chair, hoping no one could see my eyes crystallizing as I moved the pointer towards the red LEAVE button and clicked on it without even saying goodbye.

I only had two things on my mind when I woke up on Tuesday: World-Media's offer—nonexistent up to that point—and the coffee meetup with Esteban, who texted me a time and place to meet after work.

I was still staring at the phone with little stars in my eyes when Mom's call came through.

Angry flames replaced my stars. What now?

"Hola Sofia. ¿Ya está despierta?"

"Si, Mami. Buenos días."

"Buenos días." Her greeting was paused and cautious, but I knew better.

"Mami, ya tienen el mes completo. No me digan que necesitan más plata, porque ya les mandé todo lo que tenía." I reminded her that I'd already sent what was due for the month, and I had nothing left.

"Ay Sofia, yo se. No se ponga así. Solo la estoy llamando para preguntarle como está. Como le está yendo en el trabajo. Siento que ya casi ni hablamos."

It took me a few seconds to realize she was calling to check on me. I was so conditioned to the usual two minutes of back-and-forth that it was hard to believe she had called so early in the morning to ask me about work and how I was.

"Estoy bien," I replied, hesitation evident in every word, "de hecho, estoy entrevistándome para un trabajo nuevo." I chose to disclose the most relevant aspect of my life lately—interviewing for a new job.

"¡Ay no me diga que se quedó sin trabajo!" Her unexpected reaction was alarmed, as if a lifeline was about to be disconnected. So I clarified that I still had a job, I was just looking at other options. "No ... no me quedé sin trabajo. Solo estoy viendo otras opciones."

"Gracias a Dios." She sighed.

There was no point in explaining anything to her. As long as the money kept rolling in, she wouldn't mind if I worked at a pretty office or did janitorial work. I wanted to believe she cared about my well-being; I did. I wanted to feel our mother-daughter connection ran deeper than money transfers and one-minute calls every week. I needed her to be concerned for me with the same intensity she worried and cared for Santiago. Still, our kind words for each other had dried off a long time ago, our calls getting shorter every month, video calls reserved only for

Navidad and birthdays. There was no money for me to visit them, and they would have preferred to receive the cash from me anyway.

Laughter broke out in the background of her call.

It was two laughs. I thought one of them was Santiago, but the woman …

"¿Santiago está ahí contigo?" I asked her about Santiago first.

"Aquí está, sí." I heard a chair screeching against the floor, the shuffling of shoes, and a door closing.

"¿Y con quién más está?" Who was there with him so early in the morning? Santiago slept every day until noon.

The silence was so long, I checked that the call was still open.

"Con Lorena." Mom finally mumbled.

"¿Con Lorena? ¿A las 7 de la mañana?" I snapped. Lorena was Santiago's latest girlfriend. I had stopped trying to get acquainted with his partners after I realized none of his relationships lasted very long. But a girlfriend hanging out at the house at seven a.m. was a novelty. Mom was so quiet I could feel my heartbeat accelerating.

"Mami, ¿Lorena está viviendo con ustedes?" Was that woman I didn't even know living there with them?

Silence.

"¿Mamá?" I pressed on, louder this time.

When she finally answered, she sounded resigned. "Se mudó aquí hace un par de semanas. Es que estaba teniendo muchos problemas con su familia, los papás no gustan de Santiago, todo era un problema. Pero su hermano la quiere mucho."

That woman, a person I didn't even know, had moved in with them weeks ago. I couldn't care less that she had family problems or that for the first time in Santiago's life, he had decided to care for someone other than himself. If she lived in the house, I was supporting three adults financially.

"¿Pero esa mujer trabaja? ¿Les está pagando algo por vivir ahí?" I could feel my volume rise with every word. Did this person even work? Was she at least paying rent?

"Sofia, usted sabe que aquí es bien difícil encontrar trabajo. Ellos están tratando—"

When Mom replied that they were trying to find a job, I lost it. I was trying to find a job myself, but unlike them, I had no one else to rely on.

"Que descaro, mamá. ¿Como así que tratando? ¡Una partida de vagos es lo que son!" I slammed the phone against the mattress.

I got out of bed and stomped my feet on my way to the bathroom, as if Mom could hear me from Colombia. My phone rang again, but I didn't pick it up. I jumped in the shower and begged for the water to cool my anger. I had agreed to help Mom when the bills at home were too high for her to manage. It was supposed to be a temporary arrangement until Santiago found a job, but two years had passed, and the only job he seemed to be good at was drinking and spending my money.

When I got out of the shower, I had three missed calls from her. I didn't return them.

That was the life I had left on pause back in Colombia. If I didn't find some means to stay, I'd pick up my story exactly where I'd left it three years earlier. The same old house, the overwhelming money problems, the everlasting uncertainty about my future. Only now, I'd be returning as the backbone of a shattered family, trying to move forward, forever pulled back by the weight of a mother and brother who were engrossed in a lifestyle I refused to live.

It's not what Dad had wanted for us. For me.

I rummaged around the kitchen for something to eat, pondering about the other, more creative options I had to avoid going back.

The obvious one was disregarding the date limit to exit the country when the time came. I wouldn't be the first or last to do it, so I had plenty of second-hand experience to draw from. Find a rental *efficiency* from a landlord who didn't mind leasing to an undocumented tenant, work por debajo de la mesa—off the books—or find other houses to clean during the weekdays and pray that I never got pulled over by a cop or needed medical assistance. I could become a ghost, invisible to the American government, absent from the Colombian one. The one setback was the permanence of that status. I wasn't ready to return home yet, but I didn't want to lock myself in the U.S. forever, to let decades pass before I could find a way to visit Bogotá or see my family again.

The other—less enticing—option was to marry someone por los papeles. But the last case I'd heard of was someone who had paid twenty-five thousand dollars to a Cuban American student, in three convenient installments. For two years, she lived the lie of a sham marriage, complete with a fake wedding, monthly meetups to take pictures to post on Instagram, and rehearsals of every possible question an immigration officer could throw their way. I could do it, but even if I could find someone desperate enough to go through the performance, where would I find twenty-five thousand bucks?

The solution—the Option A, Sofia-like solution—was to find a new sponsor company before Sunset kicked me out.

Chapter Six

I read Esteban's message about twenty times while on my way to meet him. *Grab a coffee.* He had only referred to it as coffee. Not a date. Just coffee with a stranger I met on the street. Yet thinking about him was the only event I looked forward to that night. Truth is, I was terrified of getting home—terrified of being alone with my thoughts, of knowing that each minute that passed meant less time to find a way to stay, of opening my email to find a *no new messages* headline. So, instead of driving home after work, I drove straight to the quaint café Esteban had suggested that morning.

Naturally, no parking spaces were available, and I spent three minutes in a mortifying display of parallel parking. I hoped he wasn't among the people witnessing me holding up traffic while I maneuvered my car back and forth with little results.

When I arrived at Café del Mar, Esteban had already texted me that he was waiting at a table. Standing in front of the entrance, I took a deep breath. What was I doing there? How could coffee with a stranger help in my situation? I paced uncomfortably around the entrance, calculating the odds of the night ending well. I was practically out of a job, and—I shuddered at the thought—on the verge of deportation. It wasn't only irresponsible—it was reckless to think about a date. I should've gone straight home to search for new job postings or research other options. Maybe even stalk Dianelys on LinkedIn.

Then again, what harm could come from a cup of coffee? I had spent the past week working my ass off, job searching, house cleaning, rethinking my every move. Didn't I deserve a short break, too?

I took a deep breath and forced my feet to cross the café and enter the patio, perusing the tables for this mysterious stranger who had shown up seconds after the crash. I had walked into so many bars, parks, and Starbucks to meet up with blind Bumble dates that I was used to bracing myself for disappointment when the picture didn't match the real-life version.

My eyes met his just as he looked up from his cell phone.

And my breath caught in my throat.

Meeting Esteban was different. Sure, I had met him before, but my heartbeat had been racing, my mind was preoccupied with the interview and my car was all squashed up. The coffee meetup felt like the very first time.

He flashed a smile that stopped my heart, and he lifted his hand in a quick, welcoming wave. I realized I was more nervous than tired. As I walked closer, I bumped my thigh against the back of an empty chair (one of those heavy iron chairs they use at fancy cafés) and I felt the color rise to my cheeks.

"Careful. You didn't survive a crash yesterday to crash into a chair today," he said as I sat.

"At least there wasn't anyone sitting on this chair, right?" I laughed, and I was surprised at how easy our greeting was. It flowed organically, without expectations.

After ordering cortaditos (I wanted to keep it as inexpensive as possible, and apparently, he liked cortaditos) and going over the mandatory first date topics (traffic, Miami weather, and how hard it is to find a parking spot in Brickell), the conversation took off. He asked if I had felt any pain from the accident, if I had been to that café before, if I lived close to the area. I loved how he paused and listened to my answers, tilting his head just a bit, ignoring the noise and the distractions around us.

The sun was at that glorious spot where hints of orange and golden streaks colored the air. A side of his face glowed under one of those streaks like a spotlight. I noticed details I had missed entirely the prior day. His skin was like toasted honey, with stubble covering his jaw. His eyes matched his hair and thick eyebrows, dark brown, and he was studying me with the same intense curiosity with which I was inspecting him. And he smiled, often. Perhaps that's what made me feel so at ease.

"Have you lived in Miami a long time?" he asked.

"Almost three years. Not sure if that counts as long."

"By Miami standards, I'd say it's above average." He grinned. "Your English is definitely better than mine, and I've been here for over twenty years." That made me happy. To have someone who had lived in Miami for so long think of me as a local. "¿Donde lo aprendiste?"

"I vacationed here with my dad when I was ten. He made us watch TV and collect books in English to bring back home. We were only allowed to talk in English when we were here." A small lump formed in my throat. The part of my heart Dad had taken with him was still tender. "When we went back, we could sing all the TV jingles in English while they played in Spanish."

"By *we* you mean ...?" he asked, not breaking the line of sight of his deep brown eyes for a second.

"My brother Santiago and I. He's still in Colombia."

He nodded. "Is your father also in Colombia?"

"He passed five years ago." I leaned back on the chair and gazed at the calm water on the bay, thinking how it had been Dad's dream to do exactly what I was doing at that moment. "He wanted to move to Miami. After he was gone, I felt like nothing was left for me in Bogotá. So, I moved here." I pressed my lips into a line, wondering if it was a mistake to share so much, so fast. But there was nothing but genuine interest in his face. He hadn't even touched his coffee yet.

"And your brother?" he pressed.

"Stayed home with Mom." The thought of them kindled the anxiety I had ignored all day. "But I had to get out. Moving here was my way of living Dad's dream." My voice broke with the last two words. The conversation had taken a turn I wanted to avoid. Talking about Dad was something I saved for a fourth or fifth date. I wasn't sure how it had slipped in so easily with Esteban.

"I'm sorry about your dad. I can tell you miss him very much," he offered. Those piercing eyes had not left mine for a second. "I think you made a good decision coming here. For him, and you."

Everyone criticized my decision—from my great-aunts to the boyfriend I broke up with before I left. At times, I had my doubts, too.

"It gets tough at times—not having my family around." I wondered briefly what it would be like if Mom and Santiago lived in Miami, and a shiver ran through me. That was a question I would rather leave unanswered.

All around us, the colors were slowly shifting to violet, and the far-off sound of traffic was replaced by wind and chatter. A pretty waitress swung by and asked if we needed anything else. He paused for an instant, giving me a quick look as if he was assessing something. That demure glance made my pulse quicken beyond explanation. Then, he asked for the menu.

My credit card balance popped into my mind. "Oh no, that's okay. I'll eat something at home."

"Really? The food's good here." He looked at me with big, hopeful eyes and waited.

I hesitated, but it lasted only a second. Surely, it'd be more time-efficient to grab a quick bite and focus on the job search when I got home. When I agreed, he almost looked relieved.

I scanned the menu down the price column for the cheapest item—a tomato bisque—and decided that would be my dinner, even if my stomach would be clamoring for something solid in less than two hours. It was already out of budget if I added tax and tip, but frankly, I could give the lentil soup a break. Also, I wasn't ready for the conversation with Esteban to be over. The waitress took our order and scurried away, zigzagging between the tables of the packed café.

It was my turn to ask the questions. "What about your family? Are they here?"

"No. They gave Miami a try, but eventually went back to Puerto Rico."

"Puerto Rico?" I exclaimed, faster than I intended to. I suspected he was from an island, given how his pronunciation thickened and how he switched his Rs to Ls when he let Spanglish take over. But even after years of meeting people from all corners of the Caribbean, it was hard for me to differentiate between Spanish-speaking islands. His answer sparked an entirely new level of interest, adding yet another reason for me to like him and to find a way for him to like me back. He was from Puerto Rico. He was American.

I took a slow sip of my coffee and nodded, trying to hide all traces of excitement by making a disinterested *Mmmm* for him to go on.

"They worked here when I was a kid, but missed the family they left behind. My grandparents were still alive back then. After a few years of living in Miami with their hearts back in Puerto Rico, they moved, and I stayed with my aunt." His eyes briefly gazed at the bay behind us as if he could see his island on the horizon. "I was eight, and I didn't remember what life was like in San Juan. I didn't want to leave my school, my friends."

"That was a big decision to make when you were so little."

"I can't take all the credit. My parents were set on returning, but even they wanted me to stay here."

When I told Mom I was moving to Miami, she was furious. She attributed the source of Dad's cancer to the work shifts he did in Miami during our vacation, which were *underpaid, like every job done by immigrants in that country*. She didn't like that I was moving away, but after I sent the first check home, she had a change of heart. All she ever questioned now was the frequency of my money transfers.

"Would you go back to Puerto Rico now?"

"No," he exclaimed, then seemed to regret his rash answer. "I might go back someday. But not now. I love it here. My parents are happy there. We're all good."

The waitress set the plates down, and I was relieved I'd decided to order, even if it pushed my credit card balance sixteen bucks closer to its concrete ceiling.

"What about you?" he asked. "Would you go back to Bogotá?"

That seemingly innocent question was enough to catapult me back to real life. Of course, I didn't want to go back, but every event in my life forecasted that I'd soon be back to sharing a room with Santiago (Um, and with Lorena?). Why was I even out, spending money I didn't have and watching the sunset from Café del Mar, instead of getting my life together? My mind started racing.

What am I getting out of this date, again?

Maybe I can ask him if he knows of any job openings!

Would that make me appear opportunistic?

I mean, he saw my ugly car, and he still gave me his card.

I don't want to ruin the evening by asking him for a job.

He's from Puerto Rico. He has a job. He's hot ...

Since he was still waiting for an answer, I put together something that wasn't a lie. Something that he might've wanted to hear. "I ... no. I love Miami. It hasn't been long, but I feel I'm more from here than there. Is that weird?" I bit my lip, worried that he might sense something was amiss.

"No, I get you. That's exactly how I feel."

I smiled, glad to feel that the conversation about life decisions was ending. Later, I'd find the right moment to ask him about job opportunities and relationship status.

Talking with Esteban that afternoon had an intense, surreal element to it. The events at Sunset were so fresh that I almost felt as if they belonged to someone else, so I could navigate all his questions without even thinking about the grace period on my visa. How weird would it be to tell a man I'd just met that I was about to lose my job, and my days in Miami were on a countdown clock? I kept the conversation flowing, enjoying that precious pocket of joy life granted me before landing hard on my real life.

"So, what do you do? I mean, besides being beautiful and avoiding driving lessons."

My stomach dipped a little when he called me beautiful.

"I work in Marketing at Sunset Cosmetics," I rushed to say. The words soon-to-be-unemployed flashed in big red font in my mind.

"Impressive." His eyebrows raised in tandem.

"You think?"

"Yeah, marketing positions are hard to come by. Too many applicants and not many spots available."

He was right, of course. The same old positions kept popping up in my LinkedIn feed night after night. My resume was probably drowning in a sea of resumes for each submission. "You are right. The market's a little saturated now."

"Do you like it?"

"You mean, do I like my job?"

He nodded.

I had no issue coming up with an answer. Other than Giselle's constant requests for favors, Rafael's creepy looks, the excess of testosterone in upper management, HR micromanaging my arrival time, and ... oh! the fact that they were moving my position to Mexico almost without warning, yes, I did like the *marketing* side of it. I liked promoting a product I loved, sending it out to the world to test if others were as excited about it as me. I came up with the answer that put me in the most favorable light. "I do. Sunset has a great product and is quite an aspirational industry."

"Are you good at it?"

I laughed. I liked his bluntness. "I like to think I am."

In between the banter, I found myself inching closer, holding his gaze for even longer periods, instinctively lowering my voice until it was a velvety sound meant just for him. The chatter, the traffic noise in the distance, and the rest of the world disappeared. And suddenly I didn't want to leave that table.

"How long have you worked at Altamira?"

His eyes narrowed. "How do you know I work there?"

"I'm one of your potential clients. Remember?" I exclaimed, a little too enthusiastically, lest he believe I had cyber-stalked him in the past day, despite the many times I had thought about doing it.

"Right. My business card." His face relaxed again. "Almost two years now."

"That's not too long. Almost the same time I've been with Sunset."

The corner of his mouth curved up in an almost imperceptible smirk. "Well, I'm open to other opportunities if you happen to hear of any."

"But two years at a company is nothing."

"They've been restructuring for a while, and I want to jump off that boat before it sinks."

I opened my eyes wide, surprised at how easy it was for him to ask for a work recommendation on a first date. I couldn't pinpoint whether his drive was crass or utterly brilliant. "I think I have a lot to learn from you."

"From me?" He laughed. "No. It's the other way around."

"What could you possibly learn from me?" I asked, curiosity flickering deep in my belly.

"I'd say it's obvious." He lowered his voice, almost as if trying to shield his words from the dozens of people surrounding us. "You're keeping the memory of your father alive. You've lived here for just three years, and you've done more with your life than most people I went to school with."

I knew better than to make a big deal about it, just like the women in the sequined dresses, who probably never responded to a compliment with giggles and blushing cheeks. I muttered a thank you, but I couldn't help the warmth from spreading through my body.

Where did he find the secret formula for the words I needed to hear?

More importantly, how would I ask him for a job after that?

I knew I had to go home, back to facing reality, but during those perfect hours, all I wished for was to be everything on his list. I wanted to be a beautiful woman with a successful career on a first date with a handsome man at a pretty café. I wanted to see myself the way he looked at me, just for a little longer.

When the waitress placed the bill at the exact center of the table, I turned to fetch my credit card—months of blind dating had trained me to do so, despite being broke. Also, I had sold my apparent financial independence to Esteban so much that night that the most logical action was for me to cover my part.

When I had the card in my hand, he had already slipped his to the waitress. I was relieved. Also, I was a little bummed that I had refrained from ordering a sandwich with my soup.

We walked out of the café together.

"So ... I'm glad your back isn't hurting or anything."

"Thank you." I was glowing. "It was nice of you to check on me."

I took a small step back towards the street where my car was parked, still looking at him.

"So, if it's okay, I can check back on you tomorrow." He ran his fingers through his hair in the most adorable way I'd seen, confident with a dash of nervousness. "You know ... sometimes the whiplash effect shows up two to three days after an accident."

I feel my lips curve. "Well, you were the only witness, so that's the least I'd expect from you." I leaned forward to kiss him goodbye by pressing my right cheek against his and blowing a kiss, the way I've done my entire life. In the process, I placed one hand on his shoulder, feeling its firmness under his shirt. The scratch of his stubble against my skin made me giddy, and it took me a moment longer than necessary to remove my hand and turn around.

I had to use every ounce of control in me not to skip to my car.

That night at my apartment, I reached entry number fifty on my application log. I figured fifty applications was some sort of milestone, and that one good YES was close. With my stomach protesting for more food, I went to bed.

Just as I was falling asleep, a text message came through.

Esteban: I want to see you again.

Rafael had to apologize. Or at the very least acknowledge what he'd done was a shitty, insecure, condescending move. The conversation with Esteban had helped me realize I deserved to be in that conference call as much as the others, especially if they were planning to take credit for my idea. I was fuming that morning as I hopped on the elevator and hit the six on the pad with more force than necessary. Traffic had given me the chance to imagine at least fifteen different versions of how I'd bring up the Zoom showdown to him—each one of them ending with a heartfelt apology. I hoped my crafted arguments wouldn't fade when I confronted him.

I switched my Havaianas for my worn suede pumps, the bare metal of the heels clashing against the porcelain floor, and rushed to the door before anyone else emerged from the elevators. I knew how much work was waiting for me that Wednesday morning. I knew that Giselle would be circling my cubicle by noon like a hungry shark to ask for help on another client pitch. And I didn't know in what mood Rafael would be in, so I took a deep breath before I pressed my badge over the entry pad.

Instead of the usual *beep* and the clacking sound of the lock, the pad was silent.

I tried again.

Nada.

I turned the badge in my hand, puzzled. The Sunset logo was still strong against the bright orange background. The *Sofia Rodriguez* was almost completely faded. Was there some emergency drill I wasn't aware of? Some reset of the entry system no one had told me about?

I stretched my neck, trying to catch if there was someone inside, and little beads of sweat were collecting on my forehead. Surely there was something wrong with the pad. My badge was working fine yesterday. Everything was fine. Yet the questioning looks I was getting from the flawless women in the reception posters, shielded by the glass doors that refused to budge, said everything was *not* fine.

A loud *ding* from the elevator broke the silence, and the hall was filled with the clack of heels and the halo of a flowery and expensive scent. I didn't have to turn around to find out who it was.

"Morning, hun." Giselle purred behind me.

"Morning, Giselle," I said, embarrassed to be standing outside the office doing absolutely nothing with a non-working badge in my hand. "Um, my badge isn't working."

I said it like it was the most common thing at our office. Like it happened to at least one employee daily. But the way she looked at me, intuitively arched her eyebrow, and the corner of her mouth curled up like she had just been granted the juiciest piece of gossip, made my heart crumple.

She pulled her orange badge out of her Chanel bag and swiped it against the pad.

It beeped immediately, and then there was the familiar click of the door.

"Mine does."

Chapter Seven

Giselle strutted in, waving her long hair every few steps like an animal marking territory with her scent. I followed a few feet behind, eyes set on the white tiles, and went straight to Rafael's office. He hadn't arrived, and José—the other director who could shed some light on the abrupt yet expected lockout—was busy in a conference call.

I hid behind the walls of my cubicle, rearranging documents, pretending to type something, going through the motions of a normal day while trying to slap the denial out of me. My computer login info was blocked, so I gingerly organized some of my belongings and packed them in a box. I did it in slow motion, careful not to let the sample glass vials clink together, or to produce any sound from papers falling in the trash bin. I didn't want anyone to know what was happening, because I wasn't very sure myself.

At ten a.m., Rafael walked in without saying good morning to anyone. I had gone through the five stages of grief at least three times by then, so I just sat and waited for his phone call. When it finally came—fifteen minutes later—I got up and walked quietly to his office, dreading what was to come, but yearning to get over it.

"Sofia, you had an exit interview scheduled at eight a.m. today." He ran his hand over his head. "They sent me an e-mail last night, but I was busy presenting the mascara plans. I just saw it now." I was taken aback when he said *he was busy presenting*, like this whole firing debacle was a nuisance to him.

"Am I out of a job?" My voice emerged distorted. I already knew the answer, but I needed to be certain. I needed to hear the words to make the idea sink in once and for all, and take me down with it.

He exhaled loudly. "Yes, Sofia. Today is officially your last day. They say they sent me a note a week ago, but I never received it."

I saw the clutter of notepads and Post-Its covering ninety percent of his desk and understood how the note announcing my last day of employment had been misplaced.

"I'm sorry things didn't work out. Please go back to your desk to pick up your things and give Maria from HR a call."

I didn't go to my desk. Instead, I locked myself in the last bathroom stall, my back against the tile wall. For a few minutes, I had the painful luxury of being alone with my thoughts, conscious that outside those doors, the news of my layoff was spreading through the office like weeds in an unkempt yard.

Sixty days. That's what the fine print said. I had a sixty-day grace period to leave the country or secure another status if my employment ended.

A chorus of approaching voices drifted through the door. I shut my mouth to keep my sobs silent and stood very still, hoping they would be quick. The clacking sound of at least three pairs of heels filled the bathroom.

"That's what Giselle said," said the first one.

"Pobrecita," answered the second.

"That's how things are here."

"Y se vá a quedar sin papeles."

Listening to those words spoken out loud shredded my heart to pieces. A tiny squeak escaped my throat.

"Wait." The first one stopped. And for a second, the restroom turned completely still. I froze, barely breathing, until I heard an exchange of whispers and the door closing.

I waited in absolute stillness but struggled to form a coherent idea. It was hard to move to the next step when the one I had been standing on had vanished into the air. I let those precious minutes creep by, accompanied only by my breathing, shuffling my cell phone. I wasn't ready to go out and face the world yet, not after listening to that conversation.

I'm unsure how much time passed before someone else entered the restroom. Evelyn's voice floated in the air, along with the faint scent of hand soap and designer perfume.

"Sofia. ¿Estás aquí?"

With a deep breath, I finally pushed against the stall door. Evelyn stood there, alone.

"I heard." Her voice was soft and reassuring.

"Does everyone know?"

"Does it matter?"

I scoffed. "Not really."

"What are you doing here?"

"I don't know ... hiding?" My voice broke with the last word.

She twisted her features into an expression that clearly communicated just how pitiful the answer had sounded, yet genuine compassion softened her eyes. "Dale, no pierdas el tiempo." *Don't waste time.* "Go pack your things. Call HR."

I sighed long and heavy. It came out ragged and uneven. Life had given me a thirty-minute break, and now it was time to reemerge.

"I don't even know where to start. I mean, what's my status now? Do I keep job hunting? Do I get a plane ticket?" I paced all over the bathroom, not letting my eyes meet Evelyn's or my own in the mirror.

"Cálmate, Sofia. You know you get a grace period, and it's much easier to find a job if you already have one."

"But I'm already unemployed."

"The companies where you're interviewing don't know that," she said while nodding, like she was giving me a very detailed set of instructions. "All I'm saying is that you don't waste a day. Make your follow-up calls now. You can always say that you found out about the lay-off at the end of the day."

I thought about it. I didn't have to lie to potential employers. Just ... twist the truth the slightest bit. It was time to give WorldMedia a friendly call. I gave Eve a tiny nod and muttered, "Thank you."

"Oh, and when you can, pass by my desk. I have a ton of product to give you." Then she winked, and I tried to smile back. Not all of them were witches, after all.

I spent the next ten minutes using the restroom as my private office, my fingers gingerly scrolling on my cell phone screen. Calling Dianelys at WorldMedia felt desperate, but I remembered Eve's advice. I was calling from the Sunset office because—as of that very moment—I was still a Sunset employee. I dialed her work number. I desperately needed to know if my best chance at a job and a visa was still alive. And she had given me her business card, which meant she was okay getting a call from me.

"I think I saw her walking into a meeting room," the receptionist said when I asked for Dianelys. "What's your name so I can tell her you called?"

"I'm Sofia. Sofia Rodriguez. It's with regards to the Senior Account Manager position." It was a mouthful, that title. I couldn't wait to tag it next to my name. "I met with her and Linda Prentice on Monday."

"So-fi-a-Ro-dri-guez." I heard her mumble, probably jotting my name down. "Right. I'll have her call you. Have a great day!" She hung up immediately after.

Pressing the phone against my ear, I froze while trying to decipher the meaning behind those words. The familiar sense of anxiety threatened to show up, but I managed to hold it at bay. That position was mine. Linda had made it practically clear.

When a text message came in, I was about to call HR for the infamous exit interview and—most importantly—to ask if I was receiving any severance.

Esteban: Have you felt any pain today?

I liked how the message wasn't prefaced by anything else, like it was the continuation of a conversation that had started a long time ago. My face softened, a flutter of joy stirring in me, then it quickly tightened up again. How could I feel excited about a message from some random man I'd just met, when my life had just been turned upside down? I decided to give him the least amount of my attention, replying with a curt,

Sofia: No pain, thank you for asking.

Dragging my feet to my cubicle, I tried with all my might to keep my head high. I ignored the reminder I had set to turn in an eleven a.m. report—not my problem anymore. I refused to sign up for lunch when the lunch delivery sign-in sheet went around the office, knowing I didn't have a dollar to spare for fancy salads. When lunchtime came, I sat down with everyone else, and answered all the questions that came my way, making sure to mention—clearly and without shame—I was looking for a job. I thanked those who said they'd keep an eye out for openings. I even pretended not to listen when the far side of the office cheered because Giselle had single-handedly secured a new client after only one meeting. The only reason she signed that client was because I had worked on her pitch deck and cut out the work for her. But what did it matter? She took the credit while I ignored the sound of her heels clacking all over the office, receiving the congratulations she had promised to share with me.

I threw everything together without caring who heard the racket, then hit Evelyn's desk for all the product samples she'd promised—even asking for extras while at it. Maria from HR confirmed what seemed inevitable: no severance pay was coming my way. After giving Rafael some pointless thank-you for the "opportunity," it was back to place my useless badge next to the laptop. With my cardboard box in arms, I walked through that office one last time, leaving behind a chapter that had obviously reached its end. The box wasn't heavy, and I still struggled to get my feet to move faster. It was as if the combined weight of all my hopes and dreams had landed with the makeup samples, which seemed to be the only inheritance I was taking with me. I could feel multiple pairs of curious eyes on the nape of my neck, but I didn't think about them twice. It was only a matter of days, maybe even hours, before they would find out that I had been hired by WorldMedia, against all odds, under work conditions far greater than anything Sunset had offered.

Then I spotted Giselle at her oversized, window-facing desk. She alternated between a PowerPoint deck and a spreadsheet on her computer screen. I recognized the same deck I had done for her the previous week. Only the cover now had a different retailer name. She switched between the table I had created to calculate growth projections and the pretty slide that presented the data, back and forth, more times than I could count. A hand flew up to her forehead, and even from a few feet behind, I heard her grunt.

I'm not sure what pushed me to move closer. Maybe it was a hidden desire to discover what made her so successful, despite relying on everyone else for the most basic tasks. I found myself inches behind her, staring incredulously at how the cursor hovered over the Excel spreadsheet, like she was hoping for the correct numbers to magically appear.

"Hi, Giselle." My voice came out cheerier than I meant it to.

She gasped, a hand with perfectly manicured nails reaching her heart. "Sofia, you scared me." Her eyes went to the cardboard box shielding my torso, and there was the same expression I'd gotten from the rest of the office, one I could only describe as *limited empathy*. That is, enough to generate pity but not enough to elicit action.

"Congratulations on signing the client," I said.

"Oh, thank you," she answered, her tone cautious.

I stood there, realizing I had nothing to say, and waited until it got awkward. Then my eyes hovered over to the screen, and a spark of opportunity shone in her face.

"I have this meeting in thirty minutes," she said with her usual confidence.

"Oh," I replied with absolutely no emotion in my voice.

"I'm trying to find where these numbers come from." She floated the cursor over the line of cells with the totals, making a disapproving face as if something was wrong with my spreadsheet.

I waited, embracing the moment's discomfort, until I was sure she was setting the tone to ask for help. I already had a foot out the door, and she was the one who'd been applauded for her latest success. I wanted her to know she couldn't have done it without my help.

"I think there's something wrong with the formula here," she offered, but her encouragement did not affect me.

"Um ... yeah, I remember that one," I said before shutting my mouth again.

She turned from her laptop to face me, and I stared right back. I could sense the steam fuming from her eyes, the silent outrage at my defiance. I stretched the silence long enough to make her uncomfortable. There was something satisfying in watching her dig herself deeper into the mud of her own making.

"Well, I have to go." I fixed my hold on the cardboard box and turned around. Then, over my shoulder, I said, "Goodbye, Giselle."

It might not have been much, but the sheer elation that came from giving her a silent NO was enough to power me for those last few steps.

She'd find another minion, of course. People like her always do. And perhaps that wasn't something necessarily bad. Perhaps her superpower (and Rafael's) was how they could delegate and ask for help, and still show up to meetings glowing confidently at presenting someone else's work. I stored that gem of experience deep in my soul, along with the few happy memories I had made at Sunset.

As I approached the glass doors, the same ones that had refused to let me in earlier that day, my resolution faltered. In some crazy way, they reminded me of the security doors right past the airport security checkpoint, with the NO RE-ENTRY warning me that once crossed, I'll never be able to return. As I got closer to the exit, I felt like Bogotá was waiting for me on the other side, with the cold, traffic, and smog, and Mom and Santiago expecting me to figure out how to keep our little family afloat.

My knees buckled and I almost lost my grip on the box. Was this actually happening? What if WorldMedia didn't call? Was I destined to return to Colombia without a second chance?

Time must have stretched beyond notice, because the HR associate suddenly appeared to offer help with the cardboard box. I managed a quick nod and a vague gesture toward the exit. I can't even remember if I thanked the person or not.

I crossed the exit at Sunset Cosmetics and didn't turn around.

"Where'd you find him, again?" Nina's eyes widened when I showed her Esteban's Instagram profile image. I had spent the entire day pacing around my apartment like a caged lion, making follow-up calls that led nowhere, and dodging calls from Mom. When, at the end of the afternoon, Nina asked me over to her place, I practically flew over. It took me an hour to bring her up to speed with everything that happened at Sunset (to which Nina responded with a string of cuss words in Portuguese), and then we spent the next hour plotting my next move. We were making a list of people to contact when I decided to mention Esteban.

"I told you," I replied with a smug smile. "I met him in the middle of the street."

"You met him," she pointed at me and then at my cellphone as she said it, "by *chance*, just before the WorldMedia interview?"

"Uh-huh." I had to press my lips together to keep a huge grin from spreading.

"And you still have the nerve to say my dress isn't lucky?!" Nina rolled her eyes as she waved the wooden spoon she was holding.

"That's under consideration. I might wear it to the next interview I get called to test its powers."

The wooden spoon slowly made it back to the skillet. A playful smile had appeared on her lips. "Did you tell this Esteban person you're looking for a job?"

"Ah ... no ... I mean, the topic didn't come up, and I wasn't officially let go then. And we just met, I couldn't—"

"Add him to the list, girl." She pointed at the notepad with the spoon that was now covered in creamy pink sauce.

"Ugh, I don't know, Nina."

"You have to do it. He might know of someone who can help."

Her kitchen smelled of shrimp and tomatoes, and every inch of the counter was covered with ingredients. Nina was not the most gifted cook, but she liked to experiment. She liked to think her inner Brazilian goddess would eventually take over and concoct a meal so delicious and rare that it would make me fall in love with Brazilian food forever. She insisted she was using me as practice for the homemade dinner she would cook for her family someday. Her camarão na moranga was one of my favorite dishes.

"I can't believe you went on a date without telling me," she said.

"Sorry. I didn't think of it as a *date*. I just needed a break so bad."

"I understand that, but you still have to tell me. What if he ended up being a psycho or something?"

"We met at Café del Mar. I don't think he'd be able to abduct me in public view."

"Right ..." She turned back to the cast-iron skillet. "Plus, with that face, you might end up abducting him instead."

We exploded into laughter. Then she went back to cooking. The scent of the shrimp stew made my mouth water.

"Seriously, Sofia. Just send me a text before you meet up with anyone. I don't care if you met through Bumble or in a parking lot."

I stared at Nina. My brilliant friend in her beautiful apartment was cooking for me. I wanted to leap off the stool and hug her. In many ways, I felt closer to her than I had ever felt with Mom. If I had to return to Colombia, Nina would be a big thing I would be leaving behind.

That thought alone cast a shadow on my face.

"Nina." I had to contain a sudden urge to cry. I couldn't pack Nina into a suitcase. I couldn't pack my independence, my security. I couldn't bring the palm trees, the turquoise artificial lakes I loved, the silver Miami skyline. "Promise me we'll still be friends if I go back to Colombia."

"Nossa! De novo com essa conversa," she exclaimed, raising her arms to the ceiling. "You aren't going anywhere, Sofia!"

"They haven't called from WorldMedia."

"It's only been three days!" she exclaimed, tasting the stew before she poured it into a roasted hollow pumpkin. She spread grated Parmesan cheese on top and returned the overflowing pumpkin to the oven, making a congratulatory clap. "There'll be more than enough for you to take home."

Nina's apartment stretched behind me. White marble floors sat flush against the floor-to-ceiling glass windows. In the far corner, a sliding door led to an oversized balcony. Twinkling lights from the adjacent buildings began showing as the sun set. An image for one of those gorgeous Miami postcards was probably taken from Nina's balcony. The interior décor was pragmatic and modern, free of textures or complicated pieces: a white sofa, contemporary and expensive, though a little stiff and uncomfortable; a coffee table with a clay sculpture of a naked woman on top; three abstract canvas paintings on the walls.

Nina was only one year older than me—*one year*. I lived like a thirteen-year-old compared to her.

"Are you okay, Sofi?" Her voice—soft and mellow for Nina's standards—snapped me back.

My shoulders slumped under the weight of the day's events. Outside, daylight was fading rapidly, with heavy rain clouds gathering along the horizon. I had to hurry before Togo made a mess in Catalina's apartment. Despite the urgency, I needed to get something off my chest first.

"I think Santiago's new girlfriend moved in," I said. I was still staring out the balcony, not daring to look at Nina.

There was a second that all I heard was the rush of water hitting the kitchen sink. It did little to mask the memory of Lorena's laughter in my mind. Nina took a long time to say something—enough time for me to worry. Quiet Nina was scarier than loud Nina.

"How do you know?"

"Mom kinda mentioned it when she called yesterday."

"And you are okay with that?" I sensed a change in her tone, a bitterness, when I mentioned my family.

"I don't know ... I don't know what to think." I finally turned around to face her. She was pulling the moranga out of the oven. A golden layer of cheese bubbled on top. "I don't live there. Do I have a say in how they live their lives?"

"Well, if you are sending them money, I'd say the answer is yes. Yes, you do have a say." She served two heaping plates, splashing spoonful after spoonful of the creamy mixture. Her knuckles had turned white around the handle of the wooden spoon. Little specks of sauce flew everywhere, but I knew her thoughts had shifted to more pressing topics.

"In any case, that's gonna stop soon." I let my shoulders slouch even more.

She rolled her eyes. "Did you talk to Santiago?"

"I messaged him this morning. He hasn't replied."

"Darn it, Sofia!" she exclaimed. I feared for the wooden spoon. "If I were you, I'd be ringing him nonstop. *Every day*. Until he picks up and gets his shit together."

"I know, but I can't ditch them without warning. Not until they have a steady income."

"Ohmigod, you realize that's what you've been saying for years, right? Has anything changed?"

"Things are different over there. And if you think about it, I was only sending *a portion* of my paycheck, and it was enough for them to live. I can't be so selfish as to be here and not help them."

"Okay." Nina took a deep breath, as if trying to summon the sample of patience she had buried somewhere in her soul. "First of all, you lost your job to someone *in Latin America*, so don't tell me there are no jobs. Clearly, some people are getting hired. Second, if you had saved the $500 you send every month, you wouldn't be so stressed now because you'd have at least some savings—something to get you by for a couple of months. And third, this is what happens when lazy people get free money. They get used to it. Why on Earth would Santiago look for a job when you made it so easy for him?"

"But that's the thing. It isn't easy for him! I feel they are always struggling to make ends meet."

"Because he doesn't want to work!" she yelled, then pressed her middle and ring fingers to her forehead while she inhaled deeply. I had seen her doing this a few times in the past, and the outcome was always the same.

She was winning this argument.

"Do you know where he was last night?" She articulated the words to her lips' fullest potential. "He was posting at three a.m. Sofia. Looking like shit. On a weeknight! He doesn't have money to pay rent, but he does have enough to get wasted. Tell me again how you are *not* making it too easy for him?"

Of course, I didn't want to admit it, but every word she said made sense to me. Had I inadvertently trained my brother to depend on me by helping Mom? They expected a deposit to their bank account on the second of every month, and they asked for more if they ran out before the next deposit.

We sat down to eat in silence. The food was delicious. I didn't tell Nina that my last decent meal had been my tomato bisque with Esteban. I wished I had more time to savor it, but the rain clouds were coming closer, and I hated to walk Togo when it was raining.

"Why are you eating so fast?" Nina asked.

"I have to go walk Togo." My voice came out like a whisper.

Nina just kept eating, shaking her head. "*Amiga,* I don't even want to go there."

Chapter Eight

The first drops of rain fell right after Togo had done his business. I patted his head, shaking off the droplets that had landed on the fur between his eyes. He looked up at me and wagged his tail. It was his beautiful way of saying thank you.

"You need to teach your owner to be more grateful, buddy," I said softly.

When the rain picked up, we ran to the building entrance for shelter. We sat on the entry steps and contemplated the downpour. I loved the rain, but I couldn't see it from my apartment, and Togo was more than happy to join me.

A text message came through, and I thought it would be Nina. I checked my phone and smiled to see Esteban's name.

Esteban: Have you been to Aura?

Sofia: I have. It's beautiful when the weather is nice.

Esteban: It's supposed to be nice tomorrow night.

Sofia: Oh. Are you going then?

Esteban: Kinda looking for someone to come with me.

My composure threatened to crack as my pulse skittered and raced. Aura was a trendy new restaurant bar that turned into a nightclub after hours. I had met a few Bumble dates there before, and none had gone well.

Sofia: What a coincidence. I'm free tomorrow night.

Esteban: I'll meet you there at 8.

Later, after Togo had been dried off and safely locked in his apartment, and I had changed into PJs and shimmied into bed, I texted Nina. I knew I wouldn't fall asleep if we were on bad terms.

Sofia: Hey

Nina: Oi

Sofia: I'm sorry about earlier.

Nina: It's ok. I'm sorry I snapped.

Nina: I just hate to see people taking advantage of you.

Sofia: I know. And I'll figure something out. I promise.

I stared at my last text, wondering how much of that promise was to Nina, and how much of it was for me.

Sofia: I'm going out for a drink at Aura with Esteban tomorrow night.

Nina: Thanks for telling me, Sofi. Be safe. Love you.

Sofia: Love you too.

The eclectic vibes of the Aura lounge, with its demure lighting and chill music, didn't match the deranged beat of my heart as I made my way through the crowd. The anticipation of seeing Esteban again had intensified with the same speed as the elevator that soared me forty flights above ground to a place that made me feel like I was on top of the world. With the city lights brightening up the terrace, and the sticky breeze threatening to awaken every frizzy strand in my hair, the rooftop exuded an attitude that was hot and irrevocably sexy. One of those locations from where I couldn't just see the Miami skyline, I was *in* the Miami skyline.

I made my way through the curvy bodies, the tight bodies, and the sweat-glistened skins in all shades of white and brown. Was I one of them? Did I fit their standards? Pretty, yes. Hot, maybe. I still felt I needed to push through some invisible barrier to truly *belong*.

The last time I was there, it took me four minutes to identify my Bumble date at the bar. The men there were all perched on their cell phones and looked like the guy on the profile image. But this Friday night was different. I scanned the bar, knowing exactly who I was looking for. I searched for a match to his shoulders, the dark hair that framed his face, and the edge of his jaw full of stubble that had grown during the day. I had revisited his image so many times since Tuesday. It was just a matter of matching it to the right contestant at the bar. Only he wasn't there.

With a deep breath, I extracted my phone and hovered my thumb over his name. A couple sitting at the bar were staring at me, most likely adding one more tally mark to the list of stranded women at Aura.

Two long tones crept by.

Just as it occurred to me how easy it would be for him to walk out of my life before even crossing the entry door, I heard his voice rising above the chatter.

"Sofia!"

I swiveled around, scanning the tables this time, until our eyes met.

Esteban stood beside a table, holding his cell phone and waving at me. He was wearing a smoky gray shirt, the top two buttons undone. Enough skin was showing to see the exact break where his stubble ended. Enough to make my pulse quicken.

A menu was laid out in front of him, and another was waiting for me. Then it occurred to me that Esteban was sitting at a table, not at the bar, at a place with appetizers starting at thirty dollars.

That's when my mind ricocheted back to my bank account.

The thing is, I knew the place well. I knew every price on the menu. I knew cocktails were twenty-four dollars each, excluding tax and tip. So, every time I had met a Bumble date at Aura, I ordered a glass of the cheapest prosecco at the bar, sipped the bubbles slowly while assessing the contestant in front of me, then closed the tab and made up an excuse to go home. I would get ninety minutes of entertainment, followed by an internal alarm reminding me to leave before I had too much to drink or spent money I didn't have.

But Esteban wasn't just there for a drink.

He stood up as I approached the table and flashed his smile, making my legs melt. "Hey, gorgeous."

He was checking the menu while listening to the server's recommendations, asking me if I had tried the Korean ribs or the grilled cauliflower, but all I could think of was how much the splurge would cost me.

"Are we having dinner?" I asked in the most detached way I could. With one paycheck to go, not a dollar to my name, and the end of the month approaching, the last expense I needed was a flashy Miami meal. There I was, perched at an overpriced rooftop bar, watching my meager savings disappear into a cocktail I couldn't justify, across from a virtual stranger. One drink, I promised myself. Then I'd slip away.

"Let me get you our specials menu," the server said while shuffling through the menus on the table. "We change them up every week. You don't want to miss the miso black cod!" And off he went through the maze of tables until I couldn't see him anymore.

"Did you already eat?" Esteban asked.

"I had a little something because I didn't know we'd be having dinner."

"Sorry, I didn't mention it earlier. If you're up for it, we can order something small."

"Yeah, small sounds good." My stomach protested. What was leftover of Nina's shrimp stew didn't stand a chance against the golden coconut shrimp platter on the adjacent table. I followed the food with hungry eyes.

"That looks amazing," Esteban said, effectively reading my thoughts. "Why don't you order that, and I'll have whatever you don't eat so it doesn't go to waste?"

I didn't have the nerve to ask if he would pay like he did the last time—ew, crass. Instead, I chose to drown myself in uncertainty until the end of the night.

The server reappeared with the specials menu ready to take our drink and food order.

"Water for me. Thanks," I said first.

Esteban took another look at the menu, then up at me again.

"Have you tried the martinis here?"

I shook my head.

"They're really good."

"We make all our cocktails from scratch," the server announced with rehearsed enthusiasm.

I scanned the drink menu, and my mouth watered.

"Come on, my treat," he said in his mellow voice.

When I looked back up at Esteban, he had tilted his head and was staring at me with eyes widened, like he was trying to match the person in front of him to the peppy Sofia he had met three days earlier. That's when I realized it wasn't his fault that my life was deep in shit. He had asked me out, and I had knowingly accepted, and now I was competing to become the most boring date ever. I decided right there that it was Friday night, and I was hungry. I was with Esteban at Aura, and he was paying after all. It was probably one of my last chances to have a fantastic time in Miami.

"I'll have the lychee one with vodka," I said.

"Two of those," Esteban added.

The server scurried off, leaving me alone under Esteban's intense gaze. Although he was quiet, he had a hint of a smile on his lips, and I could tell he was studying me again.

"How was your week?" I asked. I had lost my usually confident tone, and I briefly wondered if he had figured out the effect he had on me.

"Work was good. We're getting ready to pitch Altamira to a new client, so I spent the past few days building a plan with my team."

"Sounds like you've been busy."

"And if we sign this client, there will be more work."

"More money for Altamira. Will they give another headcount if you sign?" I knew I was heading into dangerous territory. If he answered yes, would I have the guts to ask him if I could apply?

But the answer was so far from yes, it sent my mind on a spiral.

"No. I'm actually trying to negotiate a raise for myself."

"A raise?" My eyebrows almost reached my hairline. "For signing a client?"

He leaned back on his seat, his elbow resting on the low headrest. *So calm*. Not the slightest hint of self-doubt. He paused before he replied, "I think I deserve a promotion, even if we don't sign. But as you said, it's more money for the company. It should also represent more money for me."

"But you've only been there two years," I observed, eager to understand where his sense of self-entitlement came from.

"Doesn't make a difference."

I had been at Sunset for over two years, and it had never occurred to me to ask for a salary increase.

"What happens if you don't sign the client?" I asked.

"I've thought of that too. I'm looking for job offers from other companies. Offers that I can use to negotiate a higher salary."

"You are looking for a job that you don't need so you can climb the ladder faster at Altamira?" I was astonished. Was this a thing? Was it as normal as he made it sound?

"You make it sound a lot harsher than it is." He chuckled. "But it's actually pretty common."

"Okay ... so how is this completely unnecessary job hunt going?" I teased.

"It's good. It's going. I've been to a few interviews. The minute I get the offer, I'll walk into my manager's office to negotiate."

"You mean you'd reject the job offer?"

"That's right." He took a sip of his water.

I couldn't believe what he was saying. Here I was, struggling to get interviewed at any company, while he was applying for jobs he didn't even need because he wanted more money from the one he currently had.

You know, I'm actually open to other opportunities, too. If you happen to hear about one. The phrase swirled inside my head and reached my mouth, but I couldn't force the words out. I didn't want to spoil a perfect date by dumping my life problems.

The server returned with our drinks, and I took a huge sip of mine—anything to alleviate the rising tension in my neck, in my head, and down my back. I let the sweet, tangy notes spread on my tongue and travel down my throat. I took another sip. The week had been a rollercoaster of emotions. Maybe a drink was just what I needed to ask Esteban to keep an eye out for me during his job search.

"Are you even tasting those?"

"Sorry, I usually don't chug them like this." I felt the vodka notes swirling in my mouth. "I had a horrible week. I need to wind down somehow."

"Don't be sorry. You work hard, and it's Friday night."

"Cheers to that." I raised my glass to him, toasted the air, and took another sip.

"But tell me what made your week so horrible." He was serious, patiently waiting to hear my answer.

I swallowed while I stared at him, convinced I didn't want to drag him down with my endless repertoire of problems. Just for one night, just for a little while, I tried to pretend those problems didn't exist. I wanted to be one of those beautiful women at the Aura foyer, whose only worries were unrepeated weekend outfits, snapping a perfectly shareable picture, and their social media follower count.

"I'll tell you some other time." I shook my head. "Tell me about the food. What's the most amazing thing to eat here?"

He leaned back. I sensed he didn't like my evasion, but he respected it. According to my dating rulebook, a second date was still too early to go into the hard stuff.

At some point during the next hour, I calmed down and assured myself this was life's crazy way of giving me the break I deserved. Life wanted me to be a normal twenty-five-year-old, to work a little and have enough money left to splurge on expensive drinks, to party and be careless and free on the weekends.

That's what life wanted, and it had sent Esteban to help me accomplish it.

So, we talked about everything but work. I listened to his stories about his aunts and uncles drinking and partying during Las Fiestas de San Sebastian on his beautiful island, while he and his teenage cousins stayed up until five a.m. drinking rum from leftover cups and getting high a block away from their house. He heard about the only time I'd been to Disney World, how, even at ten, my eyes got watery watching the fireworks. It must have been the liquor talking when I told him how my parents first stopped at the dollar store to buy us Mickey souvenirs, because everything was too expensive at the park.

We talked about those two skinny kids we left behind all those years ago in Colombia and Puerto Rico, all their misfortunes and childhood dreams, until it felt like we were discussing two lives that didn't belong to us at all, like loose pages out of a storybook. With every story and every look, I felt more drawn to him. I craved a crash course on Esteban. I wanted to learn who he was and who he wanted to be, and how I could participate in the process.

One hour, two cocktail refills, and three meal courses later, the server announced the kitchen was closed, and so was the rooftop area where we were sitting. He mentioned the bar would be open for a few more hours and left the check right in the center of the table. My brain was so fuzzy it took me a few attempts to focus on the menacing black envelope. I have no idea how much our dinner and drinks cost that night, but the mere thought of the number was enough to sober me up.

I wanted to pay half of the bill—I really did. But behind all the noise, the lychees, and the music, I was still very much aware that I didn't have enough to cover the tip. When Esteban picked up the envelope and placed it back on the table with his credit card on it, I mouthed a thank you and smiled at him.

We moved to the bar, but we could barely hear each other over the music and the noise, so he took my hand and pulled me away from that area. His touch was electric, activating every nerve on my palm and sending goosebumps shooting up my arm. My fingers melded with his as he guided me through the maze of vacant tables, under a canopy of twinkling lights, behind the clusters of sweaty dancers, their collective energy pulsing through the floorboards. Midnight was a distant memory now, yet I felt no pull toward sleep or responsibility—only toward him. The warmth in his gaze told me everything I needed to know: he felt it too.

Plus, I had no cleaning duty the next morning.

We reached the veranda on the far side of Aura. An open area with glass walls overlooked the tops of the glimmering buildings, where the smell of weed and sweat from the bar dissipated and was replaced by the faint scent of morning dew. The light shows were fully displayed, painting Miami with silver and teal dancing lights. I stood there contemplating the nighttime beauty of the city (*my city?)*, and the flicker of hope I kept hidden in my heart grew into a flame. Miami welcomed me with open arms when nothing left for me in Bogotá. I refused to believe the same city could be so cruel as to kick me out. I hoped that in the same way Miami had put Esteban in my life, it would produce a solution for me to stay.

"Sofia?" His voice slashed through the music.

I turned around. Esteban was inches away, looking intensely at me instead of the view.

"Are you okay?" he asked.

"Sorry." I shook my head and turned back to the glass wall. "It's so beautiful up here."

And it was beautiful, but I couldn't help but wonder how my life would change if the image were replaced by a sea of brick buildings surrounded by mountains covered in fog.

"But?"

"Do you ever miss Puerto Rico?" I blurted out.

"Of course, I miss it. I was born in Puerto Rico. My family is there."

"Would you say you are from Miami, o de la isla?"

"I'm both," he said without losing a beat. "I'm a Boricua raised in Miami."

He said it with such confidence—a local in both cities and free entry to both places. Exactly what I wanted for myself.

"What about you?"

And there it was. The question I couldn't bring myself to answer. The constant agony over my migratory limbo. Too attached to Miami to want to return to Colombia. Too Colombian to live permanently in the United States.

The melody of a 90's song that had been remixed and relaunched at least three times boomed off the rooftop. The crowd slowly approached the secluded veranda, covering the floor with tourists, mini-dresses, and fake IDs. Esteban waited for an answer, but all I could think of saying was *I also want to be both.*

Instead, I pulled my hair up in a ponytail and turned to him.

"I think I need another drink."

The thing about having one too many cocktails that night was the hypersensitivity infused into my senses. My emotions were heightened, from the vibration of the music causing my skin to tingle, to the glow from all those lights casting violet shadows on the floor, to the warm scent emanating from Esteban's skin. The vodka twisted my perception of reality. My laughter was a little too loud, my movements were exaggerated, and my date was a little too funny. The perfect moment crystallized around us, and I knew instantly I wanted to capture it. My hand found my phone, and I pressed my lips close to Esteban's ear, shouting over the music that we needed a photo to remember this moment. He smiled and obliged, making sure he was in the picture with me. As he flipped the phone into selfie position, circling my waist with his arm so my ass was flush against his leg, I could feel the grit of his stubble against my cheek, and warm air caressed my neck. He waited for me to approve the picture before he set me loose. The separation made me feel like Esteban was standing yards away. I desperately wanted to close the gap between us.

We were moving to the same beat when the crowd closed in, decreasing the distance between us and the glass wall. When he put his hands on my lower back, I let him pull me closer, until we were breathing from the same pocket of air. My fingers interlocked behind his neck, closing the space between us even more. I could make out his features with absolute clarity. He had a subtle grin; his eyes locked with mine. He was taller than I, even with my heels on, which I had not realized until I felt my neck arching back.

And then he began to move.

He could dance; of course, he could. He was from Puerto Rico *and* Miami. He had it in him. He had probably grown up listening to the phrase "para levantar mujeres tienes que tener dinero, ser bonito, o saber bailar." To pick up women, you need to have money, look good, or know how to dance. He had two of those nailed down. Possibly all three.

I let him guide me, following his movements, and melting into his arms some more. We danced to some reggaeton-salsa-techno fusion until the floor became so crowded that I had no choice but to press my body against his completely. I don't have a small frame, but Esteban's body felt massive against mine. He emanated this energy I craved. I exhaled slowly to control my heart from beating so hard, leaning against his chest and turning my head to avoid facing him. I felt that if our eyes met again, I'd fall for him right there.

I was getting comfortable when the crowd shifted and cleared a path of vision. There was a tall table with a small group of people. They looked eerily familiar, though it was hard to tell. It was dark, after all, and my surroundings were distorted from the vodka. I zoomed in on one of the faces that looked most familiar and realized it was Eve from Sunset. Then, the other faces came into focus, including all Sunset employees. They were laughing and toasting, and one of them turned and made eye contact with me.

"Oh, shit."

"What is it?" Esteban pulled back to face me.

He'd want to say hi if I told him my work colleagues were there. Two dates with Esteban were enough to deduce that much. If I stayed where I was, one of them might come over, and I had no control over how the conversation would go. I was too tipsy to form coherent thoughts, and if Eve were to bring up my layoff, if she were to say something as innocent as *I miss having you around*, or *I'm sorry how it all went down*, well, I didn't have the mental clarity to explain anything to Esteban.

"I don't feel very well. Let's leave."

His hands had not left my lower back until that moment, and when they did, I knew I wanted them back.

"Are you okay?"

The one who made eye contact with me said something to Eve, and I felt my stomach twist. "I am, but it's getting so crowded in here."

When Eve turned to face our way, I grabbed Esteban's hand and pulled him in the opposite direction. To his credit, he didn't say much. He must have guessed I felt like crap, because he followed me straight to the exit. I kept going until we were safely inside the elevator with closed doors. I didn't know whether Eve had seen me or if she had searched for me in the crowd. But now that I was far away with Esteban, I felt safe.

We descended the forty floors on a packed elevator, the light pressure of his chest against my back keeping me from falling. He offered to walk me to my car a block away, parallel parked because it was the cheapest option I had found. My mind was a blur. It was hot, I was sweaty, and what little conscience I had was split between staying close to Esteban and keeping the vodka down.

When we reached my car, I fumbled in my bag for the keys.

"You can't drive," he said.

"I can't leave my car here. It'll get towed."

His fingers wrapped around my hand, holding the keys. "I'll drive you."

"You mean in my car?"

"Yeah. I'll drive you to your place."

I tried to process the idea, but my thoughts were like bumper cars at a carnival. I pictured Esteban behind the wheel of my *transportation*, which didn't even have a working A/C.

"It's the least I can do after I let you chug those drinks like water." His mouth tilted up, but his eyes showed a hint of guilt.

"What about your car?" I asked.

"I took an Uber. I live close by."

"Oh."

I let him slip the key from my hand, walk me to the passenger seat, open the door, and watch me drop ungracefully into the seat, despite my best efforts to appear sober. I hated that he was about to drive my crappy car, but I didn't want the night to end. Also, I was vaguely conscious of my inability to drive in such a state.

In those few seconds that it took him to walk around to the driver's seat, my heartbeat began to race, out of nerves or perhaps trying to get rid of the alcohol. I brought my hand up to my forehead, which did nothing to keep it from spinning. I would've preferred that he hadn't seen the poor state of my car so soon. I had left the fuel gauge arrow precariously hovering over the red E, and the speedometer hadn't worked in forever. I mentally begged my car to *please start and don't make any weird sounds*. It might have been the crazy energy I was emanating, but it started at the first try, and then I was in my car with Esteban driving it.

The date had gotten a lot more interesting.

If only my head would stop spinning.

"Is the A/C working?" he asked after turning it on and being blasted by a tornado of hot air.

"Haven't had a chance to fix it," I replied, then closed my mouth to keep the nausea down. The car started moving, and the entire world spun around me.

"I have a good mechanic I can recommend, if you want to." When I didn't reply because I couldn't open my mouth, he added, "Sorry, last thing you probably want to talk about is mechanics. I'll send you his contact."

I nodded, feeling the world expanding and collapsing around me.

"You do remember where you live, right?" He chuckled while he looked at me like I was a child.

Instead of attempting to direct him, I gave Esteban my address—a concession to my impaired state. He eased my old carrito into the late-night traffic, beginning a journey that would later exist in my mind only as scattered memories. The world around me had become a mush of sounds and lights. My mind was slowly shutting down, incapable of processing the signals around me. I ebbed in and out of consciousness, but there was an intense awareness of what little information I could take in: The glare from the traffic lights cast a red glow on Esteban's face; the loud music coming from a car on Brickell Avenue; Esteban's hand turning down the radio volume, then gently tucking some loose strands of hair behind my ear. The simple graze of his fingers on my skin was enough to send chills down all corners of my body.

Even in my state, I realized the decisive moment of *say goodnight and go to sleep* versus *fuck it all and ask him upstairs* was getting closer. A part of me didn't want to arrive home. That part—carnal, longing, lonely—wanted Esteban to drive forever. For his hands to venture further.

The other part of me was busy trying to keep the liquor from coming up my throat.

It was a miracle that I managed to keep it down while he parked my car, then guided me across the parking lot and into the lobby.

And then it was decision time.

"Thank you for dinner," I said while fumbling behind me to grab a handrail or a wall or something to keep me steady, "and for driving me home." I looked up at him, trying with all my might to focus on his eyes.

"Are you sure you don't need help getting to your apartment?" He grabbed my free hand, like he was afraid I would end up lost in the maze of corridors inside the building. It was warm and reassuring against my own. My entire body craved the moment we had at the rooftop, when our lips were just inches apart and we were breathing from the same air pocket.

Yes, I needed him. I wanted to get lost, disappear down a corridor, and have him rescue me. The need to have him carry me to my bed was overwhelming.

I looked down at our entwined fingers.

He didn't want to let me go.

He wanted me. Maybe even more than I wanted him. So I decided to stop fighting against my instinct. To let my body win.

I flipped my hair to the side, the same move Giselle did before work presentations. It always caused the men in the room to stir in their seats. Then I bit my lower lip and lowered my gaze, enough so that I had to look at him through my eyelashes. Then—to finish up my femme fatale combo—I said in my most seductive voice, "Is that what you want? To come up to my apartment?"

Only it didn't come out the way I intended it to. It was more croak than purr, with a hiccup at the end to top it off.

He opened his eyes very wide and shifted back a little. Then, to my absolute horror, he dropped my hand.

"Um ... Sofia. I just want to check that you make it okay."

The lobby's massive mirror ambushed me with my own reflection. My mascara had abandoned my eyelashes, leaving dark smudges around my eyes; my lipstick was a vague memory of its former precision; my hair bore no resemblance to Giselle's perfect flip—instead, it told the chaotic story of the night. I glanced down, surprised to find my shoes dangling from my fingers, with no recollection of when I'd liberated my feet. I wasn't a femme fatale.

I was a hot mess.

My head whirled as more hiccups appeared. When I gagged, and I had to hold my hand hard against my mouth, I knew my wish to pin Esteban against the elevator wall was a recipe for disaster.

"Are you okay?" I heard his voice between my hiccups.

For the love of God, keep it down. Don't let him see you like this.

"I'll call you tomorrow." My throat constricted as I clamped my hand over my mouth. Feeling Esteban's gaze burning into me, I lunged toward the elevator, slipping through the narrowing gap just as the doors were about to seal shut.

I crashed into my bed as if I had a sobriety elixir waiting on my pillow, but the room kept shrinking and expanding around me. The sour taste in my mouth reappeared, more intense by the second, then bubbled up in my throat.

My stomach yanked me up from bed, and I flew to the bathroom. I made it just in time to jet out buckets of the tart substance—swirls of miso black cod and shishito peppers with a vodka aftertaste—in the toilet.

To think I wanted Esteban to sleep over.

Chapter Nine

The buzz in my head woke me up the next morning. It took me a few tries to lift my head towards the dollar store clock on my nightstand.

It was noon. I had lost half a day of job hunting and solution seeking to a vicious hangover that refused to leave my body. My mouth was dry, and my head pounded with the slightest movement. When I closed my eyes again, the flashbacks appeared in no particular order: Hints of violet and crimson in the sky just before entering the garage; a table covered in empty cocktail glasses; Esteban's hand slipping the car keys off my fingers.

Esteban.

My eyes fluttered shut again, searching for the sensation of his hands on mine. I replayed every word we said, every song we danced to and every story we shared. My head burned, but a smile formed on my lips. The elation lasted a whole minute, until the vivid memory of a disgraced Sofia in the lobby mirror appeared.

Did last night really happen?

Oh yes, it had, and there was no better proof than the throbbing sensation in my brain, the shakiness creeping into every muscle in my body, and the faint notes of vomit swirling in my mouth.

Two messages waited on my cell phone.

Esteban: Hola Corazón. How are you feeling? Let me know when you wake up.

Nina: Should I send a search party for you?! Just tell me if you are okay, please.

Corazón—a sexier version of sweetheart. Really? We were on corazón terms already! If I hadn't had the killer headache, I'd probably done a happy dance around the room.

My fingers moved sluggishly across the screen as I forced myself to respond to both messages—reassuring Nina that I was functional despite my hangover, and confirming to Esteban that consciousness had been achieved, though not without consequences. The phone beeped exactly a minute later with a string of texts.

Esteban: Happy to hear.

Esteban: Last night was fun.

Sofia: Yeah I had a great time. Did you get to your house ok?

Fantasy images of what Esteban's home might look like popped into my mind. Fancy midtown loft? Townhome at the Grove? Coral Gables rental with roomies?

Esteban: I'm catching up with work today. Are you free tomorrow?

My weak smile bloomed into an uncontainable grin. Despite the blur of words and actions from last night—most still eluding my memory—something had sparked his desire to see me again. It was only noon, but I knew I'd spend the rest of my day counting down the hours until Sunday, reliving every delicious memory of him, and shaking off the alcohol from my system.

In the hour that followed, I managed to use the restroom, drink a full glass of water, and plot the rest of my Saturday.

Follow up with WorldMedia

Apply to at least four more jobs

Check bank account and credit card balance

Survive hangover

Not my favorite things to do on a Saturday afternoon, but better than removing sweat stains from Mrs. Garcia's Peloton.

I opened my laptop and drafted a polite follow-up e-mail to the WorldMedia recruitment person, silently praying before hitting send. Then I moved on down the rest of the list, thinking that the sooner I got to the end, the sooner I'd see Esteban again.

I've always preferred the beach over the mountains. My happiest memories come with the feeling of waves crashing against my legs, toes buried in the sand, sun warming my skin, and miles of deep blue stretching on the horizon. And Dad is always in them, a soothing presence caring for me and my brother in the water. I still cherish the feeling of safety that came with my arms firmly grasping his shoulders when I ventured where my feet no longer reached the bottom. Or the many times we built small forts and moats out of wet sand and then sat next to each other until sunset. Miami was his dream, and his dream was a reality during that glorious summer vacation he gave us.

"Papi ¿Tu prefieres la playa, o las montañas?" I asked him the first time we went to the beach together. Growing up surrounded by mountains, I wanted to know if Dad thought the sea was as magical as I did. I was ten, and it was my first time at the beach. After hours in the water, my lips were already cracked from the sea salt, and the skin on my forehead and cheeks had turned the color of toasted honey. But I didn't want to leave. I had created so many versions of that infinite pool of water in my mind, but nothing compared to the real thing—the sizzling sound of the little waves washing the shore; the smell of salt, so dense that I could taste it every time I inhaled through my mouth; the moist air that picked up now and then and tangled my hair into a thousand knots.

"Uy, la playa. Toda la vida," he said in his beautiful Andean Spanish while staring into the vastness of the sea. The beach—one more line to add to the growing list of things we both loved. "Las montañas te encierran. El mar te libera." Mountains lock you in, but the sea sets you free. I thought of the gray mountains blocking my view in Bogotá, and the sea stretching in front of me, and I understood what he meant.

I smiled and leaned against him, my head finding that little nook on his chest. We stayed there until it was so dark that the colors of the sea and the sky blended together, and the horizon line disappeared. And then it was a mission to find our flip flops in the sand. Mom had suggested that staying at a fancy resort with beach lighting would have been much more convenient. She then complained of exhaustion from too many hours under the sun all the drive back. And then she found another long list of things to nag about, until I was forced to block her voice so I could focus on the city's beauty at night.

I was exhausted, too, but I could feel the *thump* of my heart at the sight of downtown Miami alive with all those twinkling lights.

We stayed at a distant cousin's house in Kendall—as far west as we could possibly go while still in Miami—all four of us crammed into a spare bedroom on the first floor, sharing one twin bed and one inflatable mattress. I knew we weren't welcome there. On the day of our arrival, Dad's cousin had given us a spare key, sneered while eyeing our luggage, and then asked how many days we were planning to stay. He then pointed to the first bedroom on the right and disappeared down the corridor to the entrails of the house. That's it. I don't recall him ever joining us at the beach or for breakfast in the kitchen. "Aqui la gente siempre esta ocupada," Dad would say. This I'd heard before—that people are always busy in the United States.

Dad's forced enthusiasm couldn't mask the shame in his eyes as he revealed the modest vacation accommodations—the best his stretched finances could manage. Even if the few people we knew were so busy that we could spend an entire week in Miami without hearing from them, I treasured those days like the gem they were. After all, it took Dad three years to save enough money to pay for the four round-trip tickets and the car rental. We could have slept in the car for all I cared; that's how excited I was to visit Dad's favorite city.

Late at night, after Santiago and I had gone to bed, I'd hear Dad quietly scurry out of the room and leave the house. The first time I jumped out of bed to go after him, Mom stopped me before I reached the door, her fingers digging deep into the fleshy part of my arm. "Tu papá tiene que ir a trabajar," she said. Dad never knew that I pretended to be asleep when he snuck out to work every night of our vacation.

That's how I found out how costly that Miami trip was. Dad working under the table overnight shifts was the only way we could afford the rest of the trip—our food, the expensive entry tickets to the attractions we visited, even the cost of those full-day parking spaces at the beach, an amount that easily surpassed what we spent on groceries in Bogotá in a week.

Dad would do odd jobs that random acquaintances referred him to—unloading boxes in huge storage facilities in Hialeah, stocking merchandise in low-key department stores, even washing the toilets at office buildings like Sunset Cosmetics. He always arrived before Santiago and I woke up, and then he'd sleep until noon. But five hours of sleep were not enough to erase the dark circles around his eyes, subside his lower back's soreness, or the painful swell in his ankles. In the darkness of that small room, I'd catch him massaging his shoulders and rubbing his temples, but when I asked if he was okay, the answer was always the same: He was *good*, and *was I ready for a surprise?* Then he'd shower me with tickles and ask us to hurry up, taking turns using the shower, because in less than one hour we would be driving around the city, marveling at beautiful sights using those crumpled twenty-dollar bills he had earned the previous night.

Years later, after Dad had left this world and I had made up my mind about moving to Miami, I reached out to that same distant cousin—the one who couldn't wait for his pesky relatives to return to Colombia—to ask for a life-changing favor. I needed someone to serve as a sponsor for the student visa I was applying for. It took me weeks of research, three expensive long-distance calls, and a lot of praying. Until one day, overcome by pity or exasperated by my polite insistence, he agreed to file the paperwork. He warned me that he didn't want to hear from me again, that I better have a plan to come up with the money, because he sure as hell wouldn't be sponsoring me, and that he was only signing because he felt sorry for Dad who always wanted to live in Miami but died before he got his wish. The phone dug into my ear as I strained to catch every fragmented word through the unstable connection. A smile spread across my face—somehow I knew Dad was up there, orchestrating this miracle, nudging this man to come to my rescue.

It was a dream that I was approved for a student visa—the first step of many that brought me closer to Dad's beach, and my ticket out of Bogotá. That's how I left the sandless city where I was born, surrounded by mountains and brick buildings, with one of the highest altitudes in Latin America, and a sky so dense with gray clouds that the sun didn't bother to show up for days, in favor of a more tropical location.

Esteban asked me to wear a bathing suit, put on sunblock, and be ready at ten a.m.

I was dying to see him, but at the same time, I was so nervous that I didn't want to see him. I craved the version of me who surfaced those few times we had been together. When he was around, the black cloud of problems that followed me everywhere seemed to disappear. I needed more of that feeling. I needed more of *myself* when I was around *him*.

The jitters escorted me down the stairs, across the lobby, and outside of the building, where the late-summer sun shone brightly on Esteban's car.

A Tesla. Of course.

Luckily, he jumped out to open the door for me, because I had no clue how to operate the nonexistent handle on his car. Once I was inside, I realized I hadn't greeted him properly. No kiss, no hug, no nothing. I was a little more than a pile of nerves hidden behind a lopsided smile. His car had that expensive smell and flawless sheen, making me feel like I didn't want to be anywhere else. By the time we were on the expressway and cruising over to South Beach, the jitters had subsided, and I was acting more like a normal person.

"Where are we going?" I asked. There was a long line of cruise ships on our right. The sun cast a golden glow over their blueish windows, the red and yellow mega slides on the upper deck, the mini shapes of people moving along the silver rails, ready to set sail. I had never been on a cruise. It was one of the forbidden fantasies of my childhood.

"You like the sea, right?" he asked, clearly noticing my sight was fixed on the water.

As a little girl, I longed to see the ocean, but there are no beaches in Bogotá. My first encounter with the sea—during that one magical vacation in Miami with Dad—made me fall in love with it. The sea represented some of the things I loved the most: Dad, vacations, and Miami.

"I do."

"Can you swim?"

The way he asked made me jump in my seat. "I can," I answered warily.

"Good. We're taking the boat out."

"You have a boat?" The thrill coursing through me was written plainly across my features—I didn't even try to temper my reaction.

"I do." That crooked smile resurfaced when he took in my surprised expression. "But it's a small one. I co-own it with two friends."

"That sounds nice. Who are your friends?" I begged him not to say the name of a woman.

"Two guys from the office. We split the maintenance and the marina. I have it this weekend."

"Oh." My heart somersaulted in my chest.

I'd never been on a boat before.

After parking and walking along the boardwalk at the marina, we reached a pier that housed row upon row of white boats. An attendant approached Esteban and gave him instructions in a vocabulary that was undecipherable to me. I pretended not to be nervous and followed Esteban when he asked me to board a gray and white speedboat that looked to be about twenty-five feet long.

My fingers gripped the edges of the seats as the boat dipped and rose beneath my shifting weight. It rocked more dramatically when Esteban moved about. I remained frozen, utterly useless and bewildered by the reality of being there. Turning back to the dock, I half expected a bunch of Esteban's friends to show up carrying coolers and towels, and to jump on the boat and send me flying to the water. But aside from the attendant swiftly untying the last rope and giving us a gentle push, the dock was empty.

"Is anyone else coming?" I asked.

He moved close, lowering his face dangerously close to mine and whispered, "No, nadie. It's just us."

The intensity of his words landed in my belly and spread like wildfire through my body. The corner of his lips curled in a delicious grin right before he turned back to the wheel, leaving me with an image of his perfect backside.

Moved by a newly sprouted survival instinct, I wobbled to a seat in the back row and dug my fingernails into the cushions. Soft brown panels covered the floor, and there were enough cup holders and space to throw one of those boat parties I had only seen from a distance—usually when I was stuck in traffic on an expressway overlooking the bay. I wondered how many of those parties Esteban had hosted on that same deck. How many corks had he sent flying into the water to spray the champagne over dancing bodies?

His confidence suggested I was hardly breaking new ground as a guest on his boat. Other women had undoubtedly experienced this same ritual, a thought that sent an unreasonable wave of jealousy through me. I was still trying to decide if I was lucky to be there, or if it was a fool's mistake to let a stranger take me out to sea. After all, we had seen each other a grand total of ... two times? Three, if I counted the car incident, but my curiosity won out. He turned around and found me sitting all the way in the back, like a child on a time-out. I must have been quite a sight: back frozen in place, knuckles drained of color, face toggling between fear and amusement. And we hadn't even left the marina. How pathetically I contrasted with those golden-skinned women in their perfect bikinis, the ones who drank and lounged and danced across boat decks as if they'd evolved with sea legs. He made a face like he didn't understand what I was doing in the back, then he pointed at the seat right next to his—Captain's orders.

With both hands securely grasping every possible edge, I stumbled into the seat as he asked.

The engine's vibration pushed us away. Esteban navigated the boat away from the docks, zigzagging between glimmering yachts and other boats.

After a few minutes crossing the calm currents of the canal, we reached the exit, and the water opened in front of us. Shades of turquoise faded into dark blues, stretching to the horizon, almost begging to be disturbed.

He barely uttered a word while he navigated. He was lost in thought, his gaze fixed on some distant point in the water. I tried—and failed miserably—to keep my eyes away from him. I couldn't get enough of the bumps and threads of muscle stretching and flexing under his shirt, the confidence with which he steered us away from the boat traffic in search of open water.

When he caught me staring, I was mortified, but I saw a hint of a smile on his lips, his cheekbones pushing his sunglasses up, which made my heart flip.

"Ready?" His low, reassuring voice did nothing to calm my nerves. *Ready for what?*

"Agárrate bien, que voy a acelerar." He instructed me to hold on tight. My response was instinctive—I wedged myself into the chair, my hands clamping down on any stable surface they could find. I felt the vibration increase, the wind hit my face harder, and the front of the boat rose slightly. The sheer speed pushed me back against the seat, and it was impossible to contain the thrill from claiming every nerve in my body.

The boat slashed through the surface, bouncing against the ripples of waves, splashing salty water on my face. The wind was doing crazy things to my hair. I tried to gather the flying strands with one hand while I held on to the edge of the boat with the other, but gave up after a few attempts.

This seemingly fun boat ride had a curious effect on me. While I was trying to relax and stop worrying about the speed, my hair, and my boat ignorance, the other problems that plagued my life appeared front and center, claiming my attention.

As I turned into the wind, letting it sweep my hair from my face, my eyes fixed on a solitary charcoal grey boat in the distance, motionless except for the rhythmic rocking of the waves beneath it. Despite the heat on my shoulders, an icy chill crept up my back as I noticed two officers in combat-ready black outfits. I ducked my head and pretended to search for something in my bag, my fingers instinctively moving to my wallet to check for my driver's license. Although I wasn't undocumented, I couldn't help the anxiety settling in my chest, wondering if border patrol could pull boats over. I knew the occupants of that imposing boat, which we passed by without incident a minute later, had the power to shatter the dreams of people like me in an instant.

Only after the patrol boat disappeared from view did I reclaim my seat, ducking back before Esteban could question why I'd been burrowing into my beach bag like a frightened child. Behind the boat, the long wake of azure and white seafoam diffused across the surface. I followed the wake with longing eyes. In the distance, the Miami shoreline surrounded us, like a collage of postcard images.

"Sofia?" We had decreased speed and approached a shallow water area where other boats were anchored. The sound of the wind blended with the sound of at least three different songs, the loud voices, and la fiesta. Instead of moving to the center of the party, Esteban maneuvered the boat and positioned us on the very edge of the sandbar.

"Are you okay?" he asked.

"I am," I lied. "This place is perfect."

"Why do you look worried?" he asked as he pulled an anchor from a compartment and dropped it in the water.

"Um, I'm not … I mean, we all worry about something, right?"

"Right." He raised an eyebrow above the frame of his sunglasses. "Are you nervous I'm gonna throw you off the boat or something?"

That made me laugh. "Is that why you asked if I could swim?"

He smiled. It made my heart flutter. I wanted to end the conversation there. I wanted Esteban to be my escape, not my reminder of all the crap going on in my life.

"Sorry, this place is beautiful." I took a deep inhale and let the salty air fill me. "Sometimes I wish I could make my problems disappear, but they find a way to show up in the weirdest places."

"What problems?"

"Oh, you know, the usual … work problems … family problems …" *Money problems. Legal status problems.*

He checked the anchor once more, then he sat beside me and pulled the small cooler he had brought aboard. Inside were mini prosecco and beer bottles peeking from underneath ice cubes.

"Drink?"

"No, thank you." Despite my body being alcohol free for more than twenty-four hours, my stomach twisted.

He laughed and dipped his hand deep in the ice, retrieving a can of lemon-flavored sparkling water.

"How did you know?"

"I figured after Friday night, you might want to stay away from the cocktails for a few days."

My cheeks started burning, and it wasn't from the sun. There were chunks of the night I could not remember, and only Esteban could fill in the gaps.

"Please tell me I didn't make an idiot of myself."

"You mean after you threw up on the street?"

"I did not!" I pushed his shoulder, mortified.

"Okay, you didn't." He laughed and raised his hands. "I was testing to see how much you remember."

He leaned back and took a long sip from his oversized water bottle. The party boats were floating behind us, so all we could see was the crystal blue expanse of the sea, framed here and there by stretches of land covered by expensive real estate. There was music in the air from the other boats, but the wind and the waves drowned most of it out. It truly was a place to leave all my worries behind.

"So ... about those *problems*."

I took a big gulp of my drink. "What about them?"

"You don't have to tell me anything, of course. But I'd like to help in any way I can."

"That's sweet, but I don't think you can help me."

Silence.

He removed his sunglasses. His eyes looked different than the night on the rooftop. They were light hazel, and they were staring straight into mine. And this time I wasn't completely drunk, but sober and alone on a boat with him.

"Here's what I think," he said. "Is there anything you should be doing now to tackle those problems you have?"

I shook my head. Sunday or not, I had applied to every open position available. The immigration attorneys I'd researched remained an impossible luxury. I'd resolved to find an employer willing to sponsor my visa rather than to find the money to pay for a lawyer.

"Do you already have a plan to solve these problems?"

I nodded. Yes. Find a new job to sponsor my visa. That was my plan.

"And you don't think I can provide any useful advice to tackle those problems?"

I bit my lip and looked at him through my eyelashes. He was determined. I was not used to the level of attention, and deep inside, I knew he was not faking his interest in me.

"So, if you already have a plan, and there is nothing you should be doing now, and you don't want to talk about what worries you ... why don't you forget about it for a little while?" He wasn't smiling anymore. He was staring at my lips, and he had moved closer. My eyes traveled down to his lips, too. And suddenly there was very little space between us, and a lot of space surrounding us.

Here's the thing: under normal circumstances, he was right. If my so-called problems had been anything else, like a broken car or a family argument (both of which I had, unfortunately), then by all means, I would have shared everything with him while sipping bubbles. I wouldn't even waste so much time with all the lip-staring.

But my situation was a lot more delicate than that.

He caught the line of my sight again. "Relax," he mouthed.

And, for once, I decided to listen.

I allowed the fresh sea breeze to caress my face and do with my hair what it pleased. My tension ebbed away as I eased back against the leather seat, finally releasing my white-knuckled grasp. There wasn't a cloud in sight, no chance of a storm sneaking in, nothing to suggest that it wouldn't be one of the best days of my life.

"You know what? You're right." I went to grab the lunch box I had packed in the morning. Anything to soften the mounting tension between us. "We are here now, and that's what matters." I took out the small Tupperware filled with guac I'd prepared that morning and passed it over to Esteban with a container of arepitas, just like Mom made them—thin and crunchy, perfect to be topped with anything left on the fridge.

"You brought guac?"

"Homemade guac," I clarified. "And homemade arepas. It's almost noon. I packed it because I didn't know what we would have for lunch."

"We'll have lunch afterwards, but I'll gladly stay here and eat your guac instead." He devoured three loaded arepas in a row, making low *Mmm* noises.

"Do you like it?"

"Corazón, best guac I've ever had," he said between mouthfuls.

When the guac and the arepas had disappeared, he stood up and peeled his shirt off.

I swear he did it in slow motion.

Or maybe that's how my mind remembers it.

He wasn't ripped, but his abs stretched and contracted as the shirt fell on the chair. The shoulders I had touched while dancing two nights before looked as full and firm as I had imagined. And he was tanned. A delicious light brown color that was equal parts his skin tone and one too many hours spent under the sun.

Since we had already agreed to have a good time, I decided that sitting there and staring at him as much as I wanted was okay.

"Let's go in the water."

"Now?" I asked, surprised at how quickly he moved from one idea to another.

He didn't answer. He stood on the boat's edge, with his back towards the water, and didn't break eye contact with me for a second. Then he did the cutest move: He let his body fall back, flat against the crystal blue. There was a loud splash, and water flew in every direction.

I peeked over the edge to check on him, partly to make sure he was okay, partly because I couldn't take my eyes off him. He emerged from the water a second later, running a single hand through his hair, sprinkling droplets around him. I quite literally had to order myself to stop gaping. Never, after all that time in beauty marketing, watching ads of male models shot on beaches, had I encountered one who was so naturally attractive.

"Get in here. You said you can swim." His deep voice rose above the sound of the water.

"Is it deep?" I asked while trying to make out the bottom through the glassy surface.

He moved a few yards to the side, and his waist appeared over the surface.

"It's like four feet here." He motioned with his hand for me to join him. "Ven. No me dejes solo aquí." *Don't leave me alone here.*

With deliberate movements, I peeled off my top at the boat's edge, acutely aware of his gaze following the contours of my exposed skin. As my clothes hit the seat, it dawned on me that it could be my last chance to do something completely reckless and impulsive in Miami. There was a high chance that I would be back in Colombia in less than two months, and when I remembered that moment with Esteban, I did not want the memory to be clouded with regrets and *should haves*.

I descended the ladder in the yellow Brazilian bikini Nina had gifted me for my twenty-fourth birthday. The freckles on my back and shoulders must have had a frenzy coming out to greet the scorching midday sun, but the burn subsided when I entered the water. It was cool and crisp when it splashed on my skin. My feet landed on the cold sand and led me to where Esteban had been standing, but he wasn't there anymore.

There was a splash in the water, and he pierced through the surface close to me. *Very* close.

Just go with it.

"It's so beautiful," I whispered, facing Miami, hoping the city would hear me.

Esteban edged closer, shifting my attention back to him.

"*You're* beautiful."

"Thank you," I muttered, breathless, wanting him closer.

"—and smart, independent, funny ... and you can cook."

"You're judging my cooking based on guacamole?"

"That's how good it was."

I'm not sure if it was the summer heat, the half-naked Esteban standing a foot away, or the ten boat parties going on the same sandbar, but I realized that moment was a snapshot of the life I had been yearning for. It was salty, sexy, and stripped of all my problems.

The snapshot became instantly addictive. I wanted to stay in it, and so I wanted to stay with Esteban.

At least for the next two months.

"You just ruined all future dates for me, you know?" I said.

"I don't want you thinking about other dates."

"Oh ... what do you want me to think about?"

"Do you really want to know?"

He inched close until our bodies connected. It was subtle, just a graze, but enough to send tingling sparks racing through my body. Our toes met in the sand, too. The cadence of the water shifted us even closer, until our lips were less than an inch apart. I could feel Esteban's breath in my mouth.

He leaned in, one hand in the same spot where he had placed it when we danced together, his lips feathering against mine. It was excruciating. Time seemed to suspend itself in that perfect instant. Just as reality began to fade at the edges, his hand found mine and our fingers wove together. Then I caught it—a distant ringing rising above the ocean's rhythm. Though my eyes remained fixed on him, my concentration splintered, part of me now straining to identify that faint melody drifting up from somewhere on the boat deck. It was my phone.

Drawing back just enough to create a sliver of space between us, I released a sharp breath. My eyes never left his as I inwardly pleaded for the sound to fade away, but it insisted on remaining. Three rings, four rings ...

It couldn't be Mom. I had just sent her the full amount for the month the previous night, which usually made her disappear, at least for a few days.

It could be Nina. She knew I was going out with Esteban, but she had no clue we had gone out to a sandbar on his boat. She would be worried, not to mention pissed, if I didn't answer.

I unlocked my toes from Esteban's, breaking that salty spell, and threaded through the water until I reached the boat. I knew he was checking me out when I climbed the small ladder. I could feel his gaze eating me up as I dried my hand and picked up my phone.

It was an unknown number. I swear, if it had been a spam caller, I would have thrown my phone overboard.

When I picked up, it turned out to be Dianelys Gonzalez calling me. From WorldMedia.

My breath caught in my throat. She apologized for calling on a Sunday and then asked how I was doing, like it was the most casual conversation in the world, like it was normal for dream bosses to call to say hi on weekends. I prayed for the wind to stop blowing so I could hear her clearly and shielded the phone with my hand to avoid the sound from filtering into the conversation.

She wanted me back for a second interview on Monday.

I was so shocked that she had to explain what had happened. She had arranged for her manager—the head of the department—to meet me, but the receptionist had forgotten to call me.

Was I available to come in? Yes, yes, I was.

Did nine a.m. work? Yes, it worked beautifully.

I vaguely registered *enjoy the rest of your Sunday* and *see you tomorrow* before we hung up.

When I looked up, Esteban was already on the boat, standing just a few inches away. I could barely contain the explosion of giggles bubbling up in my throat.

It was happening. WorldMedia wanted me.

"Woah! Tell me what made you smile so I can do it too." He flashed a smile that made his eyes crinkle on the sides. His entire face lit up.

I figured it was okay to share the good news with him.

"I got a call for a work interview tomorrow," I squealed in absolute joy.

"Just now? On a Sunday?"

"Yes! She forgot to call on Friday and had already scheduled an interview with her manager."

"Congratulations, corazón." He moved closer, our bodies connecting again. "We need to celebrate."

A smile of relief spread across my face as I silently thanked the universe for orchestrating that precise moment—my collision with the drunk driver's car happening at the exact instant Esteban was passing by. He wiped his hands methodically on a towel before retrieving his cell phone. "Oh, shit," he said, phone in hand, as he scrolled with his thumb, his eyes locked on the screen.

"What is it?"

"I have like four missed calls from this number." He shook his head. "You don't mind if I call back, do you?"

"Not at all!"

Feeling like the luckiest woman in the sandbar, I watched him as he moved away to the other end of the deck. Talking, nodding, smiling.

He was hot, smart, caring, and he was interested in me.

He was also from Puerto Rico, which meant a long-term relationship with him could result in my getting los papeles I desperately needed. I despised the idea of marrying an American citizen out of convenience, but I couldn't help it. The thought popped up by sheer instinct, mainly if things flowed organically like they were with Esteban. Was it a sin to think of myself when choosing who I wanted to spend time with?

With a mental shake, I dismissed the unwelcome thought. I detested how my circumstances had programmed me to evaluate a new date's legal status in the country almost immediately after meeting.

When he returned, there was a shadow of a smile on his lips, and I momentarily put all my visa thoughts aside.

"Guess what? I also got called for an interview tomorrow."

"You did?" I asked, a little perplexed.

For a second, I was happy for him—I really was. I wish I could have bottled that beautiful second so I could have drank from it when things went awry.

Because dread set in almost immediately, something that Mom would call un presentimiento—a premonition.

The question left my mouth before I had a chance to catch it. "Where are you interviewing at?"

"It's just some media manager position at WorldMedia."

Chapter Ten

The late summer wind picked up, swallowing every sound in its path, then liberating them individually. First, the waves' splash against the boat's exterior, then the reggaeton beat of the now-out-of-control party next to us, and finally, Esteban's voice.

"What is it?" His gaze locked with mine. Dark brows lifted with curiosity. Tanned, full muscles inches away and getting closer. This time, I didn't allow the warmth to spread any further.

"Is it for the Senior Account Manager position?" I asked.

"That's the one." His smile faded away. A light frown appeared between his brows.

"It's the same position I'm interviewing for." I waited for a reaction.

I wasn't expecting what came next.

"Sofia, that's amazing." His full grin reappeared. "It's a great opportunity ... and man, what a coincidence."

"It is, right?" I chuckled.

"Is that the meeting you were running late to the day we met?" he asked, the realization glowing in his face.

"Uh huh." Flashbacks from that morning played in my head. My teal dress, the clock ticking like a time bomb, the squashed bumper of the car I hit ... and then Esteban appearing like a mirage, his crisp shirt and freshly shaved, angular jaw. How relaxed he was, how sure of himself, how cool even as he aided that flustered girl dealing with a drunk in the middle of the street.

They would give him the position over the candidate who arrived late, for sure.

Then I remembered our conversation at the restaurant. His situation was nothing like mine. He had a job. He had never said he was unhappy with it. His only complaint was he thought he should be making more money.

"Is this the job you said you were interviewing for, so you could negotiate a raise?" My words escaped with unexpected force, landing with an accusatory edge I hadn't intended.

"I thought you'd forgotten most of that night," he replied.

"I wasn't drunk for that part." I waited for his answer, crossing my arms before me, trying to conceal my unease.

"I'm always open to opportunities. Company shifts are the fastest way to grow." His tone shifted from flirty to business in a snap. "But to your point, yes. This interview is the closest option to getting a job offer I can use to negotiate with my manager."

The physical pull I had felt just minutes earlier completely evaporated.

"What about you?" he asked. "You said you are happy at Sunset."

It was a question I wasn't prepared to answer. I bit my lip, trying to organize my thoughts as he contemplated me. The job would be mine if everything went well in my second interview. If Esteban received an offer, he would negotiate his raise and stay at Altamira, at which point they would give me the position. I would maintain my work visa, and he would never discover the circumstances behind it. It was part plan, part wish, but the best I could come up with in those two seconds I had to think under his gaze.

"I am. I saw the opening and applied without thinking much about it. Like you said, keep your eyes open for opportunities, right?" I replied, imitating his confidence.

"Right you are," he replied. Then he added, "I'm glad I'm going against you for the position."

"What?" I snapped back.

"Yeah. I mean, I wouldn't want the offer to go to anyone but one of us."

My eyes traveled from the edges of his bare shoulders up to his neck, where the first hints of golden suntan appeared over his already light brown skin. Just as my hands were about to reach his shoulders, a new thought popped into my head.

I had a follow-up interview in less than twenty-four hours and was up against *him*.

"Do you think we should head back to prep for tomorrow?" I asked, hoping he couldn't sense the anxiety in my voice.

A furrow appeared between his brows. He slightly lowered his chin and said, "You don't need to prepare for a job interview. You're either ready or you are not."

"No ... I mean, yes. I get it. But I'd like to ... I don't know, print a few more copies of my resume?" My interview prep list began to fill up with new to-dos appearing by the second.

"Resume copies? Corazón, you don't need those. Relájate. You'll do alright tomorrow."

What he didn't know was *alright* wasn't enough. This was perhaps my only chance to stay. I grabbed my phone and browsed my emails to check if I had missed anything while living my *Miami life* in the water.

"Okay." Esteban raised his hands, as if admitting defeat. "I want you to have a good time. If you feel more comfortable, we can cut it short and head back earlier. Say, two more hours? Would that work?"

In one swift move, he appeared right in front of me, zipping our bodies back together, just like we were in the water. He leaned close, fast, and I tilted my head to kiss him back. But he stopped just as his lips feathered against mine and whispered, "May the best one win."

The rest of the morning was not the steamy scene I had fantasized. We talked about boating, swimming, cruises, and almost every other unrelated topic to jobs or interviews. I was thankful to be there with him, but I couldn't help feeling that an invisible wall had appeared between us. There were no more side glances, subtle electric touches, or inquiries about what we were doing later. I was awkwardly shy, double-thinking every answer, wondering if and how I should reveal what was happening. But just how crappy would it be to spit out the truth I had so swiftly concealed?

Later that afternoon, when we pulled up in front of my building, I leaned over to kiss him on the cheek and felt my bikini straps digging into the nape of my neck. My shoulders and upper back started to burn from the midday sun exposure. I should have been excited; I was getting the opportunity I had prayed so much for, but a wave of dismay washed over me instead. When I returned to my seat, I found Esteban's eyes were locked on mine, the space between us hot and dense with anticipation.

He was perfectly fine with the situation, while I was nervous.

But I couldn't get myself to say it. It wouldn't have changed anything, right?

The room was hot when I woke up on Monday morning, my pillow moist with sweat. I got out of bed in a haze and stumbled to the A/C vent perched on the ceiling, waving my hands in front it. I was met with a soft breeze—definitely not cold or fresh. Just hot Miami air spitting out into the room, threatening to turn the apartment's interior as hot as it was outside.

I groaned and went straight to the shower, still sleepy from a restless night, and let the cold water do what the A/C was supposed to. It was refreshing for a few minutes, but I started sweating when I walked out of the bathroom. Throughout the night, my shoulders had gone from hot pink to toasted, the tanned skin peeking from the sides of the white collared shirt. Still, I pushed through the morning mechanics a little faster than usual to escape the rising heat, making a mental note to reach out to the landlord about the broken A/C as soon as the interview ended.

I waited to be called in at the WorldMedia reception, crossing my ankles under the chair to keep my heels from tapping erratically on the floor. WorldMedia employees paraded through the front door, hoisting their laptop bags and lunch boxes, concealing the spark of curiosity in their eyes, muttering polite "buenos días" as they disappeared down the corridor. I smiled at each of my future coworkers and tried with all my might to hide how terrified I was.

I knew they were analyzing me. That's why I arrived at 8:42 a.m. for my nime a.m. interview. This time, there was no drunk driver in the street, and I knew exactly where to park and how to find the WorldMedia office. Armed with a fresh stack of resumes I had printed at the business center in my building the previous day, I waited to hear my name called.

As if the interview wasn't enough, my heart halted every time the glass door opened, knowing Esteban could show up any second. I could picture him in a shirt like the one he wore the day we met, his presence filling every corner of the room, a relaxed half-smile on his lips, as if he was holding a secret that only he knew about.

Would he acknowledge that we knew each other? Would he disclose that we were in the same boat when we received the call?

At 9:05 a.m., I was called into the conference room with the huge window overlooking the Miami Bay. Dianelys was sitting, placing a cup of coffee and her laptop in front of her.

"Oh my! You got a tan," she said when she saw me.

"I did." No need to disclose where it happened.

"Your freckles came out."

"They always do with the sun."

"They must love Miami, then," she said with a smile.

Oh yes, they did. Like their owner, the Miami sun was vital to their happy existence. I failed miserably at keeping my mind from flashing the image of Esteban, shirtless on the sandbar.

"Linda won't join us. She helped narrow down the decision, but you will only meet with WorldMedia today," Dianelys said.

My nerves tingled with anticipation. I had made a good impression on Linda, but I had no idea what to expect from the rest of the team.

One by one, they arrived: two managers and one director, until I was convinced this was life's way of telling me I had enjoyed my freckles for far too long, and nothing—not even Esteban declining the offer—could secure me the position. Two of them were middle-aged men who vaguely reminded me of Rafael. I hoped things would be different at WorldMedia while I answered the questions they shot from every corner of the room. None of them asked for my resume.

My memories of the interview are as blurry as those from my drunken night at Aura, but I recall the sweet relief I felt when Dianelys asked the magic question: *Do you have any questions for us?*

Then the interview was over, almost as quickly as it had started. Was it as nerve-wracking as being questioned by a U.S. customs officer? Definitely. Could I confirm that I would get a job offer the next day? Probably. Did I verify that they would sponsor my work visa? Absolutely not.

I didn't think of Esteban again until I left the interview at 9:45 a.m., long after I had stopped worrying about the sweat stains that were probably visible in my clothing. He was there when the elevator doors opened, wearing a blazer over a white shirt and jeans. *Jeans*. I'd never considered showing up for an interview wearing something even remotely comfortable.

While drops of sweat traveled down my back, he walked out of the elevator and leaned over to kiss me on the cheek.

"Hola corazón," he said with the slightest hint of flirtation in his voice.

"Hi," I said.

"How'd it go?" he asked like it was the most normal question, like I hadn't been half naked on a sandbar with him twenty-four hours earlier.

"Um, okay, I guess." I could sense some employees looking at us from inside the office, but I didn't turn around to find out who.

"Will you tell me all about it later?"

Later. There was a later. His casual demeanor bewildered me—approaching interviews with the lighthearted ease of a weekend hobby. With a nod from me, Esteban disappeared inside. The young receptionist welcomed him with a smile she didn't give me—then he entered the conference room and greeted all the managers with a firm handshake and a smile, like they were old pals or something. My eyes never left him, not until the elevator doors clamped shut between us, leaving the key to my uncertain future outside in someone else's hands.

At the dog park that night, I absently watched Togo romp with another lab while my mind retreated to the interview. Each detail resurfaced with painful clarity, spawning endless alternative responses I should have given. Some answers returned with such force I buried my face in my hands, unable to face even the memory of my own words. The interview had drained me of everything I had to give, and now it was up to them to decide if I was enough. But the more pressing question haunted me: would my best outshine Esteban's? I pictured his interview, bolstered by Altamira credentials, that self-assured smile, and his overachieving attitude. Envy crystallized inside me, sharp and undeniable.

Nina's texts popped up on my cell phone screen.

Nina: "Where are you?"

Sofia: "Downstairs with Togo."

Nina: "Almost there. How'd it go today?"

Sofia: "Hard to tell."

Nina: "It's yours. You're staying."

Sofia: "I hope."

Hope was an understatement. I dreamt of that position. I bet my future on it.

As the sun set, and the clouds became tinted in beautiful pinks and oranges, I wondered when I had convinced myself that Miami was the only place I wanted to live. I was raised in Bogotá in what many consider a normal childhood, surrounded by little boys who played fútbol in back alleys, disturbed by the occasional temblor that shook our shabby house and everything in it, surrounded by the silence that swept over the city during elections, when a toque de queda and ley seca—a mandatory "no alcohol" curfew—were enforced.

My parents struggled to make ends meet when Dad was still alive. Every month, I was called in front of the class as part of a group of students who were late on their tuition payments. Somehow, Dad would come up with the money every month, right before I was expelled. He worked so we could afford the school uniforms that we were constantly growing out of, insisting that if we focused on our education, he could guarantee our lives would be much easier than theirs had been. What

Dad didn't know was that we would lose him only a few years later, when I was in my last year of Bachillerato.

Mom had her way of dealing with his passing, pouring all the devotion she had for Dad into a teenage Santiago, who suddenly found himself experiencing all the liberties that came after suddenly losing his main role model. It's not like Santiago and Dad didn't have a good relationship—they had the typical dynamic of a strict father attempting to educate an unruly son, in a society where one mistake could alter the rest of your life. But with Dad out of the way, it was easier for Santiago to lose his way in the dark alleys that had called to him for years. Mom never found the resolve to control a young man set on his ways. It was as if their aspirations and spirit had died with Dad. I remember the first phrase she said when we left the funeral, as we walked silently to the bus station, "¿Y ahora que vamos a hacer?" *What are we going to do now?* Burdened by the idea of being left alone with two teenagers, she was never up to following through with Dad's wishes. She let herself drown in grief and rum, in laziness and excuses.

Sometimes I think she wanted to take me down with her.

Maybe that's when my life in Bogotá became unacceptable. Or perhaps it started earlier, after all those nights listening to Dad talk about the palm trees lining the expressways, the clean streets, and the abundance of everything in Miami. Or maybe it happened when we returned to Bogotá after our vacations, when that first cloud of cold fog and smoke enveloped us after exiting El Dorado airport, and we were welcomed into our city by children a few years older than us selling candy and cigarettes.

The truth, I came to realize, was that the idea had grown in me throughout the years like a climbing vine.

Throughout my childhood, I absorbed the complaints of the previous generation—más de lo mismo, more of the same—their shorthand for the depressing cycle of repetition. Their narratives haunted me: bombings that shattered communities, civilians caught in the crossfire of drug wars, and the persistent shadow of guerrillas who preyed on the poorest children for recruitment while kidnapping the wealthiest for ransom. While I didn't experience it firsthand, I had to deal with the aftermath, with the guilt complex they carried from being a Colombian in the 90s, when the international perception was that nothing good could come out of the place where I was born.

I also grew up trying to avoid the fate of the middle class: to know I'd never rise above the estrato I was born in, but forever fear falling in disgrace to the one below. I could not picture a life back there anymore after three years of receiving a direct deposit to my checking account, even when payday landed on a holiday. I purchased my car, albeit beat-up and pre-owned, and a used laptop just a few months after my arrival, and was able to take the college classes I had financed through a student loan, with minimal assistance from others.

Would I fit into the life cut out for me in Bogotá? The girls I graduated with already had one or two kids or had found low-paying jobs as assistants or salespeople. A few lucky ones worked at family businesses they would later inherit, or had found a position at one of the international companies in Bogotá through family ties. My family didn't have any connections, and a job as a sales associate could barely allow me to afford a motorcycle after three years of savings.

Nina arrived at the dog park and snapped me back to reality.

"Why do you have so many freckles today?"

I shrugged. "I forgot to wear sunblock yesterday."

She let Dante run over to the area where Togo was playing with the other dogs and sat beside me on the bench, inspecting my shoulders like a concerned dermatologist.

"Meu Deus, Sofia. Put on some aloe or you're gonna start peeling."

My skin is the color of café con leche, and my cheeks turn pink under the mountain sun. The freckles first appeared at age ten in Miami, when my Andean skin was exposed to a cloudless summer sky and ninety-five-degree heat. We became addicted to Miami at the same time.

"I think I have some Sunset samples. I'll apply some tonight."

To change the subject, I delved into my interview experience—how I'd meticulously prepared the day before, navigated to the parking lot without my usual vehicular mishaps, showed up ahead of schedule, and still produced armpit sweat patterns that outlined a map of South America. I also told her about Esteban being a candidate for the position.

Her jaw dropped. "You are kidding."

"I'm not. He got the call right after I did, and I saw him at WorldMedia just as I was leaving." I didn't mention that he walked in like he owned the place.

"Shit."

"I know."

Nina was quiet for a moment, which packed a lot of words, her being Nina and all.

I answered the question I knew was lurking in her mind. "He has a job. He needs an offer to negotiate a raise."

"I don't know, Sofi ... if they are interviewing him, they are probably interviewing other people."

A cloud of pessimism descended on me. Not only did I have Esteban to worry about, but possibly a queue of candidates who also wanted *my* job.

"Have any other companies called you?" Nina asked.

"Oh, I have companies behind my ass alright ... the electric company, the water company, the cellphone company ..." We burst out laughing—my first real laugh in the entire day.

Togo returned, leaping for joy, tail wagging, and placed his big paws on my lap, leaving dusty brown footprints on my sweatpants.

"Your neighbor's dog looks happy," she said as Togo curled on my feet, panting with exhaustion, his tongue hanging from the side of his mouth. "I bet that bitch never allows him to run like that."

"She's always working." I defended her almost by instinct.

"She is *not*."

"Alright. Time to go upstairs," I said as I clasped the leash onto Togo's collar, not wanting to jump into another heated conversation topic.

"I'll come with you to drop off Togo, and then you can show me what you wore for the interview this morning," Nina announced as she stood up.

I imagined the heat wave attacking Nina's face as soon as she crossed the threshold and thought about stopping her. I did not want her to be sucked into the chaos of my daily life. But she was already standing up, expectantly waiting for me to peel my ass off the bench. Making up an excuse to Nina was little more than a waste of air. She would find out one way or the other, so I tackled it the way you rip a Band-Aid off.

"I'd love to, but my A/C broke."

"What do you mean *it broke*?"

"Stopped working."

"Why hasn't the landlord fixed it?"

"I called him after the interview, and he was stressed out. He dropped off a fan in the afternoon."

"A fan?!"

I nodded in silence.

"Sofia, it's ninety degrees outside. Your landlord has to fix it, or accommodate you in a hotel, or something." She shook her head; a furrow appeared between her brows. "You can come to my apartment, of course, but the landlord still needs to fix it."

"I know."

"Then what are you waiting for?" She cocked a hand on her hip, her signature Nina scowl on her face.

"I don't want to pressure him. The contract renewal is coming up, and I'm hoping he doesn't increase my rent."

Her jaw dropped, shock in her eyes. Then she shook her head and took a breath. "You need to start looking out for yourself, Sofi." She called Dante, who ran over, his little ears flapping in the wind.

"What am I supposed to do, Nina? If I don't get a job, I'll have to use my last month's deposit for rent. I won't even have a place to live before I go back to—"

"*If* it comes to that." She jumped in before my rant spiraled out of control. "You'll stay with me."

It was a relief to hear her say those words. "Thank you." I could not picture myself pacing around Nina's apartment, counting down the days I had left before returning to Colombia. "I wish I had some hope with another company. Plan B. Some certainty of where I'm going to be in two months."

"We should've been roomies when I told you." She scowled. "You wouldn't have wasted all that money on that ridiculous rent."

"I know." I bit my lip. "I messed up."

"You know I can lend you some money. At least to get you by."

"You'd seriously do that?"

"I wouldn't do it for anyone else." Nina squeezed my hand. Suddenly, her voice switched from gentle to fierce in her unique Nina fashion. "Of course, you'd use the money strictly for rent and student loans. Not a penny to your bum of a brother who hasn't worked a day in his life."

I was surprised she only mentioned my brother and not Mom. It seemed like she was deliberately avoiding bringing her up in the discussion, though she knew it was Mom who sent me bi-weekly reminders about money and how much they struggled. Then, she posted pictures on Instagram of her having carne asada and aguardiente at the house with people I didn't recognize.

"I can't just ditch them. They're my family." I tried to keep my voice low and assertive, but even I could feel the doubt seeping into my words.

"Please don't be mad at me for telling you this, but that's not what family is about."

"All families have problems." I snapped back.

"They are a problem because you are allowing them to be." Her hand left mine.

She ducked to pick up Dante when my cell phone rang. Sure enough, it was Mom, and I felt the pressure on my chest expand. I didn't dare admit that it was becoming harder to feel the same excitement as my first year in Miami. Back when Mom and Santiago called every week to thank me for working so hard and not forgetting about them.

I used to swell with pride every time I signed the Western Union slip, and later, when I clicked *send* on the screen, knowing that seconds later Mom would receive a notification that money had been deposited. That feeling lasted until they started calling to complain because the cash I sent was not enough.

Nina stretched her neck just enough to see my screen, raising her eyebrow until it almost touched her hairline. "Sorry to tell you this, amiga. But your problems are calling you."

Chapter Eleven

That night, I kept my distance from Esteban. Nina's warning echoed relentlessly through my thoughts—a stark reminder of all my missteps. I questioned whether my growing connection with him might be undermining my own candidacy. The reality was unavoidable: he'd advanced to a second interview, placing him on equal footing for an offer. Despite his reassurances, what guarantee did I have that he would actually decline? And beyond him, unknown competitors likely circled the same opportunity. My Sunday at the sandbar had been a complete waste of time. I was days away from receiving a nice letter from the U.S. ICE reminding me of my exit date, yet I was thinking about dating and Esteban.

Bumble notifications popped up on my screen throughout the day, yet I deliberately ignored the app. The reason remained frustratingly elusive, even to myself. I crafted a convenient explanation about prioritizing my career search, but I couldn't escape the simple truth: Esteban had made the prospect of meeting anyone else seem boring. While I maintained my digital distance from him that Monday, my phone became an object of compulsive monitoring. I craved a message from him.

I loathed how much I craved him.

The fan was on at full speed in my bedroom, aimed at my bed, while I filled in the job search filters on LinkedIn. I had stopped sweating after taking a cold shower, and it was not the living hell Nina had described, especially after I opened the door to let the cold A/C from the hallway in. I also let the small bedroom window half-open for added circulation.

Windows are always closed in Bogotá to keep the cold air and the burglars out. In Miami, we keep the windows shut to keep the A/C in. But that night something was refreshing about the air in the bedroom and the low hum of the fan. The temperature had surprisingly dropped a few degrees, and a gentle breeze came from the bay. It reminded me of the boat, the sea breeze, and Esteban's body leaning closer to mine in the water.

Naturally, when the phone pinged at 9:37 p.m, I almost broke my wrist to check it. My body physically relaxed when I saw his name.

Esteban: Hey.

Esteban: How'd your interview go?

Ay of all possible topics, he wanted to tackle the one that hurt the most.

Sofia: It was good. Tougher than the first one.

I stared at the string of text before I hit send. It was so vague, but just the thing to keep my expectations guarded.

Sofia: HBU?

Esteban: Chill until they asked details about my accounts. They grilled me for like thirty minutes.

Shit. They had discussed his account management. They had devoted thirty minutes to the one skill I lacked. The twisted thought spiraled around in my mind.

They were picking him, for sure.

> **Esteban:** Hardest part was when the Latam VP showed up. I swear the mood in the room changed. It's like they're scared of him.

And he met with the VP.

My heart crumbled into tiny pieces. Was I out of the race? A World-Media rejection would take me back to square one, filling out applications and checking the few empty cells on the Excel file that had not sent a rejection yet.

I read the messages a few times, astonished at his ease and casual tone, like he was discussing restaurant choices or Bumble profiles. I didn't feel raw resentment towards him. After all, he was making the career moves he thought were right for him. Deep inside, I wished I were also job hunting for sport, my position secure and untouched at Sunset.

> **Esteban:** Can we meetup tomorrow, after work? I can tell you how Dianelys Gonzalez spilled her coffee all over the table when the VP walked in lol

Meeting with Esteban could count as market research or competitor analysis or a strategic move in my job hunt. Right?

> **Sofia:** Sure.

> **Esteban:** Here's my address. I'm cooking

My stomach dipped, and then it fell some more. A warm flutter spread from my belly in all directions.

Of course, my phone rang ten seconds after I announced Tuesday's dinner plans to Nina.

"Sofi, don't."

"Um, hey, how are you?"

"No te hagas la loca," she warned. *Don't be silly*. I loved how her singsong Brazilian accent slipped into the Spanish phrases I had taught her. "Unless you plan to take me with you, you shouldn't go."

I pictured Nina showing up with me at Esteban's door. My mom had never been overprotective, and here was my friend wanting to play chaperone. If Nina ever had kids, she would become one hell of a helicopter mom nightmare to her teenagers.

"Why shouldn't I?" I asked. "We've had dinner before, we've been out on his boat, and he said it's to discuss the interview."

"That's why!" She snapped. "You shouldn't be discussing anything with him. You are still competing for the same position."

"There's no policy against being friendly to the other candidates."

"You are more than friendly to him. You like him."

"So?" I was being altanera—*haughty*—but I also knew when Nina was holding back, like that moment when she let the silence stretch too long.

Several seconds of silence stretched between us as I glanced at my phone screen, checking if the call was still connected. Her voice surprised me when it returned, softer and more gentle than before. "I don't think it's a good idea, Sofi."

"Why would you say that?"

"I don't want you to get hurt. I know it's none of my business, obviously, you can date whoever you want. But you really want two things and I'm afraid of how it might turn out for you if you lose one or the other." *Or both.*

"I also think he's making you lose your focus. Like, if he's not helping you find a way to stay, he doesn't deserve your time. Not to mention, he's going for the same position you are."

She was right. But I still didn't see the danger of a free dinner with Esteban. After all, he wasn't the one making hiring decisions at World-Media.

"I'll be fine. I do need a break from all these applications," I said while scanning the blueish glare of the laptop screen, searching for the last entry I had filled out.

"I get it," she finally conceded. "Be careful, okay? And let me know when you are with him."

"I'll message you before I get there, and after I leave his apartment." I smiled. I liked that someone cared about me so much that she would never be bothered by my late-night messages.

"You know what? If you like him so much, I wanna meet him," she added, almost as an afterthought.

It caught me off guard. "Oh. Okay." I had no real reason to say no, though asking him to meet Nina made me nervous. What if he wasn't interested in meeting her? What if he thought I was being pushy?

"Let's see if he lives up to the hype," she mumbled.

"There's no hype—"

"There is. Just arrange something."

I sighed. "I will, amiga."

The next day, I received a call from an unknown number. I was stir-frying garlic and onions to make fried rice in the kitchen when my cell phone rang. My intuition screamed that this was a potential employer. The wooden spoon clattered against the counter as I darted toward the couch, handling my phone with surgical precision to prevent an accidental hang-up. I composed myself briefly before offering my first cautious "hello."

"Hello, Sofia. I'm Lucy Paredes with Lincaffé. I'm calling about your application for Digital Coordinator. Do you have a minute?"

There was no time to check out their website or to pull up the Excel file with all my notes; I only had myself to recall every piece of knowledge I had about Lincaffé. Having applied to so many companies, the ideas stacked in my mind: *Coffee. Ad campaigns. Latin America.* But one thought shone above all others: I would dump WorldMedia for Lincaffé in a heartbeat. Isn't that what happens when a possible employer calls about a job opportunity? Twist reality until convinced that the position is a perfect match and the solution to all of life's problems.

"Hi, Lucy. Yes, now it's a good time."

"Great! This is an HR screening before we set you up for an in-person interview. I see you work at Sunset Cosmetics. What's your position there?"

I had submitted the Lincaffé application weeks ago, when I still had my Sunset job. Explaining this would open a whole new set of questions, or worse yet, exclude me from the in-person interview. I answered as fast as I could, not giving myself the chance even to consider that I was masking the truth. "I've been a marketing manager for two years."

"Sounds good. We are looking for someone with that number of years of experience. And you also have a bachelor's degree in business admin, right?"

My heart was pounding, violent pumps that made my face tingle and my voice shake.

"That's right. I graduated last summer."

"Good. When would you be available to start working?"

I was ready to start the next day, but that wouldn't align with my supposed employment at Sunset. "I can start in two weeks."

"Fantastic. Thank you so much, Sofia. One last question, and I apologize beforehand, but they make me ask this one. Can you confirm that you have a permanent U.S. work permit?"

I lost my chain of thought, my words, my breath.

"Hello?" She said.

When my brain decided to unfreeze, all the words blasted out. "I don't. I mean, I do now, but I'll need sponsorship soon. The posting says Lincaffé can process a work visa for the right candidate. I think I'm a great match and can add value to your team."

"Oh ... right." A long pause followed some keyboard sounds, and when the woman spoke again, all the enthusiasm from her tone had disappeared. "I need to ask them to delete that from the website. We are not providing those anymore. I apologize for taking up your time."

I had to swallow a huge lump in my throat to talk. "Please, if something changes, I'd be happy to come in for an interview."

"Okay. Have a good day."

I sat with the phone to my ear for a long time after the line went mute. I replayed every word, trying to catch my errors, though there weren't any. I waited until smoke from the burnt garlic and onions filled the kitchen. Only then was I able to snap out of my trance to check if there was anything in the frying pan I could save.

But nothing could be saved from that mess.

Before knocking on Esteban's door the following night, I opened Bumble. I hadn't opened the app for days, and it occurred to me that I could use the location to refresh the profiles and see if he was in them. I swiped left to see if his picture appeared. My finger was getting numb when he opened the door.

"Hey!"

Of course, I almost dropped my phone, and he was this close to seeing the Bumble profile picture of some other guy on the screen.

He looked different. For once, he had changed out of his work clothes. He wore gray sweatpants and a white V-neck that looked mouthwatering on him—tight on his shoulders and loose over the abdomen. His hair was a tangle of dark spikes falling in all directions, but it looked *so* good on him. I greeted him with a kiss on the cheek and confirmed that he smelled as good as he looked. Then he placed a hand on my lower back to guide me in.

The hand stayed a little longer than necessary—and that was okay.

No, it was *great* for me. That simple movement tore down whatever personal space rules we had been observing up to that point. When he finally removed it, the tingle lingered for a long time, and I found myself hoping he would touch me again before the feeling evaporated.

I was initially shy, politely lingering close to the door, watching from a few feet away. Nina's warning about growing closer to my competition still echoed in my mind, yet that lingering warmth on my lower back craved his touch again. His apartment defied my expectations—a spacious two-bedroom, two-bathroom loft perched on the forty-fifth floor of one of Brickell's gleaming luxury towers, mere blocks from where we'd shared lychee martinis under the stars. The off-white walls and sand-colored furniture created an atmosphere of understated elegance. His home contained nothing superfluous; each element, save the couch and wall décor, served a clear function. The space was practical yet unexpectedly inviting. Like Esteban himself. When he saw me looking at the abstract pieces of carved wood decorating the wall, he said, "They were a gift from a work colleague. She knew I had just moved in and was looking for something to put up on the walls."

"That was generous." I wasn't very comfortable with the idea of another woman walking around his place. If this so-called work colleague gifted him those pieces, then she had probably been to the apartment to see them. She had walked that same living room, stood right where I was standing, maybe even flirted with him.

He continued, "I recommended her for a position in operations a year ago. So, she got me a thank-you gift."

This moment. This was the perfect moment to ask if he knew of any job opportunities. He had recommended someone a year earlier, after all. I let the idea hang for a moment before I dismissed it. I had been on Altamira's company website many times, checking for any openings, and they weren't hiring. What was the point of bringing it up, then?

"Have you heard from WorldMedia?" I asked, trying to sound as uninterested as possible.

"Nada. You?"

I shook my head.

"I stayed with the VP for a while after everyone left. He's a really cool guy."

"Mmm ... how so?" I asked, regretting having brought up the subject, but desperate to know more.

"He's young. He can't be more than five years older than me and is already a VP with ten direct reports. He's been to Formula 1 races in four countries, has been to two World Cup finals—"

"Well, you also said his team is scared of him," I reminded him, not liking the conversation's turn. Cold drops of sweat slid down my back. I wanted him to stop praising this man I didn't know.

"Yeah, I mean, it's hard for me to report to someone I don't admire somehow."

"Oh."

"Let's see what happens." He walked toward the glass sliding doors. "All I'm saying is that after getting to know WorldMedia better, Altamira will need to come up with something amazing to get me to stay."

I pretended not to dread every word he said and stepped out to the balcony. Still trying to organize my thoughts, that first glimpse of the city overpowered my senses. The sun was beginning to set, and the buildings were slowly coming to life with their pink and blue light shows and sparkle. It was such a pretty sight that I yearned to wake up to it every morning.

Esteban, much like Nina, had made it in Miami. He was a beautiful man with a beautiful apartment overlooking this beautiful city. He was kind and independent. He was the male version of everything I wanted to be.

As the city lights replaced the last rays of sun, embarrassment grew about my situation, my family, and my status. Was there room in his life for someone carrying all my baggage? Would he be willing to share all his success with someone who wasn't even *close* to the lifestyle he had created?

I hadn't noticed how hard I gripped the railing until he placed one of his hands over my fingers, slowly prying them open.

"Are you scared of heights?" That deep, masculine voice vibrated against the skin on my neck, sparking chills at a place that was too warm to chill anything.

"No." I turned to face him, and to my delight, he didn't move back one inch. "It's beautiful out here. I love your apartment."

"I'm glad you like it." He gave me a shy smile, and his modesty made me like him even more. I loved that he could achieve all of this and still be humble about it. "Let's see what you think about my cooking."

He entwined his fingers with mine as he guided me to the kitchen, which was a vast contrast from the living room's earthy and cozy textures. White cabinets covered the walls, and four stools were aligned against a gray slab of stone that served as an island. On it, he had placed plates and utensils. He filled two glasses with white wine and handed me one, then served what looked like a Mediterranean salad and breadsticks.

"A salad?" I asked, my eyes opening wide. I teased. "Fancy."

"Don't laugh." He dumped an entire bag of croutons over the greens. The oven beeped, and he turned to check on a rack of chicken tenders he was roasting.

"Okay. So, what's your favorite meal to prepare?" I asked, mesmerized by the sight of him moving around the kitchen.

"Well ..."

"Well?"

"You got me on that one. I'm not very good in the kitchen."

Seeing this grown man admit he wasn't good at something, yet attempt to put together a meal for me, warmed my heart. I tried some of the salad directly from the bowl, and it was delicious.

"For a salad, this is quite good," I said as I dipped my fork in the bowl again.

"Now you are just being nice."

"It's true!" I laughed as I helped myself to more salad and wine.

By the time dinner was over, my shoes were off, and we had moved to his couch. I didn't check the time, because I didn't want to realize it was getting late, and I had to leave. The truth was that I didn't want the night to be over. Every start to a new story felt like bliss because it meant I had a pretext to stay for another little while. The wine warmed me in tiny sips, but his complete focus generated a different kind of heat. I savored how his eyes followed my every movement. His laughter became my favorite sound, a reward I sought repeatedly. That empty stretch of couch between us became my silent obsession—each repositioning of my body deliberately erasing a small portion of the distance. Everything was perfect until the conversation boomeranged back to job prospects and interviews.

"You never told me how it went for you yesterday," he asked. I didn't detect the slightest hint of malice in his voice, but I was bummed that he wasn't making any moves. Maybe I had read him all wrong, and he wasn't into me, like we had somehow ended up plugged into two separate outlets. Upset as it made me, I let him change the topic. But the wine kept flowing freely in my system, making me breathe in shallow puffs of warm air, urging me to close that last square of space between us.

"It wasn't that much different than the first one." It was a struggle to focus on the conversation, but I took the chance to check that his interest in WorldMedia was still as minimal as I hoped. "Are you waiting for offers from other companies?"

"I got a call from a software company. They want to meet me next week."

"Oh. That's really great. I hope that one goes well."

"Thank you. Have you applied anywhere else?"

I bit my lip, my brain too hazy to even come up with a good lie. "I've sent some applications out there."

"That's good. I think you are in the perfect moment to search for something better. Two years into your current job."

"Yeah." I took a long sip of wine, enough to placate the voice telling me to come clean. Enough to loosen up the last shreds of inhibition that pulled me together.

"But if you really like Sunset, remember you can always use another job offer to negotiate something better."

How did he manage to sprinkle his seriousness into almost everything he said? I sensed the honesty of his words. It translated into guilt because I was reminded of how much I was keeping from him.

"Thank you for the advice."

"But?"

But it's not that easy for me. I'm out of Sunset.

"But I have to get an offer first! Then I'll weigh my choices. I like to dream, but I don't like to plan on things I can't control." Bullshit. All bullshit, like that other perfect version of me possessed me. I was terrified of his reaction if I were to show him how crazy my life was, but he must have liked my cover, because when I looked up, he was smiling at me.

"What?" I snapped, already intimidated by his piercing gaze.

"There are so many things I like about you."

"Really? Like what?"

"Well, for starters, you are beautiful." He moved closer. "Like, breathtakingly beautiful." His fingers laced with mine. "Like, can't-stop-staring beautiful."

I enjoyed every word, yearning for more.

"But even that doesn't come close to the main reason why I like you."

"Which is?"

He ran a hand up my cheek and leaned in very close. I could smell the wine on his breath and longed to know what it tasted like in his mouth.

"Your drive. The way you have sorted out your life. That's hard to find."

Remorse set in my belly, but I dismissed it. I refused to ruin a perfect night with my problems and insecurities. Instead, I let him continue.

"I see it in the big things. Like what you did all those years ago, coming to Miami on your own and getting a degree and a job you love ... but I also see it in the little things."

I nodded because I couldn't bring myself to say anything. If I just let him talk, then I wasn't technically lying. And most of the things he was saying were true, anyway.

"Like showing up for a job interview minutes after crashing into a drunk driver. You were so nervous. And you managed to get a second interview."

"And now here we are, competing for the same job." It was a cheap joke, but he laughed.

"Yeah, but I know that interview is nothing for someone as smart as you."

Somehow, that conversation made me want him more. Accurate or not, it was the external validation I'd been craving. When he slid the empty glass off my hand to refill it, his fingers did that thing again—that spark on my skin. Perhaps it was the wine, but every sensation was heightened now. The heat rose to my face and left my mouth in a gasp of air.

I had to stop.

Breathe.

But I couldn't stop my eyes from following him to the kitchen, exploring every curve and nook of his body. He sensed my gaze upon him and turned around, flashing me a deliciously tempting grin that made my entire body melt.

My hand trembled when I reached out to receive the glass he had just refilled.

"I ... I don't think I should have another one." I heard myself mutter, sounding unconvinced. I knew I couldn't risk getting pulled over after drinking three glasses of wine. I also knew that it was easier for me to keep hiding the truth if I was sober.

He eyed the half-empty glass in my hand. "If you think you've had too much to drink, you can always rest here for a while."

And then the wine took over, and the last shred of inhibition came crashing down.

"I can't possibly think of sleeping if I'm here with you."

His eyes didn't leave mine for the next minute, while I took a long sip of the wine, placed the glass back on the table, and leaned back the length of the couch. He leaned close.

Closer.

Until I felt the heat of his body hovering over mine.

"Can I kiss you now?" he said, as if he had been holding the urge to kiss me for years. What little air was between us was warm and dense, bursting with energy, and a scent that was irrevocably his.

I nodded and let out a soft *uh-huh* as I laced my fingers around the nape of his neck, tugging his hair to pull him closer, until there wasn't any space between us. We let our lips graze for a moment, and they parted just as they were about to meet. We moved slowly at first, our breaths steady, taking the time to explore and taste the faint wine notes that lingered in our mouths. Our tongues followed the cadence of our hands. Then the light beard I had longed to touch so many times was grazing down my neck.

Faint notes of music hovered in the background. I couldn't determine whether the soundtrack had been present since my arrival or added later in our evening, but now I recognized its subtle presence. Those whispered melodies perfectly enhanced every sound between us. In those moments, his apartment eclipsed every other place in the world. My hands slid down his back, then over his abdomen, and felt his muscles contract under the thin fabric of his shirt. I reached to peel the bottom, uncovering a strip of skin, and he pulled back and took it off completely.

The air between us vanished as Esteban's half-naked body suddenly dominated the space above me, his skin radiating warmth. My touch wandered across his chest and arms with intentional slowness, preserving each moment of contact. I pulled him toward me, wanting to feel the weight of his body on mine. Our movements rapidly combusted into something fierce and impatient—restraint abandoned for raw urgency. I wanted him. I wanted everything from him.

The music faded away, and the only sound that mattered was our breathing, shallow and uneven.

I could feel his erection against my jeans when my phone went off.

Once.

Twice.

About a minute of ringing later, he stopped for an instant and looked at me. His eyes had gotten darker.

"Can you turn it off?" he asked in between shallow gasps of air.

My cell phone was vibrating on the table right next to us. With Esteban's lips an inch away from mine, I turned my head around to see the glowing screen. It was an unknown number. Instinct suggested an HR screening might be on the other end of the line, and though my thoughts remained muddled, I knew that I needed to answer.

Chapter Twelve

"I'm sorry. I need to pick up."

Esteban leaned back to his corner of the couch. His lower lip was a little swollen, his hair tousled, his eyes impatient. He looked beautiful in his corner, all bare chest, impatiently waiting for me. The urge to switch off my phone and straddle his body tugged at me, but practicality prevailed; an unknown number could mean the difference between staying in the country and leaving it.

"Hello?" I contained the panting in my voice as best as I could.

"Oh, Sofia!" Catalina barked on the other side. "I need your help."

Ugh. I rolled my eyes until they hurt. Leave it to my neighbor to interrupt at the most inconvenient moment. I considered hanging up, but she was so loud that Esteban had probably heard her voice. He was looking at me intently.

"Today is Tuesday, Catalina," I murmured. "We agreed to—"

"I know. I'm sorry. But I'm stranded here, and Togo hasn't been out of the apartment since last night."

I didn't know what she meant by "here." Heck, I didn't mind if she was stranded in the middle of the sea, but I thought about Togo. All hollow eyes and tummy waiting for someone in the darkness. Then I looked at Esteban leaning on his side of the couch, all muscles and lust, waiting for me to hang up.

Catalina's explanations faded in the distance. I didn't care about her excuses anymore. Whatever they were, I had known for a long time she wasn't fit to keep a dog.

"I'm in the middle of something. Can you ask someone else?" My voice was strained. My head was a conflicted mush of thoughts. What was my plan, again? Part of me wanted to finish what I had started with Esteban, whatever that was. I also wanted to help Togo but knew he wasn't my responsibility. The rest of me was still processing that the call hadn't been from WorldMedia or another company, as I desperately wished.

Esteban tapped my knee. When I looked up, he mouthed, *I'll go with you*.

"*What?*" I mouthed back. He picked up his shirt from the floor and put it on, then took hold of my hand and gestured with his head towards the door.

Confusion washed over me. Had Catalina's voice carried to his ears? Was this his polite method of showing me the door? A weak "yes" fell from my lips before she ended the call. Nina's reproach for helping someone like Catalina echoed in my mind, though poor Togo hardly deserved blame for his unfortunate owner. I trailed after Esteban—my cheeks flaming, movements uncoordinated, thoughts scattered—while pretending everything was normal as I tugged my top back into place.

Only after I'd begun slipping on my shoes did I summon the courage to ask, "Did you hear what she said?" He stopped in the hallway, inches from the door. "Not all of it, but what I heard sounded important." Then, without any warning, he turned and pinned me against the wall, pushing his body against mine and whispering in my ear, "And I'm not ready to say bye to you yet." He brought his lips so close to mine that they were almost touching, and I actually closed my eyes and leaned in—enthralled and forgetting about Togo and Catalina. He froze briefly and whispered into my mouth, "Let's go."

Flushed and woozy as I was, it took me almost a minute to compose myself and walk out of the apartment. I was hooked. Physically, if not emotionally. And I knew he knew it, because of how his gaze now rested on all the areas of my body that had been off-limits a few days earlier with a half-smirk in his face.

The ride to my apartment was delightfully familiar, the sun setting over the same roads we had passed on our first night out. This time, Esteban just slipped the keys out of my hand and got behind the wheel. He didn't even ask for directions. I didn't complain. I was still smitten from all the touching, worried about Togo, and buzzed from the wine. I liked the confidence that he exuded in everything he did, and how it seemed to have everything under control. I liked how he kept one hand on the wheel while the other searched for my fingers and closed tightly around them.

Togo's eager whimpers penetrated the closed door, carrying all the way to the corridor where I stood. His ability to detect my approach remained a mystery. A pang of jealousy surfaced as I wondered if he greeted Catalina with the same enthusiasm when she returned home. "Is he friendly?"

Esteban asked. I could tell by the spark in his eyes how much he was brimming with anticipation.

"You'll see," I answered as I twisted the doorknob.

Out came an overjoyed Togo, tongue hanging out from thirst, wagging his lower body. He came up to me first, pressing his paws on my belly to reach my face, then checked out Esteban for an instant before he ran back inside to show us his empty water dish.

"Is this the dog you walk?!" I could feel the joy in Esteban's voice.

"Yup. Meet Togo. My responsibility three nights a week."

"Wow ... I never got why you did it, but now that I've met him, I don't see how you'd stop."

We waited for Togo to gulp an entire serving of water and food, then refilled them both and watched him devour them again before we walked out to the park.

Togo ran for ten minutes, stopping only to check that Esteban and I were still sitting on the bench. I rubbed the spot behind his ears just the way he liked it, and when I looked back up, Esteban was staring at me with a smile on his lips.

"You have a gift, you know?" The last ray of sunlight was illuminating his face, making him look dreamy.

"Oh, really? And what is it?" I probed.

"You make everything better. You have this ... light in you. You can't hide it, even if you want to."

Lately, my so-called *light* had been slowly fading away, until it was little more than a speck of glitter in the darkness. "I don't know. If you are thinking about Togo, then let me tell you, it's a lot of work, and nothing comes out of it."

He was quiet momentarily, then his gaze shifted from the dogs to me.

"I disagree," he finally said. "I think there's a reward in everything we do. Or that's the way it should be."

"What's the reward here?" I asked with cynicism.

"Doing this for your neighbor must bring you some joy or purpose. At the very least, you should enjoy spending time with Togo. Otherwise, what's the point?"

The streetlights lit up just as the darkness blanketed the park. It was late summer, that time of year when the day stretched to no end, and night came well after eight p.m. I called Togo over. He was dark brown, and I was always afraid he'd get lost in the dark. He ran over and placed his head on my leg, waiting for another rub.

"Sometimes it's hard to find joy when life gets messy," I said.

"Sofia—" He moved closer on the bench, and the tickle in my belly intensified. "Not gonna sugar coat it. Life can be a total shit show. I don't know a lot about you—yet." My stomach did a full somersault. "But you gotta learn to find joy in the little things."

"Even work and unpaid dog sitting?"

"Especially unpaid dog sitting."

That made me break with nervous laughter, in part because he had absolutely no idea how impossible it had been for me to enjoy my job at Sunset and, in part, because I knew he was right. He opened his mouth to say something else, but my phone rang. It was Mom.

"Do you have other dogs to walk?" he joked, but the call had taken all the humor out of the conversation. He caught on and mumbled, "Go ahead, I'll keep an eye on him." Togo followed him, wagging his tail.

"Hola, Mami."

Silence.

"¿Aló?" I said, a little louder this time.

I heard a raucous of voices, then feet shuffling and doors closing. Finally, Mom's voice blasted from the other side. "¡Mija!"

"Mami, ¿estás bien?" I asked if she was okay, because I feared something had happened to her. Something terrible and irreversible, while I was in Miami, walking my neighbor's dog with Esteban, incapable of helping her.

But the music in the background indicated the exact opposite.

"Mija, te extrañamos." Her voice was slurred, and it was eerie to hear her say she missed me. I covered my free ear to shield from the noise, but the racket was coming from her side.

"¿Donde estás?" I asked while I tried to paint a mental image of whatever low-life block party she had gotten herself into. It was impossible to place the voices over the vallenato blasting. A male voice called out to Doña Carmen, the sound of beer bottles clinking. And laughter. Boisterous laughter.

Esteban was waiting nearby, probably pretending he couldn't hear me. I raised my voice as much as I could without alarming him. "Mami, si estás en la casa, pásame a Santiago." Put Santiago on the phone.

"Su hermano está ocupado afuera," she muttered that my brother was busy outside.

Another ghastly male voice blasted in my ear, thick and garbled. I couldn't distinguish the words, but they made Mom laugh again.

"Pásame a Santiago ahora." I demanded to talk to Santiago again, more assertively this time. My words had lost all tact and patience. It wasn't the right time, but I had avoided a confrontation long enough.

There was a grunt, followed by the sound of steps and doors, more music and traffic noise, and Mom's voice calling for Santiago. I could feel my phone sucking me in and transporting me to the other side, to that front porch packed with people I didn't know. People who didn't care about me, beyond the money I sent.

"¿Sofia?" Santiago's voice was slurring worse than Mom's, and he seemed to be in three simultaneous conversations with all the chatter in the background.

"¿Qué está pasando allá?" I barked at him. *What's going on there?*

"Nada, Sofia. Vinieron unos amigos." He replied that they had friends over.

"¿Un martes?"

"Uy, ¿apenas es martes?" he mocked, and my blood boiled. Their having friends over on a Tuesday night wasn't new, but my recent unemployment was, and that made all the difference.

"Dios mio, Santiago. Yo aqui trabajando, viendo como hago—" I started to complain that I was all the way here working, when he interrupted me.

"Mira, Sofia. No me vengas con tu mierda capitalista ahora." Always the asshole. Santiago could be kind and charismatic when he wanted, but alcohol had a way of removing all niceties. The beliefs he safeguarded came out in full force, like his disagreement with the life I had chosen for myself.

"¿De que estas hablando?" I asked.

"Tú te fuiste porque quisiste." *You left because you wanted to.* "Ahora no vengas a quejarte que estas aburrida, o que te hace falta aquí, o que trabajas mucho." *Don't complain that you're bored, or that you work too much.*

His unexpected accusation froze me in place, my thoughts temporarily suspended. I searched desperately for a reply that wouldn't reveal how deeply he'd caught me off guard.

I'm glad I left!

My life is not ...

There was a woman with him. Lorena, perhaps. Who knew? It was impossible to keep track of his relationships. He could've broken up with her and started seeing someone else in the past week. His voice reappeared a moment later, as if he had forgotten he was on the phone with me.

"Me tengo que ir. Le digo a mamá que te llame mañana." *I'll ask mom to call you.*

"Que mierda, Santiago. ¿Así es como se gastan la plata que les mando?" I snapped just as the sound faded away. *Was this how they spent my money?*

His voice returned. It was loud, and full of bitterness. "Tu fuiste la que te gastaste lo que quedaba de los ahorros de mi papá para irte. No me vengas con que yo me estoy gastando la plata ahora."

His words made me freeze. He blamed me for spending Dad's savings to move to Miami, but the worst part is that he made me sound selfish, reckless. My stomach twisted every time Santiago made me question my choices and spoil my most sacred memories of Dad.

"You know there's nothing for me there." My voice came out weak when I wanted it to be strong.

"Igual te fuiste." I could picture him holding my old iPhone close to his mouth, covering it with his hand. "Tú no tienes ningún derecho para decirnos como vivir." *You left, so you don't get to tell us how to live.*

I stood there, phone still to my ear, the lively chatter on the other side getting louder. Is that what they thought about me? That I'd left them? That I'd spent what little we had left to fulfill my American fantasy? My body drained of all heat, and a heavy weight settled in my chest—that ever-present guilt they were able to stir with just a few short phrases.

"I ... I don't think of it like that, Santiago. You know, I—"

"Sofia, no puedo hablar ahora." *I can't talk now.*

"Oh, okay. It's just ... le dices a mi mamá que me llame mañana, por favor."

A few seconds of noise ticked by. I was about to hang up when he suddenly exclaimed, "Oye, aprovechando que llamaste—¿te acuerdas de los tenis Nike que me mandaste? Se están pelando en la parte de arriba. Como ya nos estas armando una caja, ¿puedes meter un par nuevo? High tops. Azules." Oh yes, he wouldn't let the opportunity pass to ask for something, and be wildly specific about it. He'd worn out the sneakers I'd sent him. He needed new ones, high tops, blue.

I was a thread away from throwing my phone against the sidewalk. The two things keeping me from doing it were Esteban—I could picture his face if he saw me blasting my cell against the ground—and knowing that I couldn't afford a new one.

It was painful to swallow the scream lodged in my throat. I shifted my body a few steps away and shielded the phone with my hand.

"You are fucking unbelievable." I hung up and struggled to keep my entire arm from shaking. My eyes tingled. The nerve! Where did he get the audacity to ask for stuff so swiftly?

Ah, but I knew the reason. I knew because it had happened time and time again. They weren't making any effort to live without my help, and succeeded at spending down to the last peso way before the next allowance was due. I would bitch about it, and they chose to ignore me. Guilt consumed me while they crafted elaborate apologies. I'd been away far too long to gauge how much of it was true.

"Sofia?" Esteban's voice behind me made me jolt. I was standing on the park's edge, so close to him that I was sure he had heard part of the conversation. I struggled to come back to my senses, to bring my attention back to where I physically was. I didn't have time to worry about Santiago's messed-up sneakers. I had enough problems of my own.

Esteban turned me around gently until we stood face to face. His gaze traveled to my watery eyes, his own filling with worry. He didn't need to ask if I was okay. He didn't need to say anything at all. At that moment, he did exactly what I needed him to do: let me steam out my anger and stand with me through it all. I was grateful he was there with me, one hand holding Togo's leash, the other one pulling me closer to his chest.

"Remember what I said about finding joy in the small things?" He whispered in my ear.

I nodded.

"It also applies to helping others. It doesn't deserve your effort if it doesn't bring you purpose."

"But I can't stop helping them." I wasn't sure how much he had heard of the conversation, whether his advice was grounded on it, but the only thing keeping me from falling apart was him.

"That's okay. You need to adjust your attitude towards it. Do it for you."

A heavy exhale escaped me. Naturally, he didn't have the full story—even my own grasp of the situation had gaps.

"Sofia?" I felt the rumble in his chest when he said my name.

"What?"

"I help out my parents in Puerto Rico, too."

I pulled myself away, only enough to look at his face.

"You do?"

"Yeah. I've done so for a while."

"Oh."

"Sometimes it doesn't feel fair to me, but most of the time I'm just grateful I get to do it."

He had found something important that we had in common, which wasn't particularly easy for us. The combination of happiness and profound relief overwhelmed me, causing my lips to curve upward when our gazes locked.

"What is it?" he asked.

"I think I like you a little more now."

Esteban's fingers grazed my chin and lifted it a little, until our lips touched. I could've stayed an hour in that position, soaking in his breath, but right there, at the edge of the dog park, we decided to close the gap.

Our first kiss quickly went from curious and chaste to urgent and passionate, a race against time to pull our clothes off. But this one was slow and tender. Every few seconds, one of us would stay still, waiting for the other to continue, as if we were taking turns asking for permission to move.

His hands were on my waist, pulling me closer. It was so perfect that I forgot about Mom and Santiago drinking my money away and about the expiration date on my visa. I even forgot about Togo, who was patiently waiting for us to finish.

When we pulled apart, he lowered his forehead against mine, his eyes closed, air escaping his mouth in small gasps.

"When do I see you again?" he whispered.

"I don't know."

"That won't work," he said as his fingers dug deeper, his hands stroking from the sides of my waist to my lower back.

It made me smile to feel wanted by a person I liked so much.

"My friend Nina wants to meet you." I let the line hang between us while I gauged his reaction. Would he run for the hills at the suggestion? Was the question clingy? Too forward?

But a soothing smile appeared on his face. "Sure. Can Nina make it to lunch tomorrow?"

When we finally pulled apart, my cheeks were dry, my shoulders were relaxed, and my scowl had turned into a smile.

Finding joy in the little things was so much easier with him around.

Chapter Thirteen

Wednesday marked a whole week since I'd walked out of Sunset with a box of samples that now strategically covered the largest stain on the carpet. My fingers traced the full-sized foundation bottles and cataloged the various lipstick shades. I would send the lot to Mom, where she could convert the neighbors into customers. Her excitement for this side hustle was uncertaain, but with my paychecks gone, Sunset's makeup offered the closest thing to an income.

It was tedious work, removing the glossy *preview sample* sticker from each product without damaging the gold letters underneath. I wish it had done a better job keeping my mind occupied and my hands away from my cell phone. My e-mail was still barren of job offers. My cell phone rested on the carpet, and every time I glanced at its dark screen, I felt gut-wrenched that no one was planning to call me. And since Esteban's happy retelling of how he hit it off with WorldMedia's VP, I knew I wouldn't have a life until I was certain I was still in the race.

I dropped the samples and searched for WorldMedia's phone number. Surely, forty-eight hours was enough waiting time to give them a polite follow-up call, especially after a *second* interview. Would they question my work ethic if I called during office hours? I had succeeded in making Esteban believe that I was at the office every day, to the point that he waited until six p.m. to call. What if I couldn't fool Dianelys the same way?

Something told me Esteban wasn't pestering WorldMedia with eager follow-ups. He was too relaxed about the outcome, and too confident in his performance to stress about Dianelys' opinion. The possibility of gaining even this small advantage over him was irresistible. I waited for the clock to mark ten a.m. to call the WorldMedia office. The receptionist transferred me to an endless hold, where office conversations leaked through so clearly, I could almost distinguish words and felt tempted to interject my own comments. My finger was already hovering over the disconnect button when Dianelys finally answered. Her immediate recognition of me registered as a triumph. "How are things at my second-favorite makeup company?" I felt like crap that she had started the conversation with the one question that would inevitably force me to lie.

"All's good!" I said loud enough to crush any room for doubt, and swiftly moved to the topic at hand. "I was calling to ask if you have any updates on the media manager position?"

"Well, between you and me, Linda hasn't stopped talking about you. You do remember Linda Prentice, right?"

"Of course, we met during the first interview." I kept my volume poised, allowing the professional version of Sofia to take over. The one who didn't have to pretend to be employed while plotting to sell makeup samples in Colombia.

"You didn't hear this from me." Her voice dropped to a whisper, "But the decision is down to you and another candidate. And that's a lot to say, because we received over three hundred applications for this role."

She didn't have to say his name. The way my stomach caved when she told *another candidate* was enough proof. How could my body react this way for the one person I was competing against?

"Oh, wow. It's such an amazing opportunity. If you need anything from me to expedite the decision, I'm more than available." Perhaps a meeting with the VP was the next logical step, and I was a second from asking her if I should meet this person, but I contained myself. No muestres el hambre, *don't show them you're hungry*, as the saying goes. Genuine interest was good, but derailed enthusiasm could come across as desperation, and no one likes a desperate person.

"We plan to send an offer out by the end of the week, so you'll hear from me by then."

"Sounds great! Looking forward to your call."

"Thanks, darling. And congratulations, again."

I hung up, and I went through the entire thing in my head. I didn't know a one-minute phone conversation could make me so happy. Friday was so close I could practically taste the sweetness of victory. The job was mine. Why else would she congratulate me? Call me *darling*? I went from pacing to jumping up and down in the middle of my apartment, shrieking into space, because finally, *finally* things were looking up for me.

For lunch, I'd arranged to meet Nina and Esteban at a tropical-themed restaurant in Wynwood. Upon entering, my heartbeat accelerated—triggered by the salsa melodies in the background and the enormous mural that claimed an entire wall, a colorful interpretation of *El Malecon* executed in yellow and blue streaks that matched the rest of the decoration. Yet what truly quickened my pulse was spotting Esteban, already waiting at our table.

He was on the phone. I stood a few feet away, taking him in. I loved how his sole focus was on that one conversation, the way his brow furrowed when he was quiet, listening to the other side. His replies were sharp and fast. Whatever the discussion was, he was winning. It took him a few minutes to wrap it up, but his smile for me afterwards was worth the wait.

"It's so nice that you made it," I said as I sat. "Taking time off work and all."

"I'm happy you asked. I didn't have lunch plans today. I rarely eat alone."

"What do you mean you don't eat alone?" I recalled how I chugged my lentil soup in the cubicle most days.

"Just that. I try to make lunch plans every day."

"Sounds intense. Don't you get tired?"

"Not really. If anything, it makes me more efficient. Tackling two things at the same time."

"Right." I nodded, but something about it made me uncomfortable. There was an intensity to it, like he had an ulterior motive for everything he did.

"I do work lunches. I catch up with friends." Then he leaned closer and dropped his voice. "I meet with people I like."

"I hope it doesn't turn into a business lunch with Nina," I teased.

"We'll see." His eyes widened. So did his smile.

He was the type of person who enjoyed his job so much that he didn't consider talking business over lunch as work. "So, what's the secret? To find and keep a job you voluntarily carry through lunch time?" It was an honest question, though it came out like a reproach. He leaned back on his seat, staring at me before his gaze softened and he chuckled. "You think I'm obsessed with work, right?"

"I didn't say that."

"You thought about it."

"Okay, I did. The whole thing sounds exhausting."

"I don't know that there's a secret—and if there is, I'm not sure I know it. But I can't afford to deprioritize work in my life."

"Go on." I stared at him with eager eyes.

"Well, you already know I help my parents, and you know I live alone. Other than my aunt, I don't have a lot of family to rely on." He shrugged, then paused like he was trying to recollect some lost memory. "A few years ago, my parents were always complaining about money. They were living paycheck to paycheck. One day, a friend connected them with a woman who was looking for an American citizen to marry; she was offering ten grand cash por los papeles. And they asked me to marry her."

My eagerness turned to dread, and my fingers shook so much I hid them under the table. I held my breath for the next part.

"I refused, but they asked me again the following year. I'm their only son, and I guess I wasn't collaborating the way they thought I should."

I struggled to grasp the meaning of his story. Did he disagree with marrying an undocumented person, or was it that he didn't like that his parents were asking more of him? If he was against doing the marriage thing for money, would he be willing to do it as a favor? Would he do it for love?

"It sounds like your parents needed your help, and those women, too." My voice came out in a squeak. I wasn't sure I wanted to know the answer to the next question. "Did you consider it?"

"No. I felt it was an easy way out, all for money that would've disappeared in a few months of rent."

My stomach dropped to my feet.

Up until that point, he hadn't noticed how still I was. It was his right to refuse his parents' proposal. However, it still hurt to learn he would never consider doing something like it, because making that same proposition had crossed my mind, and those women were probably like me: on the verge of desperation.

"So, what did you do?" I asked through the knot in my throat.

"I worked. I worked my ass off for years to contribute how they wanted me to. Eventually, I helped them sort things out in San Juan and set up their business there. I still manage their marketing. I step in when they make money decisions. I like what I do, but I like the stability that comes with it more. For my parents, too. And I learned early that the more I enjoy it, the easier it gets."

"You are lucky. Not everyone enjoys the same circumstances you had." It came out harsher than I meant, but it was hard to keep up the admiration façade when he inadvertently rubbed his endless possibilities in my face. He was instantly taken aback, and a furrow appeared between his brows.

"I don't think so. I made choices that got me where I am today. Some of my friends became parents in their early twenties, got into debt, got married, got divorced; now they're stuck paying alimony and attorney fees. I wanted something different for myself." He paused. When he spoke again, his tone was softer. “I couldn’t afford to make mistakes. My only choice was to focus on work and get ahead.”

“You make it sound as if having a life and forming a family were bad things.”

“If the timing is wrong, it is.”

We were quiet, and I could feel the tension mounting. The conversation had taken a weird turn, and it was hard to back out of it.

“I’m surprised you reacted this way,” he finally said. “You’re as focused on your career as I am.”

“Yeah, whatever. My situation is different.”

The furrow between his brows reappeared.

He opened his mouth, but whatever he was about to ask got lost in the moment. Nina’s voice screeched from a few tables away. “You guys. I’m so sorry I’m late. My last meeting went over by twenty minutes!”

Nina could make an entrance. She dumped her bag on the empty chair and stretched her hand towards Esteban.

“Nina dos Santos, prazer.” She shook Esteban’s hand with purpose, and I was filled with pride. “I’m famished! Did you guys order already?”

That’s how Nina’s entrance saved me from disclosing God knows what information to Esteban. I didn’t know if I was relieved or pissed because I had lost the opportunity to find out more about what he thought about marriage. But the moment was gone.

Lunch was served, and the topic was forgotten. Nina told Esteban how we met and basically praised me for the next twenty minutes. I smiled, nodded, and felt utterly fortunate to have my best friend and my crush getting along.

That was, until they started talking business.

"Sofia told me you do new client acquisitions at Banco do Rio." Esteban leaned in, his tone drifting seamlessly from casual to work mode.

"That's right. I'm part of the marketing department. Why? Do you have a new client for me?" For Nina, asking snappy comeback questions was a good sign. It meant the other person was worthy of her attention.

"Who runs your media?" he asked without missing a beat.

The water I'd been sipping nearly sprayed from my mouth. The realization that his lunch invitation wasn't merely social—that he actually intended to pitch his agency to Nina—seemed too outrageous to be serious.

"C&C does our media."

"Oh." It was his only answer. He let it hang there, then turned back to his poke bowl. Nina shot me a look. My motives for arranging their introduction were twofold: I wanted Nina to witness firsthand what drew me to him, but this lunch might also reveal an entirely new dimension of Esteban—his business persona discussing deals and competitors. It was a golden opportunity to assess how much of a threat he was as an opponent for the position I couldn't afford to lose.

"What about C&C?" I chimed in.

"Nothing." He shook his head. "How's it going with them? Are they helping you reach your goals?"

"I like to think so. Yes," Nina replied.

"Mmm." Another spoonful went into his mouth.

"I'd very much like to hear your opinion about them." She wasn't even looking at her food anymore. Her attention was fixed entirely on Esteban.

"Their team is not very experienced." He shook his head as he said it, dropping the phrase like bait on the center of the table, waiting to see if she clicked. "I bet most of the money you invest is wasted on third parties and fees."

"Is that so? Enlighten me." Nina gave me a side look, one that said *brace yourself* and *oh, this is gonna be good.* I realized she didn't need me to hold her by the hand, and I wanted to see how they fared without me mediating. I stayed quiet and took the chance to learn something from them.

"They tend to run the same cookie-cutter campaigns for all their clients," Esteban said without missing a beat.

"You are only saying that because they're Altamira's competition."

"I'm saying it because I've seen their proposals, and you asked my opinion."

I was mesmerized by him—by the confidence of his opinions. It was exactly the kind of self-assurance I longed to have. If he had brought this same energy to his interview, my chances were screwed.

"I think their proposals are brilliant," Nina replied. "They just presented a creative pitch for a seasonal campaign to attract high-end clients."

"Sounds like a great opportunity." He opened his eyes wide and nodded a few times, but his face didn't have the slightest glint of belief. "What are they suggesting?"

"Digital media ads with an emotional twist."

"It won't work," he said.

I stopped eating. God, he could be obnoxious. Would it kill him to sugar-coat it a little? Still, a part of me was wildly turned on.

"Excuse me?" Nina recoiled in her seat.

"It's the same plan they use on every client."

"Okay. What would you do differently?" Nina didn't sound as spirited anymore; her confidence had shattered a little in the last few seconds.

He cleared his throat and leaned into the table, lowering his voice, like he was about to drop the secret to every successful marketing campaign. "For starters, you need to know your audience. The client you are targeting won't respond to a banner with a cheesy ad."

I looked at Nina. Nina stared at Esteban. Esteban had a glimpse of a grin forming on his lips. He knew he had struck a chord.

"What works with high-end clients is relationships and word of mouth. Perhaps a partnership with a local bank at one of the cities you are targeting?" he added.

Nina's eyes opened very wide. "And I suppose your agency knows just the perfect bank looking for a partnership?"

"Give me a call when you are ready to talk." He flashed a satisfied smile at her.

Nina opened her mouth, then closed it again. There was a hint of admiration in her eyes. "Oh, you're good," she said as she nodded.

He took one last sip of water as he checked the time. Then he slipped an Altamira credit card to the waitress. Nina complained, but he argued that lunch would count as their first meeting if they ever did business together.

I couldn't unglue my eyes from him. He made confidence look natural and oh-so-hot.

"It was great to meet you, Nina."

"Yeah ... you too," she replied, apparently too dumbstruck to come up with anything better.

When he turned to say goodbye me something magical happened. He moved his face to the side and planted a soft peck on my lips. It was so unexpected and sweet, and caught me off guard. I couldn't wipe off the smile on my face for the rest of the afternoon.

After he disappeared, I turned back to Nina. She stared at me with a mischievous look in her eyes.

"So? What'd you think?" I asked, near-swooning and flushed.

"Other than he is a smart ass and a workaholic?" she replied, then her expression turned serious. "I don't think there's anything wrong with him."

"That's a relief to hear ... because I really like him."

"I can tell. So, what are you planning to do about it?"

"Meaning ...?" I braced myself for a Nina pep talk.

"I know you are not telling him the full story, and I get that. You just met. But he seems like a great guy, and I think something good can come out of this. A relationship, for once."

"We are still far from that." Although I secretly hoped we were getting close.

"And you'll never get any closer if you don't let him in."

It was crucial that Nina understand—Esteban wasn't part of the formula to help me make it in Miami. Rather, I viewed him as the ultimate prize, the finishing touch to the carefully crafted existence I was building.

"He thinks I have my life figured out." My voice came out shakier than I intended.

Nina looked at me with big brown eyes, "You don't have to dump your entire life story on him. But I'm sure he'll appreciate a little honesty. Tell him what's happened at Sunset. Just say it happened this week. Tell him about your student loan. Tell him about your job hunt. What if he comes up with some ideas?"

"You are right—" Of course, she was right. "I just don't wanna break the spell yet."

"What spell?" Nina asked.

I shifted around in my seat. "Oh, you know ... the first two weeks spell. When everything is rosy and enchanting, and he likes everything about me."

"Well, it ain't gonna be rosy if he gets the WorldMedia job, right?"

"I thought about that. I spoke with Dianelys this morning. From her feedback, I'd say the job is mine." I smiled, but even I knew how much uncertainty came from my statement.

She was quiet for a moment before she replied; her lips were straight. "I hate that your entire plan to stay depends on that one job offer."

"Not as much as *I* hate it," I said. "But what other option do I have?"

She leaned across the table and whispered, "You know, he could marry you and give you residency."

"Shut up, Nina ... you know I'd never do that," I said, matching her volume.

"And why not?" She fell back on her chair, raising both hands. "I wouldn't sack the idea. You like him, and it's obvious he really likes you."

Nina had verbalized the idea that had been spiraling in my head for the past week.

Esteban wouldn't marry me to give me papers. Besides, how would I approach the topic without completely butchering my chances? How would I ask him to do something that he had already rejected twice in the past?

He wouldn't consider it a favor. His entire concept of me would be belittled to what he once thought of his parents.

But what if he fell in love with me?

Chapter Fourteen

My resistance finally collapsed. I had reached my limit—worn down by the ambiguity surrounding my work status, by job sites that served only to remind me how elusive visa sponsorships were, by immigration attorney websites advertising fees that eclipsed my entire savings history. When I started receiving notifications about a storm gaining power and speed over the Dominican Republic, I felt life was giving me a way out, a respite. The chatter between the security guards and the valet boys in the building lobby slowly transitioned to hurricane preparedness. I set the TV in my room to its highest volume and watched the traffic intensify just outside my building. Suddenly, people were in a frenzy to aid friends who had shutters to close, kids to pick up, and water bottles to horde.

I didn't have anything, or anyone, to protect, and I certainly didn't have anywhere to evacuate. But I was grateful to see that, just for a day or two, I wasn't the only one dealing with the stress of uncertainty.

Later that afternoon, I texted Esteban.

Sofia: There's a storm coming.

Esteban: Yeah. They just turned on the weather channel at the office.

Sofia: Should we reschedule?

We hadn't seen each other since that lunch with Nina, but even two days was starting to feel too long without him. I was practically counting down the hours to see him again, but the cone-shaped model of the storm didn't seem to agree with our restaurant plans. I stared at the phone, waiting for his reply. I stared a little too intensely, hoping with all my might that his answer was a *no*.

Esteban: I think we should reschedule the restaurant. They might close, anyway.

My heart plummeted a few floors. Then the phone vibrated again.

Esteban: We should eat in. You did say you can cook.

That simple moment transformed my despair into something weightless and hopeful.

Esteban: And I've never been to your place.

My place?

Oh, shit. He wanted to come over.

I imagined Esteban walking into my crummy apartment, taking in the second-hand furniture, trying to reconcile his image of me with his surroundings ... and being welcomed with a slap of hot air.

I searched for the landlord's contact in a frenzy. Surviving Miami with a floor fan was acceptable under my standards, but I wasn't ready to pull

Esteban into my mess. Not when it involved my greenhouse apartment. Not after seeing where he lived.

The landlord picked up after the seventh ring, and I asked him if it was possible to fix the A/C by the end of the day.

"¡Oyé, niña, viene un ciclón!" he exclaimed in his thick voice. "¡Nadie está trabajando!" His reminder that everyone's mind was on the hurricane rose above the noise around him.

I tried to remain as assertive as I could. "Luis, I've waited a whole week already. Me estoy asando aquí." *I'm burning up here.*

"I'll call you after the storm," he mumbled something else to me or whoever was there with him. Then he hung up.

Four deep breaths later, I texted Esteban.

Me: I'd love for you to come over, but my A/C broke.

I clutched my phone, not allowing my eyes to move away from the screen.

> **Esteban:** I'm sure it's tolerable. Plus, the temperature is dropping a few degrees tonight.

I stared at that text message for over a minute while I pictured Esteban in my apartment, taking in the simple kitchen, the plain walls lacking any décor, the tell-tale signs that my life was a work in progress. There was no way around it; I couldn't fake where I lived. So, I decided this would be good for me, for us, because it would bring me one step closer to the truth.

And I wouldn't spend the storm alone.

I've always thought couples are formed in a series of steps. There's a first date, followed by some formal dinner, a first kiss, first time having sex, running an errand together, the day you get to meet each other's friends, a first argument, make-up sex, and then—somewhere along the way—*Poof!* A couple is born.

In my case, the entire process would usually crash and burn somewhere between having sex and being introduced to his friends. Because introducing your new love interest to acquaintances usually implies some commitment. And that's when—*Poof!* They disappear like ghosts.

With Esteban, I had kept my expectations grounded, forbidding myself from fantasizing beyond the current step, carefully guarding my feelings, and delaying sex as much as I physically could. And perhaps it was the right approach. Because there I was, entering the grocery store with him by my side, searching for ingredients to cook mushroom risotto hours before a tropical storm made landfall.

I pretended to know my way around the upscale Whole Foods Market I'd never visited before, reading the overhead aisle markers as fast as possible. I normally did my shopping at a discount supermarket where prices were normal. I could buy the ingredients to fix myself a sandwich every night of the week, for the same price as one of Whole Foods' deli sandwiches. It was the sensible choice for me, although I had to admit the place paled compared to the high ceilings and chic market feel of this gourmet grocery store, with its colorful crates of organic everything and bright deli areas. When I suggested it to Esteban, he agreed as if it were the only acceptable option. So, there I was, holding a tiny container of baby bella mushrooms that was three times more expensive than what I usually paid.

As we walked down the aisles, I struggled to hide the mix of jumpiness and giggles bubbling up in me. Could he tell how nervous I was? Could other people tell?

Not that anyone would be interested in us. The supermarket was packed, as is expected when there is a hurricane warning. One thing I had deduced after a few years in Miami was that the population secretly loved the *idea* of a hurricane—the possibility of a mandatory break from the everyday routine, and the unhinged need to overspend on supplies, like the end of the world is near. The checkout queues stretched down some of the aisles. The heated voices of two women arguing over the last can of tuna rose above that of a store clerk announcing that they were out of water.

But we were not there for the canned food or the bottled water.

"Damn, people are going crazy over this storm." He shook his head, but there was a hint of confidence there, like he had received some secret intel that the storm was not happening.

"Should we not worry about it?" I asked as I saw a man wheeling a cart of milk formula and baby food. In the past three years, I had experienced countless storms and hurricane watches, but never an actual hurricane warning.

"People just love the drama of it. It's not the first time it rains in Miami." Then he leaned in and whispered so close to my ear that it sent chills rolling down my neck, "And I get to spend the storm with you."

I bit my lip, probably blushing every shade of pink as I kept pushing the cart forward, trying to keep myself as composed as possible.

"Have you talked to your parents?" I asked.

"I have. They live away from the coast. It's raining nonstop, but that's about it."

We walked down the aisles like a normal couple grocery shopping, like we had recently moved in together or were restocking before the storm. And it was its sheer normalcy that sent my emotions haywire. Had our relationship inadvertently skipped a few steps?

I grabbed the smallest bottle of olive oil I could find and noticed the miniature sizes of truffle oil on the top rack. My eyes lingered on them for an instant. Six ounces for $25. Permanently banned from my budget was an understatement. I'd cleverly proposed risotto as our meal to circumvent the meat department completely. Blowing my budget on truffle oil would defeat the entire purpose of my frugal planning. In went the olive oil, and I started pushing again. Then I heard a soft thud coming from the cart. Esteban had placed the truffle oil inside.

"We don't need it." We were in that awkward stage where I hadn't mustered the audacity to ask *who's paying?* Would he pick up the check, like he always did? Or was this one on me, since we were grocery shopping for my kitchen? My mind was already running the numbers against my credit card balance and confirming that I could not spend $25 on truffle oil.

"You were looking at it." He teased.

"It's optional," I said.

"Will it make whatever you are cooking better?"

I nodded. I'd tried the earthy mushroom concentrate before at Nina's; it tasted like nothing I'd ever had growing up in Colombia. That inconspicuous little bottle was the difference between average and exceptional risotto.

He smiled and gently moved my hands aside so he could continue pushing the cart.

I froze in the middle of the aisle for a moment, scanning the contents of the cart as it slid past me. The cart was already half full of more food than I had in my kitchen, and surely it was worth more than what was left in my credit line. I was cutting it close. Too close.

Esteban entered the wine aisle, asking if my surprise meal paired better with a white or red. Under different circumstances, the whole scene would've been incredibly romantic. My hot date was pushing a shopping cart down the wine aisle and planning to spend the storm at my place. And there I was, too chicken to tell him I couldn't afford a $100 shopping run. I grabbed the only $11 bottle of white I saw, but he beat me to the cart holding *two* glimmering bottles with impossible-to-pronounce French names. They clanked at the bottom of the cart, but all I could hear was the cashier saying *Your card is declined.*

My anxiety built with every slow and painful step of the checkout queue. I could barely focus on Esteban's recounting of Hurricane Maria years earlier, when he could finally fly down to Puerto Rico to aid … neighbors? Relatives? I was busy developing a plan before we reached the cashier. It was simple: I would wait until the end, when the cashier announced the total, and then I would pull out my credit card *very slowly* to give him a chance to pull out his. If that didn't happen, I'd turn every shade of crimson and say, "Shall we split?"

Yes, that would work. It would bring me up to my limit, but at least it wouldn't be declined. I rehearsed the phrase in my head a few times while he eyed the contents of the cart skeptically and asked me—yet again—if we had everything we needed.

The cashier finished ringing all the items and sang the total. My hand was shaking when I searched inside my bag, but I quickly realized I didn't have to sweat it anymore because Esteban had already tapped his credit card—his personal one—on the pad. He thanked the cashier and didn't turn to me once, like picking up the bill was the expected thing to do.

"Thank you." I hoped he couldn't read the relief on my face.

"You're welcome ... but you are cooking, right?" he said as he loaded the heavy bags into the cart.

"Only if you help." I winked at him, despite the stress that had plagued me for the last thirty minutes. He smiled and pulled me close in front of him, and I realized how—without notice, without a lot of effort, really—we had become a couple.

Right there, in front of check-out lane eight, next to a cart full of gourmet mushrooms and wine, surrounded by stressed South Floridians and annoyed store employees, we kissed.

Bringing a hot date to your place for the first time is supposed to be an exciting experience, right? Well, it wasn't for me. While Esteban hauled the grocery bags down the corridor, I took in the last few breaths of cool air, convinced I'd start sweating the minute I crossed my apartment threshold. How I had agreed so easily to the idea of Esteban spending the storm at my place was a mystery. Maybe I was in a rush to skip a few of those relationship steps. All I could think about as I pulled the key out of my bag was in what state I had left my apartment earlier that afternoon. As the squeaky door swung open, and I braced for the hot air to blast my face, I felt a fresh wave of panic.

"Wait here," I said as I pushed the door just wide enough for me to pass.

"Here?" Esteban looked around the empty corridor like he had been kicked out of his house. The heavy bags he carried—one of them holding two bottles of Sauvignon blanc—were already making dents in his hands.

"I'll just be a minute." I closed the door behind me, knowing I was making the situation even more awkward by having him stand outside, but I couldn't let him into the apartment without checking it myself first. I couldn't remember if I had left the stack of unpaid bills on the kitchen counter or dirty underwear on the floor.

Once inside, the air felt stuffy, but it wasn't the living hell I had envisioned. The storm was closing in, and the temperature had dropped a few degrees outside, making the unit airy and fresh. I rushed to my bedroom and turned on the oscillating fan, then sprinted to the ugly couch to ensure the accent pillow hid the crusty cigarette burn. The box addressed to Mom and Santiago sat by the door, and I ensured its flaps remained tightly folded. Having to justify sending basic toiletries like deodorant, razors, and bargain-priced Hanes underwear to Colombia would have been mortifying. As I confirmed the Sunset samples were concealed, the door creaked open. I whirled around with the startled guilt of a caught thief to discover Esteban's face appearing in the doorway. First his head, then his entire body followed, bags and all.

"Um, Sofia? Are you married?" He looked at me intently, one side of his mouth slightly curled up, like he already knew the answer was no, but still wanted to hear it. He was looking for an excuse to catch me doing whatever I didn't want him to see me doing.

I was perplexed, the blood rising quickly to my face, then leaving in a rush. "Um, no."

"Oh, okay. I was starting to worry out there." He walked in like it was the most normal thing to do—as if it was his apartment he was walking into. Then he placed the heavy bags on the kitchen counter that had been covered by unpaid bills just seconds before. "What was that about?"

"Just wanted to check everything was in order, that's all." I struggled to keep my voice from shaking. If he realized my nervousness, he did a beautiful job of disguising it. He moved to the center of the living room and mentioned that he couldn't tell the A/C wasn't working. He was right.

"We can always leave the door open and open the window," I suggested, knowing that the entire apartment would turn into an oven once I started cooking.

He agreed, and we opened the only window to let some of the storm breeze in. It had just started raining, a mellow drizzle of tiny drops. The apartment became cool and fresh, and we didn't even have to bring the fan out to the kitchen.

He came up behind me as I took the groceries out of the bag, and his scent filled the small kitchen space. "Let's see what all the rage about your cooking's about."

"Go easy on me. I might not be as gifted as you think," I warned him, too nervous to come up with anything else.

"You know, the more you say it, the less I believe it to be true."

He wanted to help. More than help, participate. Not the type of help that stands on the side and never gets his hands dirty, or is simply there to taste the food. He was washing the cutting board, picking up a mushroom that had fallen on the floor, and putting away the groceries. He complimented the scent of the garlic and onions from the skillet, then served two heaping glasses of wine and slipped one into my hand.

I didn't have wine glasses, so we used Ikea tumblers. My kitchen was the opposite of fancy, but he was unfazed by it.

After a few sips of wine and more than a few occasions when our arms touched or his face moved tantalizingly close to mine, my apartment started to feel different. The small kitchen, which I had always loathed, was now the perfect size for us to move around. It felt cozy, warm, and inexplicably sexy. Suddenly, I didn't hate my place as much as before. I loved having him there. His mere presence felt natural, effortless. Letting him see an aspect of my life without filters was liberating. I had been carrying a heavy lie on my shoulders, and a tiny but powerful part had been lifted. And as time passed, I realized how nice it would be to let him see more of that life I'd been shielding from him. I was a step closer to coming clean.

I added the rice to the pan and took a long sip of wine while I waited for it to turn golden.

"How much wine goes in it?" Esteban asked.

I poured what was left of the bottle, which felt like half a cup, and stirred it to help the rice absorb it. The kitchen was now rich with the fragrant aroma from the pan, and the sizzling sounds were louder than the storm outside.

"I told you we needed to get two." Esteban stood behind me, close. Very close. Until his chest was flush against my back and his breath was sending goosebumps down my neck. He removed the empty bottle from my hand and placed it on the counter.

"So you did." I added some of the broth to the rice and stirred it with a wooden spoon. "The trick is to add the broth little by little and give it a stir each time so that the rice absorbs it." I have no idea how I was able to sound coherent. It was maddening to have him so close in such a small space.

He gently grabbed my hand, the one holding the spoon, and brought it close to his lips, then he twisted it and planted a kiss on the inside of my wrist. The oddest and hottest sensation, this game we were playing, prolonged the inevitable.

"Can you switch the spoon to the other hand?" His tone changed; it was lower now, velvety smooth.

"No." I was also out of breath. "The other hand is to hold the wine."

His deliciously deep laugh filled the kitchen. Then he grabbed the bottle and poured the last few sips into his glass, without detaching his body from mine. That's when I decided I'd had enough subtle touches and demure kisses. I placed the glass on the counter and reached for his head with my empty hand. I found the nape of his neck and let my fingers tussle with his hair, pulling him closer. He marked a trail of tiny kisses down the side of my neck until he reached my collarbone.

Maybe it was the sound of rain picking up and trickling inside the living area, or the spicy notes of Esteban's scent hovering over me. Or perhaps I'd had a little too much wine. But the atmosphere changed between us. I felt something inside me give, a barrier falling, a need to disclose everything about me—down to the physical. I turned around without losing any body contact, practically rubbing my entire body against his, until I ended up facing him. Something had changed in him, too. I could see it in his eyes. The way his lips were slightly parted with just a hint of a smile.

The wine was sweet on his tongue. It tasted so much better than it did in the glass. His hands stroked my back, then traveled up to my shoulders, further up the nape of my neck, tussling my hair. And it was all quite lovely until I decided it was enough of the censored touch. I guided his hand over my top to let him know he was allowed to explore any part of my body he wanted to, and then I felt those parts swell under his touch.

Things would've escalated pretty fast if it hadn't been for the risotto bubbling behind us.

"Turn it off," he mumbled.

"Can't," I exhaled into his mouth. "It's almost done."

My focus shifted back to the stove as I leaned into him, a movement that felt as natural as breathing. Every few seconds, I stole another glance, still disbelieving yet thrilled by the evidence of his wanting me, specifically me. I loved having him all to myself, knowing that at that moment, I was the only thing that mattered to him. Delayed gratification works especially well when the thing you desire is within reach, reserved for you, and wants you to take it away. That's when it turns into a game that you know you'll win. It makes the entire wait more delicious.

I let him try the risotto directly off the wooden spoon, and his eyes opened wide.

"Corazón, esto está delicioso."

"I guess I'm not so bad." I dipped the spoon in the risotto again. "Definitely not as bad as you."

"Hey!" And then we were both laughing, drinking, and eating straight out of the pot. Kissing, nibbling, touching. We couldn't get our hands off each other for a long time, always venturing a little further. I briefly wondered how much longer I could prolong the foreplay if I kept stroking his front the way I had for the past ten minutes. Not that he was complaining at all.

The storm finally reached us. It came alive with the beat of the rain rattling the small window, the occasional lightning illuminating my entire apartment, and, less than a second later, the heavy crash of thunder drowning out all other sounds. We stopped kissing to look at it, facing the window. I let my fingertips graze his neck and rested my ear against his chest. For the first time, I saw a more beautiful view than the usual concrete wall. I saw all the power of nature, beauty, and anger pounding over my dream city. Esteban held me close, and I felt both the relief and the attachment that result from finding a protector, someone to—quite literally—join you even on the rainy days.

A violent thunder caused the lights to flicker for a second.

"Should I turn on the TV to see what's happening?" I asked.

"That sounds like a good idea."

"It's in my room."

"Even better," he whispered into my hair.

We set the TV on the local weather channel. The hurricane had lost so much power that it barely qualified as a Category 1. The weatherman tried to appear thankful, but the false excitement was evident. He probably hoped to report a more dramatic event than non-stop rain throughout the weekend.

"He looks bored, not relieved," Esteban scoffed.

"I know! Isn't that terrible?"

I'd never tease those who prep before a storm, those with families and homes to protect. But it's impossible not to laugh at those who think of a storm as a holiday, or a chance to submit an insurance claim.

"I knew it'd lose momentum," Esteban said.

I nodded. "Should I turn it off?"

"Nah. Just mute it, so we at least know if anything changes."

"Okay. It doesn't look like a hurricane anymore. Just a lot of water."

Another bolt of lightning filled the apartment, painting his face silvery-white. He no longer had the collected look that I had grown used to. His eyes were filled with expectation and lust. The bed was inches away, and we were both fully aware of it.

"I'm still spending the night with you."

Chapter Fifteen

His shirt was the first to touch the floor.

I needed this. Of course, I needed it. I had delayed my gratification for far too long. I had done so much more with men for whom I cared so much less. I let him peel my top away and join his on the floor, my hair cascading over my shoulders, and then his hands traveled down again.

Most people would surrender completely at this point—all boundaries dissolving, consciousness narrowed exclusively to emotion and physical sensation. But despite the wine and the foreplay, one part of me remained stubbornly anchored in reality. Tonight would be exceptional, but tomorrow morning would arrive with inevitable clarity, and all my problems would be there waiting, staring accusingly at the foot of the bed. I simply couldn't bear adding another complication to that lineup. In other words, the thought of returning to Colombia pregnant or with an STI was enough to snap me out of the moment. That would be a shit show for sure.

"Esteban, wait." My breath was ragged and uneven. I knew I had condoms stashed somewhere. I pushed him gently against the wall, still panting, still digging my fingernails into his shoulders, trying to push him away but simultaneously missing the sensation of his skin against mine, and turned to my bedside table to look for them. And then he did what any respectable gentleman would do. He pulled out a strip of condoms from his back pocket and entwined it in my empty hand, pulling my mouth against his again without any words or second thoughts. Warmth set in my belly, then spread down, between my legs, to all corners of my body.

His fingers stilled when they reached the edge of my jeans—thumbs sliding in, his hands spread over my hips, then stopped abruptly and waited for an instant before I nodded and whispered *sí* into his mouth.

It took us a while to get out of our clothes. We were too eager to touch and taste to waste time on inconvenient zippers and buttons. But eventually our clothes covered the bedroom floor, and when there was nothing else between us, I realized this wouldn't be the slow, romantic session I had envisioned. By now, we had both waited so long, touched so hard, teased to our very limits, that instinct and lust drove us. He lowered his mouth until it met mine again, and we just let our tongues glide and our lips stroke, and eventually slide down our bodies to discover which spots made us moan and which made us tremble.

If there was ever a moment when the field was exactly even between us, it was right there in my bedroom. Being completely naked in front of him was the second sincere action I was doing that night. No coverups. No lights off. Just me in my bedroom.

I made him walk back until his legs were pressed against the edge of my bed. His hands were on my ass when I teasingly pushed him, making him land in a seated position. And then I wrapped my legs around him, straddling him, increasing all the friction between us. I arched my back to let him see me, to reach all the spots I wanted him to kiss.

I could keep him in this position longer, but I should've known Esteban wasn't the type to lie still. In one swift movement, he rolled me onto my back. We were still facing each other, but this time he was controlling all the movements, his fingers slipping in and out between my thighs.

We switched a few times, as if neither of us was ever entirely satisfied having the other one take the lead. We took turns until we couldn't hold it anymore, and my tiny apartment was filled with the drumming sound of rain, gusts of wind, the tear of a foil wrapper, and careless, deliciously loud moans.

When I opened my eyes, our breaths were still heavy. Esteban was lying next to me, one arm over my waist, his face buried in the nook of my neck. I pressed my body against him so that once again, there was no space between us, and let his warmth envelop me.

It seemed the weather reporter had given up on injecting some enthusiasm into this hurricane, because the screen only showed a computer model depicting a tropical storm that would run parallel to the peninsula. It would only be rain to serenade us through dawn.

I stretched my arm to turn off the table lamp, and then heard Esteban mumble something behind me. It sounded sweet and gentle, and he followed by kissing my bare shoulder and falling back asleep.

His words floated past me, their meaning secondary to the perfection of the night. I was willing to wait until morning to overthink it.

Morning arrived with shy rays of sun attempting to break through the clouds. The room was slightly warmer than the previous night, despite the fan oscillating all night. But we had slept uncovered, with the gentle breeze directly on our skin, and we were still naked when I turned to check on Esteban.

Images from the previous night, hot and vivid, burst into my mind.

Was that really me? Or did the wine take over? Is that how sex feels when all inhibitions are lost? If it hadn't been for Esteban splayed over half of my bed, I'd probably think I imagined the entire scene. But he was there, alright.

The golden glow from those first rays of dawn washed over his body, and I let my eyes wander and explore every inch of his flawless light-brown skin, barely even moving so I wouldn't disturb his sleep. His eyelids were shut, and his chest slowly expanded with each breath. He was beautiful, though he didn't fit a pretty-boy profile. His features—thick and angular—were relaxed in his sleep, giving him a boyish—almost innocent—appearance. So different than the sharp version that he showed to the world.

The previous night had been a perfect taste of what I wanted my life to be, if only for a few hours. Esteban had chosen to spend a stormy night at my apartment. We had gone grocery shopping like it was something we did every day. He had pulled out his credit card without missing a beat, giving me a brief taste of how it would feel to have someone to share the load with, how liberating it would be to stop attaching prices and balances to every single decision I made. We cooked together, drank together, and slept together. He seemed to like all the aspects of my life I had shown him, down to the cramped apartment. And if that isn't the beginning of a relationship, then I don't know what is.

But even while floating in the delicious haze of the morning-after, I could feel the weight of all the bits of my life that he was ignorant about. I didn't know him enough to guess whether his opinion of me would change when he heard my story. The full story. The small details I had avoided here and there. I wasn't lying by omitting the truth, but that depended on his sensitivity to the truth. Frankly, I had done a pathetic job of bringing up the subject to test his tolerance. I was in the blind. So lost in a lavender haze that I had lost all track of my plan.

Or maybe I was right on track after all. Perhaps I had unconsciously created my very own plan B, and I was already in a couple with an eligible bachelor who could help me stay by showing up at a courthouse and signing his name next to mine. As tempting as the idea sounded, I still felt the churn of guilt settling in. Like this so-called relationship was a means to an end. Like my body had taken over the situation and attempted to correct what my brain and mouth couldn't. Like I had inadvertently sold myself for papeles. Like this had been the plan all along.

He shuffled around in the sheets, ending with one lean bicep covering his eyes and leaving his mouth uncovered. He looked so good, so at ease, even in my small bedroom. This was our bed, and this is how we woke up every morning.

My cell phone marked 7:15 a.m. I had missed calls and messages from Nina since seven p.m.

Nina: Hey girl! I'm spending the storm at my parents'. Lmk if you wanna come over, or if you'd rather stay at my place.

Nina: Sofi, the streets are flooding. Are you staying at your apt?

Nina: Sofia, I'm at my parents. Please tell me u are okay so I can stop worrying about your ass.

She had sent the last message at one a.m. I couldn't even remember at what time we had fallen asleep.

Sofia: Hey. I'm so sorry I didn't text you last night. Esteban slept over. He's still here.

She replied with a whole string of emojis that ranged from angry red faces to eggplants and hearts.

Nina: Next time just let me know so that I don't stay awake thinking you are drowning somewhere.

Sofia: Love you.

Nina: Let me know when you're free so we can meet up!

My laughter transformed into something else entirely as his hand traveled up my leg—squeezing, drawing me toward him—awakening the sensations I'd been longing for. When my backside was flush against his body, he took a long whiff of my hair, kissing my back, and then his hand moved to the front, making me moan, and I naturally pushed my ass against him. His touch made me forget all the doubts and fears that had plagued my mind minutes earlier, and I allowed the storm to silence out my inhibitions again.

While Esteban showered, I focused on all my apartment's flaws. In broad daylight, he would soon discover the mystery stains on the carpet, the rancid smell of a Miami home without A/C, and the bare cupboards. There was no wine to blur the reality. He was probably used to waking up in the homes of beautiful women, to find himself in bright and airy rooms, open-floor layouts covered in shiny white marble, and an open closet door revealing a collection of sparkly dresses.

Yet there was nothing I could do in these minutes to change my reality. I had arrived at a dead end where it was tricky to conceal the pieces of me I didn't want him to see. So, I left everything exactly as it was. I put on a T-shirt and shorts and pulled my hair back in a ponytail, and finally, I sat on the edge of the bed, trying to appear casual and confident and completely at ease with having him see what I had worked so hard to conceal.

"It hasn't stopped raining, huh?" Esteban walked out of the bathroom, freshly showered and wearing only boxer shorts. His hair was spiky and wet, and I suddenly wanted to run my fingers through it.

The storm continued to pour inches of rain over Miami's already flooded streets. The sun had given up struggling against the heavy clouds, the palm trees curved to the wind's will, like wild manes of hair let loose. It felt as if the day was coming to an end, but it was only ten a.m. This storm was not in a hurry to go anywhere.

"Do you have any plans today?" he asked.

I looked at the storm outside. "Wait for the storm to pass?" I chuckled. Then I almost immediately regretted how I was making myself so available. "I had to cancel all my plans because of the storm. How about you?"

"I have a brief to work on, but I can do it tomorrow."

"Oh." The butterflies in my stomach were throwing an after-storm party in there.

"I guess you are gonna be stuck with me today." His half smile dimpled his cheek and gave me the slightest wink.

Here's the thing: I had expected to have sex. I hoped for sex and an overnight stay. I dreamed about him wanting to have breakfast with me. But to have him stay an undisclosed number of hours stuck with me? My heart melted. I felt myself blushing so much that I was tempted to cover my face with a pillow.

He was right in front of me when Mom called. I wasn't going to pick up, but he looked at me intently. "Just pick up. She's probably worried."

I contained myself from rolling my eyes and answered the phone.

"Mija, ¿Cómo le está yendo con el huracán?" She wanted to know how I was dealing with the storm, a first.

It was hard to focus with Esteban parading to the kitchen in boxers, but after a few undecipherable mumbles, I got the words out. "Bien, Mami. Solo mucha lluvia. Estoy en mi apartamento." I reported I was in my apartment, and it hadn't stopped raining.

"Quédese ahí, que estoy viendo en las noticias todas esas calles inundadas." She had seen the flooded streets on the news and had called to check on me. We talked for an entire minute without her asking for anything. I was cautious until the end, waiting for the inevitable request to be dropped, but after the last *chao* was said, I knew she had called out of genuine concern for my well-being.

I was touched. It felt so nice to have her reach out without a second agenda. I floated out of the room, elated because I didn't have to lie to Esteban about Mom's call. It was the motivation I needed. When he asked about the cardboard box I used as an entryway table, I explained I was putting together some gifts and clothes for my family in Bogotá. It sounded more innocent than it was, but there was no need to unload the entire truth at once. I could spoon-feed the situation to him, disclose piece by piece, and assess his reaction, until he had the full picture and could conclude how he could help.

When he heard that I sent my family a box of essentials every three months, he smiled. A big, proud smile. He mentioned how much he loved how involved I was in their lives, despite whatever misunderstanding I had with them. The heated conversation I had with Mom while we were at the park came to mind. I hadn't known how much of it he heard. I smiled back at him but still felt uneasy. He was picking up on all these little cues to form a particular image of me that was more like the person I wanted to become. But what option did I have? I couldn't just start complaining and ranting about their truths, their thoughtlessness. So, I politely smiled back and thanked him.

Esteban didn't react once about my apartment in daylight. We chose an avocado to smash over toast, and I set up my small stovetop coffee maker. Then we sat down, as if we had done this every morning for years, to have breakfast and wait for the storm to pass.

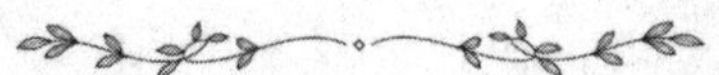

Like most Miami storms, things went back to normal at record speed. On Sunday, Nina invited me to have dinner at her place. She was back from her parents' house and couldn't wait to hear all the juicy details about my Friday night and Saturday morning.

"I just can't believe things are moving so fast with him!" Nina pulled two poke bowls from a paper bag and set them on the table. Relief washed over me at the thought of escaping a fourth consecutive meal of mushroom risotto in a single weekend.

"I know!" I squealed. "And we've been texting all day today."

"Did you talk to him about you-know-what?"

I shook my head as I walked over to Nina's fridge. "Do you want some water?"

"Yes, thank you." She scowled. "When are you planning to be—you know—upfront with him?"

"Jesus, Nina, you sure know how to spoil the fun out of everything."

She stared at me, pursing her lips. I wasn't expecting to receive a sermon, but I should've known better.

"He knows where I live now," I said as I brought a heaping spoonful of rice to my mouth. "He saw that my apartment isn't fancy. Spent the night despite the A/C not working. He knows I send money to my family and stuff. I've been pretty upfront with him in the past forty-eight hours."

She nodded, though she didn't look convinced. I wasn't convinced myself.

"How's the job search coming along? Have you received any calls? Tried applying some more?"

"Nina, I've practically applied to every open position in the greater Miami area. If LinkedIn was a dating app, you'd think I was desperate to sleep with someone."

"Have you asked Esteban if there's anything over at Altamira?" she asked.

She wasn't giving up on the topic. "I checked their company website. There's nothing available."

"But have you asked him?"

"I haven't. I'm planning to." I looked down at my half-eaten poke bowl. "I don't want him to feel forced to recommend me just because ... you know. Like I'm using him or something."

"Are you seriously telling me that you are sleeping with this guy, but you can't ask him if there are any open positions at his company?!"

I couldn't get myself to reply. She was right, of course, about this, and so much more.

"You need to start looking after yourself."

"I mean, what can he do? They aren't hiring," I mumbled.

"It's not just that, Sofi ... he probably knows a shit load of people, and the only way you can solve the mess ahead is by speaking up and asking others for help."

I nodded, though I kept my eyes fixed on the table. I couldn't even look up at Nina anymore.

"Are you nodding because you agree, or because you want me to shut up?"

"Both." My lips flattened into a sad smile. "Now that you put it that way ... yeah, I guess I should ask him."

We were quiet for some time. Nina turned on the TV and set it to a local weather channel. The storm had moved north, leaving behind streets covered in water puddles and palm fronds.

"So, what's the next step?" she asked.

I hesitated before I answered. Not because I didn't trust Nina, but because I feared my plan wouldn't be enough.

I took a deep breath first. "I have to follow up with WorldMedia again. Dianelys told me they would call me by the end of last week."

"That was probably before the hurricane."

"Right. They never called, so I'm calling her." Though Dianelys had hinted strongly that the position was mine, I held back from repeating this to her. Only an official offer letter would make it real enough to celebrate.

"Sounds good. What else?"

"I think I'm calling FIU admissions." I was hoping I wouldn't need to. "I'm asking what the process is to enroll in another international student program."

"But you'd need financial aid for that one."

"I know," I replied, thinking how much I already owed the bank for my undergraduate degree. "And I don't even know if I can go back to being an international student after working with an H1B visa. But it's worth a try."

She nodded in silence, approving. Or at least *not* disapproving.

"What else?"

"Okay, now you are just being pushy."

"That's my job." She smiled. "And this is important. I want you to be prepared for whatever comes." She cleared the table, but I held on to my almost-empty poke bowl, scooping out the last grains of rice.

Two weeks had passed since I lost my job, which meant I was two weeks closer to my exit date. I had interviewed with WorldMedia, slept with an American, spent every dollar I had, and done little else. Was I deliberately sabotaging my dream?

Chapter Sixteen

That night, alone in my apartment, I found myself recalling how my life changed the moment that Dad received his diagnosis. He used to keep a stash of money hidden under the mattress—a white envelope wrapped in plastic bags taped to the wooden planks of the bed. "Este dinero es Sagrado, por si algún día estamos muy apurados, o por si algo me llega a pasar." He reminded us that the savings were there in case of an emergency or if something were to happen to him. The thought of Dad not being present to handle that money was enough to shatter me. But that was nothing compared to the despair at hearing the words *there's nothing we can do* coming from the mouth of a doctor, or to watch Dad—his strength, his dreams, his love of life—fade away in front of my eyes in a few short months.

The holiness of Dad's lifelong savings died with him, when a few weeks after his passing, we found the torn plastic bags on the bed and the white envelope missing half of its contents. "Tomé solo la mitad," Santiago mumbled when we confronted him three days later. As if taking only half of it turned it into half a sin. He peered at us with bloodshot eyes, and the body odor of someone who had spent way too many nights en bares de mala muerte filled the room. "Es lo que me corresponde." *It's my part.* While Mom's rage erupted, something in me clicked. An idea

I had nurtured for a long time, but hadn't quite found its way to the surface.

The following week, I announced my intention of moving to Miami.

"Si, cómo no." Mom rolled her eyes, like moving to Miami was the most ridiculous thing she'd ever heard. "¿Y qué piensas hacer para mantenerte? La vida en Miami no es lo mismo que cuando yo te llevé de vacaciones." *What are you planning to do there? Life in Miami is not the same as when I took you on vacations.*

It was the arrogant *yo* that cemented my need to fly out of that house. The complete disregard of all the sacrifices Dad endured before and during that magical trip. The idea turned into determination, and when days passed before she realized I was being serious, it morphed into stubbornness. After weeks of insistence, Mom ran out of arguments, and Santiago ran out of money, and Mom had no other choice but to give me my share before Santiago consumed all of it.

I never felt like a foreigner in Miami. How could I feel like I didn't belong when surrounded by people who had arrived from all corners of the world months after I had? I thought my accent would be an obstacle, until I realized how often I had to switch back to Spanish because the person I was talking to didn't speak English at all.

Complaints never passed my lips, regardless of how difficult things became. Every weekday after classes, I waited tables, then worked from opening until closing on Saturdays and Sundays at the campus dining facility. My living situation added another layer of stress—my roommate frittered away her allowance on weed, then grumbled about my six a.m. weekend alarms. Each B grade that appeared on my transcript sent me spiraling, knowing my partial scholarship depended entirely on maintaining my academic average. Losing it meant an increase to my international student loan that I could not afford. That would've led to quitting school, cancelling my student visa, returning to Colombia, and failing Dad in that specific order.

So, I persevered. I was the best waitress, the best student, and—when I sent the first chunk of money home—the best daughter. I figured this was the American Dream Dad had been referring to all those years ago. I was working hard and getting paid for it. I had a plan for my future.

My biggest accomplishment came when I was taking my last required college class, when it became imperative that I find another way to stay. My favorite teacher suggested the Sunset position. I went from having a student visa to an H1B visa in less than a year. A life turnaround, considering that I went from waiting tables at murky restaurants—where patrons thought it was okay to engage in small talk, leave a tip, and let their hands run up my thigh while asking what time I'd be off—to the bright corridors and cubicle mazes at Sunset, where male managers allowed their eyes to do what their hands couldn't, and effectively blocked all women from reaching leadership positions.

Mom was right about one thing. I had never worked so much and so hard in my life. Sunset Cosmetics observed six holidays and allowed employees to take two weeks of unpaid vacation a year. The first year at Sunset, I took night and weekend classes to finish my degree, and what little time I had left was devoted to studying. I couldn't afford to miss work or skip class. The former was a direct hit to my already meager paycheck; the latter could escalate into being kicked out of the program that protected my status. It was more work than I had ever seen a person my age experience, and it certainly didn't feel like a vacation. But the independence that came with it, the feeling that I was *making it* in Miami, knowing that if Dad were alive, he'd be proud because one of us had accomplished what he had always dreamt of for the family, gave me the strength to keep going.

When I started sending money back home, it felt like I was secretly slapping Mom in the face. *Ha! Look at me, Mom! I* can *make it in Miami. I live on my own, I pay taxes, and I have enough to take care of you and Santiago. I am never going back.*

There were days when I couldn't escape from the nostalgia—Navidad by myself, or the anniversary of Dad's passing. Only then would I walk into one of the many Colombian restaurants spread across the city. Stepping into one of those felt like crossing a magic portal back into Bogotá. The vallenato soundtrack competing in volume against the loud voices of the patrons, the scent of freshly brewed coffee and pandebono, and the thick accents that transported me back to my street were all reminders of the brick and graffiti urban maze that was waiting for me, nestled among the Andes mountains.

"I'm taking you to this new place in Midtown I've been wanting to try." Esteban drove down the streets flanked by puddles, trash cans, and glossy buildings. The storm was a distant memory, and people were already out and about, as if it had never happened. I loved that he picked me up in his car instead of asking me to meet him there. I felt wanted, cared for. I loved how he opened the door for me, placed his hand on my lower back to guide me inside the restaurant, and said, "We have a reservation," to the host. I loved how he picked up the wine list and chose something based on the country, not the price. I loved being the woman he wanted to spend his time with, not just on weekends, but on a Monday night. I knew the time was right to merge the two versions of myself: The one I had shared with him—confident and in control, successful yet humble, and the one I had desperately tried to avoid—the desperate person clutching on to a dream.

A soft breeze swept through the restaurant's terrace, caressing my neck and collarbone. The storm had left behind a hint of cool air. I took in the smiles from the people sitting in the adjacent tables, the string of outdoor lightbulbs swaying above me, and the soft melody of the lounge music in the background. And when my eyes met with Esteban's, my stomach dropped with pleasure, my mind already racing ahead a few hours.

I would tell him everything today. And tomorrow, I would call Dianelys again.

Esteban approved the wine, and the server left us with two crimson glasses of Malbec. I gave mine a swirl the same way he did and took a sip. All money pressures had lifted because I knew from experience, he'd be picking up the check.

"Do you like it?"

"Yes, absolutely. And this place," I looked around briefly, taking in the soft lighting, the romantic ambiance, "It's beautiful. Thank you for inviting me."

"You're welcome. I ..." He inched closer, like he was letting me in on a secret, "I just wanted to say how much I loved spending the storm with you."

"Me too." I squeezed his hand in the center of the table, feeling the roughness of his skin under my fingertips, and he reciprocated. There was nothing sexual about it, just two people holding hands, but I was acutely aware of the intensity of the gesture, of the intense connection we shared, which had not weakened after we slept together. The realization struck me then—how lucky I was to share this all with him.

"There's something I want to tell you."

Anticipation told me his next words would matter deeply, but my confession couldn't be postponed any longer. I took a huge sip of wine to gather courage.

"There's something I need to tell you, too." He opened his eyes wide when I placed the almost empty glass on the table. "But it's work-related."

I scrunched my face like I was dismissing the news before I shared it. There was no need to make a big fuss about things. My plan was to downplay it, tell him I found out I'd lost my job today, and then mention the winning conversation with Dianelys. Briefly mention the visa, drop it like a problem that had nothing to do with him, that he held no possible connection to, and then let the idea simmer the rest of the night.

"My news is work-related, too. How weird are we?" We laughed together.

"Really? Then you go first." I said, losing my initial excitement. I felt the anticipation bubbling in me. Something wasn't right.

He placed his glass back on the table and flashed me a playful grin. "I hope you are not too disappointed, and we can celebrate together."

"What is it?" The image of us in bed in a few hours evaporated, replaced by nervous expectation.

"I want you to be the first to know." He straightened and took a deep inhale. "I'm the new Senior Account Manager at WorldMedia."

A cold breeze hit my bare back, but my eyes were fixed on Esteban's proud gaze.

"You are the ... what?" Surely, I had heard him wrong, but a lump had formed in my throat already.

"The account manager position ... at WorldMedia?" he repeated, raising his eyebrows. He thought I didn't know what position he was talking about. He didn't know it was all I'd been thinking of for weeks. He didn't know how his news would break me.

"You mean they *offered* you the position?" The lump grew more stubborn by the second, my voice already shaking. I pictured Esteban finding four missed calls from WorldMedia—the calls *I* was supposed to receive.

"Yes. They offered me the position."

"And you accepted it?" My voice came out coarse and low.

"Yes. I accepted it. It did take them a few days to come back with a counteroffer, but they met what I wanted."

I shook my head in disbelief. "You mean, you asked them for more than they offered you?"

"Um, yes." He was measuring his words now, trying to understand my irrational reaction. "They came to me with an offer for ninety, but I wanted a hundred."

One hundred.

One hundred thousand dollars. I wanted to laugh at its irony. At how ridiculous my situation was. There I was, begging God that they would approach me with an offer for sixty. Heck, I'd have settled for much, *much* less.

"When did they call you?" I asked.

"Um ... last week, I think. But I just accepted the new offer today." He took a careful sip of wine without ungluing his eyes from me. He must have sensed something was off, but he likely couldn't pinpoint it. He probably thought I'd be so happy for him, expecting us to toast through the entire bottle of Malbec and have celebratory sex afterwards. I'd resume my job search, and nothing would change between us. I could read the *why are you acting up like this?* all over his face. He was probably wondering why I didn't just say *Congratulations on your new job* and move on to another, non-work-related topic.

"You knew I was out of the running all this time, and it didn't occur to you to tell me?" I couldn't control my volume anymore. I was sick of trying to fit a mold that I would never fit into—exhausted of pretending that everything was okay when I had lost control over my life a long time ago.

"Yeah. I negotiated with Altamira, like I told you I would. It didn't go well. I spoke with WorldMedia again this morning, and they came up with everything I wanted."

My nails dug into my palms, marking them with small half-moon creases.

"It wasn't my plan, but that's how things worked out. Why are you getting all—"

"I wanted that job."

"But you said you were only shopping around—"

"I *needed* that job." I banged my hands against the edge of the table. The glasses, the wine bottle, and the breadbasket jumped with the impact. Some heads turned while others pretended not to listen. I didn't care about either.

His expression turned stern. The surreal glow that had welcomed me just minutes earlier vanished. Realization hit me from all directions—the position, like my dream to live in Miami, was gone.

It was never mine to begin with.

Meanwhile, Esteban—a person who can switch jobs like underwear—had beaten me to the finish line, and he still had the luxury of complaining that the trophy was too small.

Something ugly started burning inside me. Hate and envy, mashed up together.

"Okay ..." he started, "What do you mean you *needed* the job? I can't be miserable because I got it and you didn't. Jesus, Sofia! And why are you making a show out of this? I thought you'd be happy for me!"

"You told me you didn't want the position. You were only using it to negotiate your salary." I failed to keep my voice from breaking.

"Yes, that was the original plan, but Altamira couldn't meet what I wanted. And WorldMedia did, and I told you how I hit it off with the VP."

"I can't believe it," I said. "They chose you, even though I would have done it for half the money."

Esteban opened his eyes in disbelief, as if there was no way he would *ever* consider doing something as stupid as that. "What's so special about *this* company? What about your job at Sunset?"

"What's so special about it?" I scoffed, the sting in my eyes getting worse by the second. "I lost my job at Sunset weeks ago, Esteban! I'm unemployed ... and broke."

He shifted uncomfortably in his seat, not knowing how to deal with the information I had thrown at him. "Why didn't you tell me?"

"I was embarrassed. Plus, would you have done anything differently? It sounds like you were pretty set on reaching your hundred."

"There were other people applying. I hate to tell you this, but it could've been any of them if I hadn't accepted."

"The decision was down to you and me," I said in a monotone.

"What?" Confusion graced his features.

"I spoke with Dianelys last week. She said they were down to two candidates, and I was one of them." I lifted my hand and wiped the tears that had formed. "It doesn't matter anymore. It was their call, and they chose you."

I could feel his gaze on me, his awkward silence, the gazes of the people around us.

"I was on a temporary work visa." My eyes were set on the hanging lightbulbs. I couldn't bear to look at him. I took a few deep breaths before I uttered the following words. "I have to leave the country in a few weeks." My voice came out surprisingly low and collected, a recounting of facts, rather than the confession I had taken too long to make. I stood up to leave, and he went behind me. It's ironic how I kept so many truths concealed for days, and now that the plug was gone, they flowed freely out of my mouth, blurted out so efficiently I had nothing left to say.

"Sofia."

I flipped around to face him. "Would you have said no?"

"What do you mean?"

"To the offer? Would you have said no if you had known?"

My pulse thundered in my ears, drowning out the noise of Miami's streets. He remained motionless, mentally assembling the fragments of truth I'd scattered throughout our time together. His expression shifted toward something that pierced me—confusion tinged with disenchantment. "I ... I don't know," he said. "Listen, Sofia, we interviewed for the same position, and I got it. It was a fair race; you can't expect me to feel guilty." He ran a hand through his hair, exasperated. "You've been keeping all this stuff from me—"

I turned back to the street and kept walking. He followed me, but I didn't stop or turn around.

"Sofia!" His voice trailed behind me. "Sofia, let me drive you home!"

A new blast of cool breeze swept over the street. My hands were cold, but I could barely feel them. I felt like hot water was boiling in my gut, smoke coming from every pore. Esteban had spent the past week debating between two job offers, setting a bidding war where he was the ultimate prize, while I had spent my week stretching the few dollars I had left, dealing with my family, and getting kicked out of a job I thought I was good at. The sheer disparity of it was maddening.

I walked as fast and far away from that restaurant as possible, until he gave up, and I couldn't hear him anymore. I walked to increase the distance between Esteban and me, despite the grief that came with each step I took. I walked until my feet hurt, but the pain in my heart was worse. And when I finally came to a stop, all I could see beyond the skyline and the fancy lights was hollow space. There wasn't a backdrop of stars dotting the sky, no silver moon illuminating the bay—just flat land covered in concrete and glass buildings. My mind drifted to Bogotá, with its brown mountains always present, hugging the city with their ragged peaks, overlooking the millions of stories of joy and hardship written within their boundaries daily. The mountains had allowed me to leave and seek happiness far away, to fly high above them, not daring to ask when I'd be returning; they remain serene, knowing that good daughters always come back. The nostalgia set hard on my chest. I knew I wouldn't miss the mountains much longer.

I was going back to Bogotá.

Chapter Seventeen

When I was little, Dad used to tell me we all have a limited supply of tears. "*Deja de llorar, Sofia. Se te van a acabar las lágrimas.*" He used this phrase when I was in a crying spell—swollen eyes, wet cheeks, and sniffles—like that time when he announced there wouldn't be any gifts that Christmas, or the time Santiago and I almost got kicked out of school because we were past due on tuition payments. He even used it when I was older, and I found him crying after receiving his cancer diagnosis. There's something heartbreaking about seeing a grown man in tears, especially when it's someone who's so deeply loved. I was not ready to accept he'd leave us soon, and too naïve to imagine what life would be like after his departure. I sat down next to him and wrapped my arms around his back, surprised to find how much his solid back had shrunk in months. And when my stream of tears was as steady as his, he warned me, once again, that they would run out, and I wouldn't have any left to spare when I was old. The warning worked when I was younger. As a little girl, I would force myself to stop crying to contain the few drops I had left.

I thought about Dad as I walked into my apartment that night, leaving the door open behind me to allow the cool air from the corridor to seep in, and the faint scent of humidity to move out. And then I wasted my tears away, in a way that would've terrified my younger self.

Morning arrived with pale rays of dusty light breaking through the blinds. I stayed in bed for a long time, staring at the ceiling, getting acquainted with the pounding headache that had set in through the night. My feet were blistered from the walk. Even my stomach complained. The only motivation I had to get out of bed was that from that very moment, every second I had left in Miami was ephemeral. My cell phone was facing down on the nightstand, and I didn't dare to flip it over, afraid of what I might find. Missed calls from Mom maybe? Rejection emails from more companies? Perhaps a voicemail from Sunset HR requesting that I return all the product samples I brought with me? But what scared me, what I was terrified of, was to find nothing. A hollow screen devoid of messages, calls, or emails. A sign that Esteban was out of my life for good, and the rest of the world had forgotten about me.

I gingerly flipped the phone, dread smothering every movement, and felt that familiar twitch of hope at the new notifications badge. He had written, around an hour after I'd left the restaurant.

Esteban: Hey

Esteban: I'm downstairs

Esteban: Did you make it home?

Unlike every message that came before, this one contained no indication of seeing each other again. There was no call to action, no sign of continuity. They seemed so ... final. And curt. Infinitely more put together than me—the crazy chick who walked out on him in front of a packed restaurant.

Esteban: I hope you're ok. I'm sorry about how today went.

I read the words a few times, picturing him in the valet queue, texting me while the women in the sparkling dresses flashed their golden legs at him. As if I needed another reason to know there wasn't room in his life for me. I dug my face into my hands, embarrassed at what I'd said the previous night.

I let the cold water from the shower run over my hair and face, hoping it could wash away some of my grief, bad luck, and poor decisions, and when I realized none of those would go away soon, I mustered what little energy I had left to start making calls.

The first one was to the landlord who had been avoiding my desperate requests to fix the A/C unit. It was probably a long shot, but I saw it as an easy opportunity to save money.

"Sofia." The landlord always answered the phone by saying my name first, followed by a loud sigh.

"Luis, we need to talk about the apartment." I was surprised at the momentary confidence in my tone.

"¿Y ahora qué pasó?" he grunted.

"The place is in terrible condition. I've been waiting for you to fix everything that's wrong with it."

"You have to wait, Sofia. There's a hurricane, and I don't have time to stop everything."

"There's no hurricane anymore, as you can probably tell from looking outside, and the contract says the apartment must be in good condition. The A/C has been broken for a week."

"Well, I don't have time to fix it today."

I took a deep breath, readying myself to deliver a blow. "I wanted to tell you I'm willing to stay in the apartment as is, but in that case, I think you need to adjust my rent payment immediately."

He was quiet, but I could hear his heavy breathing on the other side. "So that's what you want? Money?"

"What I want is for you to maintain your end of the contract."

"You talkin' about contracts?" He scoffed, and my blood started boiling. "I'm already doing you a favor by renting to you. You have any idea how many people I have on a waitlist to live at that apartment? If you think I'm gonna reduce your rent, you're dreaming, niña."

The room lurched around me as acidic bitterness rose from my stomach into my throat. "I think it's only fair." My voice was no longer loud and determined.

"You know what? Every month, you find something new to complain about. I'll give you your deposit back, but I want you out of there by the end of the week."

My body seized up as shock overtook me—the discussion had veered into territory I never anticipated, leaving me longing to erase every word I'd uttered.

"But ... but I've made all my payments on time. I haven't done anything wrong." My back leaned against the wall, the only surface that could keep me from collapsing on the floor. Each item in the apartment materialized in front of me, from the couch to the full-size bed, the pieces of the life I'd built that I'd now need to dispose of, and I felt my eyes swell. "*Usted es un tramposo!*" I bellowed, trying to keep my voice from breaking.

"Salgase de mi apartamento, o yo le llamo a la policía." *I want you out of my apartment, or I'm calling the cops.*

No one had a reason to do this to me. The sheer thought of facing a cop, an immigration officer, of having the word *deportation* tied to my name, of being kicked out and never allowed back in, was enough to shatter me.

"Why would you call the police?" I cried out.

There was an eerie silence before he replied, "Sofia, I'm renting that place to you way below market price. This is business. Money is tight for everyone, not just for you. Your end of lease is coming up, and if you don't have enough to pay an increase, then I need to start showing the unit next week."

The silence in the apartment clashed against the street noise coming from his side of the phone. His words struck hard on my chest, crumbling me from the inside.

The phone stayed glued to my ear well after his voice disappeared, my mind unable to comprehend the conversation that had just unfolded. *What spectacular disaster did I get myself into?* When standing became too difficult, I collapsed onto the couch, which protested my weight with a loud squeal—an unwelcome reminder that I now needed to find a new home for my belongings.

I sent Nina a hasty message.

> **Sofia:** Amiga, I need you. Can you please come over?

Slowly, afraid to make any other wrong moves, I opened my laptop to check the status on all the open job applications. My fingers navigated through digital debris and promotional spam until I spotted it—an email from WorldMedia. Though Esteban had already revealed what it contained, I couldn't simply ignore the subject line I'd been hunting for these past weeks. I clicked it open, fighting to suppress the instinctive flicker of hope that it ignited.

Re: Your application to Senior Account Manager.

Dear Sofia,
Thank you for your interest in working with WorldMedia. We have reviewed your qualifications and are unfortunately pursuing other candidates whose experience and skill set more closely match those outlined in the description.

In the meantime, we hope you continue to review our job openings in the career section of our website.

We wish you success in your career search!

Regards,
Global Staffing
WorldMedia

I wished Dad had been right and I had run out of tears all those years ago.

By mid-afternoon, I had managed to control the panicked outbursts enough to make short calls and knock on doors I'd been avoiding. Anything that could result in some extra dollars to bring back to Colombia, or to exhaust every possible employment opportunity. I called Mrs. Garcia and asked if she was interested in a weekly cleaning service, or if any of her friends were looking for a maid, remarking on my new weekday availability. I didn't mention that I'd only be around for about another month. I also called Evelyn, one of the only friends I'd made at Sunset, and explained the status pretzel I had gotten myself into, begging her to ask her acquaintances if they knew of anyone willing to sponsor a headstrong woman who refused to leave Miami without a fight. I even called Catalina and left her a voicemail asking her to call me back. I had little hope of landing a position at BanLatam, but I'd reached that point where shame jumps out the window and boldness takes over. *Patadas de ahogado*, as Mom might say. The last task I completed before the headache I'd ignored all day claimed every space in my head was a list of immigration attorneys who managed cases like mine. I knew I couldn't be the only person who had lost her H1B visa. There had to be options out there for people like me. I just wasn't looking clearly enough.

When Nina's message came through, it felt like a godsend.

Nina: Just left the office. Going straight over to your place.

I stared at it for a long time, thinking everything wasn't lost if I still had a friend by my side.

Nina was sweating the minute she walked in. "Your apartment's a sauna." She twisted her curls into a top bun and kicked her heels to a corner. "You know you can sue your landlord for making you live like this."

I told her everything—how Esteban had been chosen over me for my dream job, how he had accepted the position and mistakenly thought it was a reason to celebrate, how I had finally confessed my situation in the worse possible way, how I had tried to set things right with the landlord and I had found myself unceremoniously kicked out. How I was so much closer to becoming an undocumented immigrant.

She was perfectly still the entire time. Other than a nod or the occasional closed question, she remained quiet, taking it all in. My words surprisingly kept Nina's mouth shut, her expression solemn, and that broke my heart a little more.

She waited a full minute after I was done, then she moved to the center of the living area, hands on her hips, assessing her surroundings with an air of authority. "If that man is letting you off the lease without a penalty, take it. Get rid of everything, Sofi. Keep only what you need."

"You mean it because I'm going back, right?" I could barely get the words out without losing all the air in my lungs.

She turned back to me hastily, her curls bouncing in all directions.

"You need the deposit money more than you need any of this crap. Even if you stay."

In less than one hour she helped me take pictures to post everything for sale: the ugly couch, the TV, even the glasses I had used to toast with Esteban a mere four days ago, the clothes I'd been collecting to send to Santiago with the tags still on, and the two pairs of soccer sneakers he'd been counting on for weeks. The items so busted that no one would take even for free went inside garbage bags—three in total. She created a new thrift app profile and loaded all the images, using EVERYTHING MUST GO as the caption under each. Then she checked the box for *pickup only* and winked as she turned on the notifications. "OfferUp, see? Now there's an app Bumble can't beat."

My arms wrapped around her, grateful beyond words for her steadying presence amid my crumbling reality. That embrace attempted to convey it all—my appreciation for the accounting project that had randomly united us four years earlier, how those fourteen consecutive late nights had cultivated our friendship, and the vivid memory I still carried of her face lighting up when our perfect grade was announced. I couldn't envision my life without her anymore.

"I'm using the rent deposit to pay an immigration attorney," I said.

Nina nodded on my shoulder. "I approve that idea."

"Now what?" I sighed.

"Now what?" she repeated.

When my phone went off, I was about to tell her I had widened the boundaries of my job search to Mrs. Garcia, Evelyn, and even Catalina. Nina said something about the offers coming in for my couch, but I barely heard her. I appreciated Nina's help more than anything, and there was something I needed to do right then and there.

"I'm telling my family."

"Hola, mamá."

"Mija, ¿cómo está?" She was surprisingly sober, her tone paused and mellow.

"No estoy bien." I took a deep inhale. "Perdí mi trabajo." *I lost my job.* There was little she could do to help from so far away, so there was no need to beat around the bush.

She fell quiet.

"Y no sé qué voy a hacer... pero seguramente tendré que regresarme a Bogotá." There. I just spit out that I was returning so there was no room for misinterpretation.

I knew she was still there because I could hear the usual street noise in the background. It took a few seconds for her voice to return.

"No, Sofia. Usted no se puede regresar." *You can't come back.* Her voice was stern and decisive. My breath quickened, anxiety creeping up from my shoulders. Did she not *want* me back? She went from being mute to rambling about the unemployment in Colombia, and what little space they had at the house, and how I'd never get used to the life I'd left behind.

Her reciting my reasons was just another way to remind me of everything I was about to lose.

"Además, usted gana en dólares. Y nosotros necesitamos ese dinerito todos los meses." *You earn dollars, and we need the money.*

That's when I lost it, when she said the unspeakable. That the money I could make was worth more than me. "¿Como así, mamá? Osea, tu prefieres que te mande un cheque, a que regrese yo."

"Sofia, usted sabe cómo están las cosas de difíciles—" *You know that things are difficult ...*

"¡No me hables de cosas difíciles! Por favor, ¡No me recuerdes lo difícil que es la vida para ustedes, cuando yo llevo tres años aquí trabajando para ustedes, enviándoles todo lo que tengo!" I spit out the words I should've said a long time ago. Yes, their life was hard, but I had tried my best to help, supporting them for three years, and I had reached a dead end.

"Lorena está ."

I was about to yell some more, but the words got caught in my throat. *Who was pregnant?*

"¿Quién?"

"La novia de Santiago. Está embarazada."

I had a sudden urge to slam my phone against the wall.

"Ah no, genial. Me parece fantástico." I made sure she could hear the spite in my tone. "¿Y la señora Lorena sigue viviendo en la casa con ustedes? ¿Mi hermanito Santiago ya encontró un trabajo para mantener a su familia?" Had she or Santiago found a job already?

"Sofia, cálmese. Él es su hermano—"

I wasn't going to calm down. "O el plan es que yo mantenga a la tal Lorena y al bebé también." Were they planning for me to support their growing family without question?

"Llámeme cuando esté más calmada." *Call me when you calm down.*

"No mamá. No los voy a llamar otra vez. Vayan a resolver su mierda de la de la misma forma que yo tengo que resolver la mía. Y ni se les ocurra que van a volver a ver un peso mío por allá."

I hung up. It was the first time I stood up to Mom and told her I wouldn't send her my money. Nina stared at me with absolute fascination on her face. She had never heard me raise my voice to Mom, or anyone. I was blown away myself. I had thought of saying those words hundreds of times; setting an economic boundary that was long overdue, but I wasn't prepared for the hollow pain that set deep in my chest, the pain that a tree feels when it's pulled out of the soil.

That night, the moist air that had covered the city for the past few days left for good. The temperature rose to the nineties, and nothing—neither the oscillating fan nor a cold shower—could tame the heat in my apartment. I was covered in sweat as I finished packing my clothes and my few belongings into an old suitcase and a bookbag.

Nina asked me to move in with her, and I said yes.

What else could I do?

Chapter Eighteen

Walking down the corridor, hauling the few belongings I could bring with me, felt like I was in a suspended reality, clipping my life in Miami from the roots. It was as if that apartment held my right to stay, and I had been kicked out. In front of me, Nina pulled Dad's old suitcase filled with my clothes and a few pairs of shoes. I dragged my feet behind her, carrying the cardboard box I had intended to ship to Colombia, which had been repurposed as a moving box. Inside were my laptop, Sunset samples, and Colombian passport containing my soon-to-be invalid employment visa. And that was it. Everything else stayed at the apartment. Nina had set up a few meetups with potential buyers for the following day. I wouldn't get much for a third-hand bed and a stained couch, let alone the mismatched utensils and random appliances, but at least I was saving on moving costs. And it's not like I could bring any of those things.

When we passed in front of Catalina's door, my stomach contracted. I'd been in a haze for the past day, and I'd forgotten entirely about Togo. I wouldn't see him anymore. Suddenly, I regretted all the times I had complained about walking or caring for him. I would never see his tail wagging with excitement when I arrived. He would never shower me with his sloppy kisses or press his body against my leg on the elevator, which I had realized was his way of saying thanks for saving him from endless days stranded in that apartment. My heartbeat quickened as we came closer to the door. I wanted to say goodbye, but I couldn't just show up unannounced at Catalina's door and ask to see Togo, right?

"Nina." I stopped in the hallway and placed the box on the floor. "I have to drop off Catalina's key."

My fingers fumbled with the keychain when we both froze at a mournful sound coming from inside—a whine that intensified as I moved toward the door, accompanied by the unmistakable rhythm of paws scrabbling against the floor. I couldn't help wondering if Togo somehow understood that this time, I wouldn't be coming back.

"Is that Togo?" Nina asked.

I nodded, feeling the familiar clench of another unexpected loss.

"Do you think he's okay?" she asked, concern rising in her voice as the whimpers increased on the other side of the door. Nina had never liked Catalina—or the absurd dog-walking arrangement I had agreed to months earlier—but she liked dogs and wasn't the type to walk away from a mistreated animal.

"Should I open the door to check on him?" I asked.

"Did you tell her you'd take him out today?"

"No, not today. It's Tuesday. But with Catalina, I never know."

"It's better if you knock or call. What if she's there?"

"I texted her yesterday asking if she could help me find a job. She never replied."

"Of course she didn't." She rolled her eyes to the back of her head. "Just knock."

When I knocked on the door, Togo stopped whining immediately. The three of us waited almost a minute until I knocked again. I was pulling my cellphone out to call Catalina when the lock clicked from the inside. Togo stormed out and ran around me a few times, wagging his tail with such force it could fall off. He only stopped to greet Nina, then bounced and ran down the corridor.

In front of us appeared a drowsy Catalina wearing oversized sweats and a bra. Her voice was husky, as if I had just pulled her out of deep sleep. It took her at least ten seconds to realize who I was.

"Oh, thank God you are here. He's been whining, and he keeps waking me up."

"Has he been walked?" I asked without even saying hi.

She made a face like she was annoyed. Like I was accusing her of doing something wrong.

"Can you walk him now?" she asked.

"I ... I will, yes, if you need me to."

Nina opened her eyes so wide I thought they'd pop out.

Catalina was already returning to her bed when I reacted, and my voice came out a little louder, "I'm moving out of the building. This is the last time I get to walk him."

She stopped, but she didn't turn around. "Shit."

I waited for her to say something, anything. A *thank you,* perhaps? Or *why are you leaving*? Or even better, *are you interested in working at BanLatam?* But she didn't say anything else.

"I'll leave the key when I bring Togo back," I said. Catalina kept dragging her feet to the darkness of her apartment. Togo was already waiting in front of the elevator, looking at me with pleading eyes, gratitude and loyalty all packed into one big furry package.

"Sofia ..." Nina said, lowering her voice and looking straight at me.

I didn't stop walking. My eyes were already soaked.

I didn't know Catalina. I didn't know her story, whether her life was easier than mine or not. But from where I was standing, she seemed to have everything—the job, the apartment, the dog ... I was the loser selling an old, stained mattress for ten dollars and couldn't figure out my life.

"I can't leave him."

"I know." Nina nodded.

I knew it was reckless and impulsive. I knew how costly it was to maintain a dog, especially that size. I knew there were insanely expensive fees associated with air travel for pets. I knew we didn't have a place in Miami and wouldn't have a place to live in Colombia. But I had tried doing everything by the book, and *by the book* wasn't working.

"Catalina!" I yelled as I rushed back to the apartment. There was still a sliver of space left before the door shut on my face. "I'll take Togo with me." It wasn't a question; it was more of an announcement to Catalina and to myself. There was a pause, and Catalina appeared and opened the door, more awake than a minute earlier.

"You mean, for good?"

I nodded, but I didn't say anything else. I knew trying to convince her would be futile. She would take the bait or reject my lunacy altogether.

"But you are moving out. Where are you gonna live?" she asked in her raspy voice.

"They'll move in with me." Nina's strong voice came from the other end of the hallway. "I have a large apartment, and my building allows big dogs."

She stared at me for a long time. She knew it was a serious offer. Three pairs of eyes—because even Togo knew something important was happening—waited for a groggy Catalina to decide. She didn't have to ask if I had any experience with dogs, or if I knew what it took to care for Togo, because deep inside she knew he'd be better off with me than he had ever been with her. Frankly, I think she was trying to delay the inevitable.

"Take him," she said.

My heart rate increased.

"He was never my dog to begin with."

I didn't say much after that. I can hardly remember if I said anything at all. Perhaps I mumbled a thank you, maybe I said something like I'll take good care of him. But the joy I felt was too much to process anything coherent. I slipped the spare key into her hand and rushed to Nina and Togo, hurling them into the elevator as quickly as I could, for fear Catalina might change her mind.

The next morning, sitting on one of the counter stools at Nina's apartment, I called immigration attorneys. A call didn't cost me anything. That much I could afford. Half of them didn't answer. Some weren't even taking work visa cases. The remaining ones had more interesting cases to represent—juicier ones, more lucrative, for clients who owned company *xyz* in Mexico or had this much money to invest from Venezuela. I hung up before they even mentioned the cost of an initial consultation.

Only the receptionist from the last attorney's office on my list had the time and disposition to hear my story.

"Yours is an easy case," she said between the clicks of a keyboard.

"Easy?" I echoed.

"Yes! Everything is in order. Never been undocumented. You don't have a criminal record. Still within the allotted time to find a solution. You have options."

"Options?" I muttered.

"Yes. You have so many options! You can reapply for a student visa. Or we can help you with a work visa if you set up your own company. Or an investment visa! Yes." On and on she went. She seemed to ignore that people usually don't disclose the whole truth when faced with attorneys, that stories are slightly fabricated, and that they are underplayed. "When are you available to come in? I suggest you don't wait too many days, sweetie, because you know ... time starts creeping up on you, and we don't want you going over your date."

Options. Options. So many options.

But they all required money. Money. So much money.

I didn't have money. Would Nina lend me all that money? Did she even have $25K sitting there in a savings account waiting to aid someone desperate? Did I even deserve to receive money after I had failed to plan for this moment?

"Oye." The lady's voice suddenly switched to Spanish and dropped to a whisper, and I suddenly felt like I was talking to an entirely different person. "También puedes casarte." *You could get married.*

The inconsistency briefly registered—it was strange for someone employed in a law office to be suggesting what was essentially fraud. "Eso es bien rápido, y aquí te ayudamos con el papeleo." *It's fast, and we can help you with the paperwork.*

I thanked the woman in English, and she also switched back to the American version of herself, encouraging me not to waste any time and to make an appointment soon. As of now, there was a two-week wait, and slots were filling up quickly. They were taking in new clients every day—clients who reached out from all corners of Central and South America, clients who were clinging to the American dream as fiercely as I was.

I hung up and thought about her suggestion. Marriage to an American citizen. So fast and easy! Too bad I didn't have a queue of candidates lined up—I knew well enough that Esteban had not gotten even close. The remaining option was to pay, to come up with the money I knew could buy anything. I'd been sending cash to my family all that time. I'd never see that money again.

"Dios te lo pague." *May God repay you*. That's what Mom said the first time she received money from me. That day, I had stood in line for forty minutes waiting for my turn at a Western Union. I heard people in front of me sending 1k or 2k to Venezuela or Argentina, so I figured *this is ok. This is normal. This is what good daughters do.* The cashier asked who I was sending the money to and in what country, and my heart filled with pride.

Dios te lo pague. That's what Mom said.

She should've added *because I sure as hell won't.*

A soft click came from the door, followed by muted footsteps. The mattress dipped a little. I didn't need to open my eyes to know it was Nina. She brushed the hair away from my face and let out a sigh when she saw me clearly. I had crusty, dry streaks on my cheeks and swollen eyes.

"Are you awake?" she whispered.

I nodded. My eyelids were heavy when I tried to open them. Nina was wearing sweats, socks, and an oversized T-shirt. It was only 6:30 p.m., which meant she had just gotten home from work and changed her clothes before coming into my room—well, not exactly *my* room.

She was trying not to make me feel bad by showing up wearing her badass work attire. I loved her for trying, but I was too low for anything to pick me up.

"How was your day?" she asked.

I shook my head.

"You know this is your home. You can stay as long as you need. As long as you want."

"Thank you." My voice was croaky and uneven.

"Has Togo been good?" I could hear the smile in her voice. Togo was lying outside of the room, belly glued to the cold tile, like a therapy dog waiting for his turn to get to work. He flapped his tail against the floor when he heard his name, raising his head in attention. He hadn't tried to enter the bedrooms the entire day and wasn't tempted by Dante's snarling because he now had to share his space. It was as if Togo was determined to show how grateful he was, to prove that he was the best rescue dog ever.

"They've both been good," I said, referring to Togo and Dante. "I took them on a one-hour walk to the doggie path close to the bay."

"One hour! Now you're just spoiling them." She laughed.

She was trying with all her might to pick me up, so I tried to match some of her energy and say something positive. She had already taken me in; there was no need to become the crappiest house guest by drowning her with all my problems.

"Today I made $90 selling some of my apartment stuff." I propped myself up on an elbow, keeping my voice as light as possible. "It's almost empty now. I have a few Offerup meetups tomorrow, and then I'll call Luis to turn in the key and get my deposit back."

She rubbed my back like I suppose mothers do when their child is sick. "Any luck with the attorneys?"

I shook my head before I let it fall back on the pillow. "There are ways, but they are so expensive. One of them suggested I get married."

She was quiet before she said, "If you want to try that option, I can ask my parents to lend you some money."

I gave her a side glance. She was serious. Deep inside, I was relieved of having a last possibility. If doing things the right way hadn't worked, I was afraid doing things *por la izquierda* would turn into a shit show.

I squeezed her hand. "It's a lot of money, Nina, even if I use the rent deposit. I'm already living with you; if I do that, I'll be in debt to you and your parents. I don't even have any income to repay you. Not to mention I wouldn't know where to start looking for someone to marry, someone I can trust to go through the entire process with me." The words suddenly got caught in my throat. "We both know I completely fucked up my chances with the one person who liked me and could've helped me."

"You did not," she lied. "The timing wasn't right."

I raised an eyebrow at her. "Ya' think?"

"Also, there's a huge leap between dating someone for a few weeks and getting that person to propose—arrangement or not, so stop giving yourself crap for it."

Ugh, Esteban proposing. Esteban helping me. Esteban anything. How did I go from spending a storm with him to storming him out of my life like that?

Nina shot me a knowing look. "Alright, girlie, let it out." She sighed. "I know you're worried about the visa and all, but I can tell when there's something else going on."

I nodded, wishing my feelings weren't so visible, hoping I didn't care so much about Esteban. But the more I replayed our restaurant argument, the more I realized how my reaction had driven him out of my life for good.

"Has he called?"

He had called, once per day, like he was meeting a quota, like he was trying to show me he cared, but not in an overbearing or obsessive way. I couldn't pick up.

I pulled my cellphone from under the pillow and read the one-sided conversation for the twentieth time that day.

Esteban: Hey.

Esteban: Are you ok?

Esteban: I don't know what to say. I feel terrible. I wish you had said something sooner.

Esteban: Is there anything I can do to help?

Then a pause that lasted all afternoon before his last message.

Esteban: Let me know when you're ready to talk.

Nina made a grabby movement with her hands, and I handed over my cell phone. She read all the messages I hadn't replied to, the glow from the screen illuminating her face, her expressions ranging from fake indifference to inevitable swoon.

"Well." She cleared her throat. "I hate to tell you this now, but you could've done something differently."

I dug my face into the pillow. "I know."

"He really likes you."

"You think he still does?"

"I do, Sofi. Though I'm not sure what you're planning to do about it."

"There's nothing to do. I'm going back. We never talked about being in a relationship, let alone a long-distance one." Was I the most stubborn woman on the planet because I refused to call him? Possibly. But I needed an edge, a plan, something a step above the desperate person he had seen at the restaurant. And the answer wasn't coming to me easily.

Nina's thick eyebrows inched closer. "Aren't you gonna reply?"

"I wouldn't know what to say now that I spilled *everything*." I looked at the single piece of luggage by the wall, my entire legacy packed into an ugly suitcase with a broken zipper, and sighed. "He had this concept of me. He thought I had my life figured out, but my life sucks. And I wish I had a way to fix it so things could return to what they were with him."

She bit her lip, then said in her most apologetic tone. "Your life doesn't suck, and if he's called you, it means he wants to talk to you."

Down to the pillow I went. "I want to talk to him more than anything, but I can't think about talking to him now. What I need is to find another job."

"Yeah, about that," Nina said. "I went to HR today and asked about job openings. We don't have anything, but I presented a formal request for a paid internship in Marketing. I'll let you know if anything comes out of it."

"You did that for me?" A twinkle of hope lit up. "Thank you, Nina. Thank you for putting up with me."

"I'm not putting up with anything. If you were some lazy ass, I swear you wouldn't even be my friend. But you are among the hardest-working, most brilliant people I know."

"If I'm so brilliant," I finally peeled my back away from the bed, "then how did I end up unemployed?"

I looked at her with pleading eyes, hugging the pillow against my chest, asking her to make sense of something that had become senseless to me.

"That's life, Sofi. Shit happens. But we don't let it define who we are. How we respond to life's mess is what defines us."

I pressed the heels of my hands against my eyes. She was right, of course. But another day of failed job searching had gone by, and I no longer had a lead.

"I'm exhausted, amiga. I'm tired of trying and not getting anywhere."

"I hate to hear you talk like that. You sound like an old lady, but you are only twenty-five, Sofi."

"So are you! And look at everything you've built!" I stretched my arms to the sides, my fingers pointing at all the beautiful things in Nina's crisp apartment.

"It's different. My family supported me until two years ago. They paid for my undergrad, my car, the deposit on this apartment." Her hand on my shoulder was warm and comforting. "Everything you have accomplished, you've done on your own. Leaving your family, coming to Miami, and helping them out for so long. You did something I could never do. You decided to take on the world by yourself. And I admire you so much for it." Her smile emerged, one of those expressions uniquely hers—beautiful but distinguished by the unmistakable touch of authenticity at its corners.

"Thank you, amiga," I said.

"It's the truth." She sighed. "Have you talked to your mom?"

"Not a word." I raised my eyebrows. Mom had been silent since I had yelled and hung up on her the previous day. "I've been sending them money every month for almost three years. If I had saved it instead, I would've had enough to pay an immigration attorney, find someone to marry, or at least go back to Colombia with some cash."

Nina nodded through all this. Of course, she knew. She had been telling me so the whole time.

"But I thought I'd feel better after cutting her off. It's not like I have any money to send, but now I'm worried they're gonna sink even more without me."

"You can't take care of them if you don't take care of yourself first. I know something good's gonna come out of this." The bed complained as she stood up and walked towards the door. "I'm going to fix us dinner, okay?" Then she stopped as if she had just remembered something and flipped around. "Now pull yourself together and come help me. You are a much better cook than I am."

We stared at each other briefly, then I shimmied out of the comfy duvet and followed her to the kitchen.

It wasn't easy to hit send on a text I had drafted and deleted at least twenty times, but I figured that if the moments I had shared with Esteban were worth something, then he deserved at least a reply. How the text string had evolved to a meetup at Café del Mar was beyond me. Maybe he needed some closure, or maybe he was curious about my circumstances. My favorite reason was that he was as eager to see me as I was to see him.

I didn't bother layering any foundation on my skin or curling my eyelashes to the sky. I chose to wear the same pair of faded jeans and T-shirt I had worn all morning while selling items at my old apartment. And I didn't touch my hair, so it looked like the morning we woke up together after the storm—frizzy waves held together by a ponytail. If I didn't have to overthink my answers, then it only made sense that I didn't have to overthink my appearance. That afternoon, I showed up as my most authentic self.

I hadn't seen Esteban since that night at the restaurant. Some unrealistic corner of my mind hoped he would brush off the entire scene, but I recognized it wouldn't be so simple. Because with someone like Esteban, everything is easy until the other person messes up, and then things are never the same. Esteban arrived minutes after me. If it hadn't been for the iron frame of the chair holding me together, I would've melted into a puddle right there. I couldn't deny the joy I felt when I saw him, like I was finally quenching my thirst after too many days without water. When he reached the table, his eyes didn't meet mine.

"Hey."

"Hi."

There was a long, uncomfortable silence. He didn't reply, of course. Like every good negotiator, he was willing to wait as long as necessary for me to go first.

"Thank you for coming." I managed to fill the silence with a prescription sentence. It was difficult to find the right words, even after the endless hours we had shared. "I know you are busy, with work and all ..."

He nodded, but his eyebrows remained low, not quite satisfied with how the conversation started.

"I want to congratulate you," I said. "On the manager position. The job is perfect for you, and it was selfish of me to react how I did."

He leaned in, and for the first time, he looked into my eyes, a sharp look, like he'd had it with my crap. I cowered further into the chair. But I also saw that there wasn't contempt, but empathy, and the vague expectation that he wasn't there to hear a girl who wanted to apologize, but a woman who had a plan.

"¿Qué pasó, Sofia?" *What happened, Sofia?* He was tired of beating around the bush. "Everything was fine and then you blurted out all these things, stormed out, stopped answering your phone ..."

My stomach plummeted when he called me by my name instead of corazón, but I figured it was the least I deserved.

"I know. I also asked you here to apologize. What I did the other night was rude, and not how I wanted to tell you."

A server appeared to take our coffee order and then scurried away. I took advantage of the momentary distraction to kick off the speech I had prepared for the night at the restaurant.

"A month ago, my job at Sunset was assigned to someone in Mexico. I was laid off. Sunset sponsored my visa, so the minute I was out of a job, I was in immigration limbo." It was painful to confess all of this in the blind, not knowing how he would take any of it.

"Was this before we met?"

"It was about the same time. I ... I don't remember anymore."

His lips quivered. It was the truth, but he wasn't buying it so easily. I figured I couldn't blame him after I had fed him a lie for weeks. "Why didn't you say something?"

"I didn't want to drag you into it. I mean, we met such a short time ago. At first, I wasn't sure things would work out between us. And when they started working out, it was too late to back up and fill in all the holes I'd left along the way. I thought I could fix the situation before I even had to tell you. WorldMedia was the closest I got." I swallowed hard before I said the following words. "I was so sure I'd get it."

"I get why you didn't tell me when we first met. But afterwards? We talked all the time while this was happening. You'd tell me about your day at work and everything. I feel like your mind was somewhere else every time we were together."

"I'm sorry I kept all of it from you."

"No. I get it. More than you think. I just wish you'd told me earlier."

And since the truth was out, I followed up with the rest of the story. "You probably guessed by now, but I'm broke. I'm supposed to help my family every month, but I'm out of money. Even if I get some more houses to clean on the weekends, it wouldn't make much of a difference in the long run. Also, I moved in with Nina."

He brought a hand up to his hair. It was likely too much information, too fast. I swirled the coffee around in the small cup, giving him a moment to process it all.

"Mira, todos tenemos problemas." *Everyone has their problems*. "Y creo que entiendo porque no me contaste lo que te estaba pasando." He understood why I didn't tell him.

The thing is that people don't just go around asking about their circumstances. The questions are vague, sneaky. *How long have you lived here?* Or occasionally *Where does your family live?* But never *What is your immigration status?* In casual conversation, people just assume everything is in order. The general sentiment is *If we are both here, the circumstances that brought us don't matter anymore*. We both belong, we both have a place. We move on and we don't ask questions.

"The things I said that I really like about you are still there." He made the briefest movement with his hand, barely a tap of his fingers, and I was tempted to reach out and grab it, but it was as if an invisible barrier had formed between us. "So, what's the plan now?"

"I don't know. I kinda reached a dead end. I looked at return flights this morning, but it's complicated back home. Other than my mom, there's not much waiting for me regarding a job or anything else."

"Have you looked into other options to stay?"

"I have." My voice dropped. "I'm exploring every possibility to stay."

He shifted in his seat. Part of me was embarrassed I had cornered him into an uncomfortable position, but I wasn't asking anything of him. He could interpret my words any way he wanted to.

"If you think there's anything I can do to help, will you let me know?" And there it was, another helping hand stretched my way. I nodded. He gave me a small smile—the first one that day—and I caught the flash of longing in his eyes, the adoration he had developed for me that I could've maintained if I had been honest from the first day.

We parted ways after a few short minutes. He had given his two-week notice and was busy wrapping up many projects at Altamira. I needed to return to my apartment to meet with more OfferUp buyers. As the space between us increased, Esteban became a little dot in the noon crowd, just like my Miami life that was slipping away. I had an urge to run after him, but I contained myself. I decided right there that if I found a way to stay, to have the stability I desperately wished for, I would reach out to him.

Life granted me another day in Miami, and with it, I had gathered a tiny bit of hope. I sat down in front of my laptop and scrolled through lists—lists of companies, attorneys, immigration programs, and contacts. I tried to keep my spirits up, to not let the weight of my problems crush me. That is, until my eyes came across a job posting that shattered me to pieces once again.

Nina entered the room—all curves squeezed into a pencil skirt—and found me frozen on the bed, my eyes drifting from her back to the screen.

"Are you okay?"

"Morning ..." I mumbled.

"What happened?"

"I found a job opening," I said.

"Oh! That's good, right?" I almost felt sorry about the relief in her voice. "Are you going to apply?"

"I don't know."

"Why not?"

I was still staring at the screen when I replied, "It's a position at Altamira."

"You mean Esteban's company?"

The sound of his name pierced through me and found its way into the open wound in my heart.

"Uh huh ... and they have subsidiaries in Latin America, so they probably sponsor visas." I didn't even know what to make of it. Should I be relieved there was another chance to apply? Or annoyed that I'd be tracing his steps like a stray dog?

"Do you think it's the position he had?" Nina asked.

"I'm not sure it's his position." I was sure it was his position. "And I don't want to talk to him again." *I was dying to talk to him again.*

"Sofia." She was trying extra hard to control her excitement. "I know you love to pour your heart into everything you do, but just this once, you are gonna have to butt kick your heart out of the room, apply for that position, and give him a call."

"I don't know if I should get him involved." I let my body fall back. "And what if I don't get it? I'd be mortified."

Nina opened her eyes wide. "Of course you'll get it! Both of you were *final candidates* for the same job ... and there was the salary increase." She crossed her arms in front of her. "If anything, I think you'd be overqualified and underpaid. But it'll do for now." She tossed my cellphone on the bed. It landed right in front of my fingertips.

"Call him," she commanded, pointing at the device. "You lost your job, and Esteban, and it's making you miserable. You might be able to salvage one or both. But you *have* to call."

She walked out, closing the door behind her. I remained still for a long time, staring at my phone like Esteban would jump out of it. The sound of utensils clanking and water from the kitchen sink filled the room. Then the tap of a knife against the cutting board, and fruit going into the juicer.

Nina was willing to open her home to me for an undefined amount of time, and I couldn't pick up my phone and make a call that could change everything. I turned to my laptop, uploaded my resume, and clicked on the SUBMIT button before I could double-think it. Then I got out of bed and stood by the window, clutching the phone in my hand. Way down, I could see people commuting to work, walking their dogs, and living their lives.

I searched for Esteban's phone number, and the picture from the night on the rooftop showed up. Our two flushed faces—mine with makeup smudges in all the wrong places, and my curls having a blast with the humidity; his sweaty and sweet, with a mischievous smile like he was thinking of all the things he wanted to do with me later—glowed on the screen. Memories of that deliciously careless night filled my mind. How I had gotten drunk off who knows how many lychee martinis, and how Esteban had succeeded at making me forget all my problems and convinced me I belonged on that rooftop more than anyone else.

God, I missed him. I missed everything about him.

I missed that time we walked down the supermarket aisles together, as if it was the most normal thing to do. I missed how he colored my otherwise drab apartment, filling it with more laughter and energy than I had ever thought possible. I missed the weight of his body on mine, the pull of his arm around my waist, how he buried his face in my neck, and the excitement from feeling that I was ready to jump into a relationship, and he was prepared to leap with me.

My finger hovered over the call button, and my entire arm shook. I was about to hear his voice again, and I had no idea what to expect. He had offered to help. Would he be relieved? Annoyed? Was he over me already?

My heart was beating out of control when another idea popped up. I let it simmer, then decided it was time to make the moves I had been avoiding. After all, I had nothing else to lose.

I searched for WorldMedia's phone number and hit dial.

Chapter Nineteen

Breathe.

Don't forget to breathe.

I heard the bustling noise from the WorldMedia reception, the heels, the voices, the sounds of badges beeping. I wondered if Esteban had already started working there, and secretly hoped to hear his voice in the background.

"I'll transfer you now," the receptionist said.

The pause that followed stretched into a never-ending loop of elevator music. Twice I thought about hanging up, but I had already given the receptionist my name.

"Hello?"

"Hi, Dianelys. This is Sofia Rodriguez. We met when I was interviewing—"

"Sofia! Yes, I remember you. How are you?" Her tone was friendly, and still I feared that I wouldn't be able to pull this through.

I looked at the time. It was 9:13 a.m. I'd give myself two minutes.

"I want to thank you again for your time and the whole interview process."

"Yes. I'm sorry it didn't work out. We had a few team members chiming in on the decision. The client spoke very highly of you."

"I appreciate you saying that." I took another deep breath to calm my nerves. "Um, Dianelys, the other reason I'm calling is quite personal, but I'm hoping you might be able to give me a minute of your time?"

It took her a second before she spoke again. "Go on."

"You probably saw in my application that I'm on a temporary work visa. Last week, there was a downsizing at Sunset Cosmetics." The words spilled out as if they belonged to someone else. I had been running from the truth for so long that it was hard to believe I was finally turning around to face it.

"I see."

"Since WorldMedia usually brings talent from Latin America, I wanted to reach out and tell you it would mean the world to me if I were considered for another position."

"I understand, Sofia, and I'm so sorry you are going through this." She sighed, and there was genuine empathy in her voice. "Right now, we don't have any openings at this office, but I will certainly keep an eye out."

"Thank you so much, Dianelys."

"Um, Sofia? Hang in there. I'm sure things will work out for you."

That's what everyone keeps saying.

We said our goodbyes, and then I held my phone against my chest, hoping with all my might she was right.

By 9:16 a.m. I was calling another immigration attorney.

Hola, Mami,

It feels weird writing to you, and especially writing to you in English. Chances are you will never get to read this, but if I can just get my thoughts in order, I might be able to say something coherent the next time I'm on the phone with you.

I wish I could tell you everything that's gone wrong, but every time I try to talk to you, you don't listen. The biggest problem I have is that the piece of paper that allows me to legally work and live here has an expiration date, and the date is coming up much too soon. I don't want to overextend my stay or choose any of the other options that are available to me. I can't. I love it here way too much to risk deportation and never be able to return.

I know what you think of this. Yo soy Colombiana. *I am not American. So why all this worry over a country that isn't mine? It's hard to explain, even for me. I have worked harder here than I ever thought I would. I have devoted two years of my life to a job that kicked me out without notice.*

I know it's ironic, but I still feel this is where I belong.

Living far from home gave me a new perspective on the way things are in Bogotá. There's something twisted about the system back home, something that makes me feel like I don't quite fit. I know people who have worked every day of their lives to survive and bring food to the table, but they're destined to die in the same house they were born in. How demotivating is it to know that if you are born poor, you will live in poverty the rest of your life? Then there are those who were born rich, so they will live a good life, marry rich, have rich children who will never be hungry. Most haven't worked a day, and the few who do have it so much easier than the first group. They stroll through life with access to capital, a top-notch education, and a successful family business they'll inherit someday. And then there's another group. The group that gave up. Deje así *as you say. This group lives one day at a time, making a minimum effort to survive while enjoying the little things in life. They are the men drinking their life away in cheap bars, the beautiful school dropouts waiting their turn to catch* un novio con plata, *or the families living off what they receive from relatives abroad. They know they're stuck in the life they were born in, and why kill yourself working if things are never going to change?*

I never belonged to any of these groups. Neither did Papi. He was determined for Santiago and me to live a better life than the one he was born into. But when he left us, I felt we lost our compass, our drive. We became part of that last group, overcome by shame and laziness, quick to spend what little we had on useless things, ignoring any desire to move ahead.

And then I had the brilliant idea of moving to Miami. Remember all those months I spent researching the student programs? All those weeks studying English and trying to get rid of my accent? All the things I sold so I could bring as much money as possible? It was a miracle when it happened. When I got my student visa, I remember thinking Papi had interceded from heaven on my behalf. I knew he approved how I was spending the small inheritance he had worked so hard to leave for us.

And now to have all of it taken away from me. To go back to a system that offers rewards based on status, and not because of work. How could I ever go back to that with a smile on my face?

Maybe that's what the so-called American dream is about. It's not so much about the picket fence and the second fridge, but believing that hard work will lead to a better life. At least that's what it is to me, and I'm not ready to give up on it.

Regarding the monthly allowance, I know you have come to depend on it. Perhaps that's my fault. It's not that I don't want to help anymore. You are my mom, and it would kill me to know you are struggling. But I need you to understand that to take care of you, I must take care of myself first.

And that's what I need to do now. I only have a few weeks left here, and I want to devote my little energy to giving it my last shot. And if I fail, then I need a plan for my return to Bogotá. Because heaven knows that I cannot spend my days waiting for un novio con plata *to show up. So, please don't expect to receive anything else from me. At least until I figure out what I will do with my life.*

I'm sorry I yelled at you, and I hope everything goes well with Santiago, Lorena, and the baby.

Tu hija que te ama,

Sofia

The clock marked seven p.m. and another business day came to a close. Even with Nina cheering for me and a long list of ideas and people to call, the last shreds of hope I had been holding on to were slipping away. I needed to keep my mind busy on that list, not only because my future depended on whatever desperate measure I could conceive in a month, but because any minute I didn't think of a plan was spent on Esteban.

I walked out to the balcony. I left my phone inside—there was no point in carrying a reminder that I haven't found an employer to sponsor me. I stared out into the buildings, my fists tight on the thin white railing, my belly and legs pressed against the thick blueish glass, and felt the pressure of the past few days bubbling up in my throat.

The scream building inside me had nowhere to go. I wanted to go back in time and slap the shame out of myself. I wanted to call Esteban to tell him I couldn't stop thinking about him. I wanted to feel the safety of his arms around me. I wanted to scream because if it hadn't been for my circumstances, I would be with Esteban at that very moment. I couldn't believe I'd been cornered into two choices: a legal return to a life in Colombia I had deliberately left, or an illegal stay in the life I had fought to build in the U.S.

A ringtone coming from inside the apartment sliced through my thoughts. When I turned around, Nina was already reaching my phone out to me. I stared at the unknown number flashing on the screen. It was way past the usual office hours that most HR reps and attorney receptionists observed.

But I was on the hunt for hope, and every single call counted.

"Hello?"

"Sofia?" A female voice—sweet, delicate, vaguely familiar—chimed on the other side.

"Yes. Who's this?"

"Sorry to call you out of the blue. This is Linda. Linda Prentice. We met at WorldMedia, a few weeks ago."

It took me a second to regroup my thoughts. Nina was standing outside on the balcony, making a thousand different signs with her hands—none I could decipher. I opened my eyes very wide and walked past her and straight to the bedroom. Both Togo and Dante propped their heads up in attention, as if they knew this was an important call.

"Hi, Linda. What a surprise! How are you?" I had to bring my free hand up to my chest to keep my heart from jumping out.

"I'm so glad you remember me. Is this a good time?"

I wanted to laugh at the idea that I could forget who she was, at the unlikelihood that a bad time for her to call could exist, but I remained poised.

"Yes, of course."

She spoke casually. I could tell she was moving, perhaps driving. I imagined her in a fancy car cruising Brickell Avenue, possibly passing in front of Nina's building that very moment.

"Dianelys called me this morning. I've been wanting to call you all day! I'm sorry things didn't work out with WorldMedia. Between you and me, you were my top choice. But it was the agency's call at the end."

I didn't know how to feel about this. Relieved that I had somehow beaten Esteban, even though he was the one now sitting at WorldMedia? Angry at the person who had marked the ultimate rejection next to my name?

"One of our brand managers is moving to Brazil. Her husband was relocated, and we don't have an office there. So, she's leaving the head-count open. She's not leaving Miami until the end of the month, but she wants to focus on the move. You know how these things are."

"Uh ... yes. Definitely." My heartbeat quickened under my palm.

"I need to move fast if I don't want HR to snatch the headcount away and give it to another department, and our recruitment process is so slow. I know you had your eyes set on the agency, but how would you feel about staying on the client side of the business?"

A burning flame of hope shone through the cold ashes.

"You mean with Lamballe?"

"Yes. I think you'd be great for the position. You have a background in beauty and supply chain; you have experience in media. Not to mention you worked for the competition." She chuckled. It was a nice, hearty laugh. "I think you are a better fit as a brand manager than as an account manager at an agency."

I had to repeat what I heard to ensure I wasn't imagining it. "So, you are saying you have a position available, and you think I'm a good fit?"

"That's right."

I took a deep breath to spit out the next words. I needed to be sure what she was suggesting was real, and not a product of my own twisted imagination.

"I'm unsure if Dianelys told you, but I need visa sponsorship to stay."

"Yes, about that. I called so late because I had to get on the phone with HR first, and it turns out they have *one* spot available, and they have agreed to go through the process with you."

My eyes were already pooling with tears when she said, "Dianelys also mentioned that you might be immediately available? If you could stop by tomorrow, we can chat in person, and I can introduce you to the rest of the team. I don't need to interview you because I already did." She giggled some more. "The position will be posted for legal reasons, but we can start your process this week, so we don't lose time. What do you think?"

After we hung up, I sat on the edge of the bed for a long time, staring at the Post-It scribbled with an address and a *10 a.m.* under it. The corner of my eye caught one of the last few rays of sun breaking in through the bedroom window. Swirls of yellow and orange were starting to paint the Miami sky, and I felt the colors slowly tinting my face.

When I walked out of the room, Nina leaped from the couch. I was half-crying, half-laughing. I was checking my phone to make sure the call had been real. Nina seemed on the verge of a breakdown if I didn't tell her whatever news I was holding.

"So?!" she squealed. "Tell me!"

I looked up at her and could barely form the words.

"Lamballe Cosmetics wants to hire me." Shrieks of joy threatened to burst through. "I'm staying in Miami."

Saying it out loud made it feel real. So, I repeated it.

"I'm staying in Miami!" I screamed at the top of my lungs—as loud as I could—so that even the pedestrians thirty floors below could probably hear me. There was no doubt that Miami was giving me another chance.

Nina screamed. So I did again.

For the next few minutes of absolute bliss, we were both hugging and jumping in that fancy apartment in my favorite city, overlooking the glorious pink sunset behind the rows of glimmering buildings and suburbs in the distance. Two friends were celebrating that all it took was one good YES in a sea of NOs to change my future forever.

Chapter Twenty

Recalling the week after *the call*—Nina's eventual nickname for Linda's unexpected after-hours appearance—creates a dip in my abdomen to this day. Dad didn't warn me about the amount of bureaucratic paperwork that this level of adulting required. Yet following those weeks staring at the entrance of immigration limbo, I was relieved every time I filled my name at the top of a form. I was gathering the fragments of my collapsed life. It was the liberation I had wished for, though I never knew how that would look.

On Sunday morning, in between sips of coffee and bites of avocado toast, Nina stared longingly out the window and mentioned what a beautiful day it was to take the dogs to the beach, and I swear Togo and Dante's little ears perked up. I was standing next to them less than two minutes later. After a week of filling out new hire forms, running visa errands, meeting team members, and going through new employee onboarding, going to the beach was the perfect reward.

Togo stuck his head out the car window when we left the parking lot. And Dante—who wasn't yet convinced about sharing his life with another dog three times his size—pushed his head through Togo's front legs, his small body tucked under his large friend. At a red light, we found ourselves stopped next to an SUV. There were three kids in the back seat, their smiling faces competing to get a better look at the two "puppies" poking their heads out.

Seven minutes later, we crossed the bridge connecting the mainland with Key Biscayne, a long and narrow road elevated above the turquoise sea. It was a beautiful, balmy morning. The sun was shielded by a thin veil of clouds, painting the blue sky with streaks of bright yellow. The sea was already dotted with the white sheets of sailboats and the colorful sails of windsurfers slicing through the water. We chose to park at one of the first beaches, just a few yards from the narrow strip of pale sand and the sea washing the shore, and set ourselves between two families. One of them seemed to be a father-son pair, sitting on folding chairs, leisurely staring at the horizon, their lips barely moving.

"Do we let them go in the water?" I asked. Togo's tail was close to falling off from the wagging, expectation building up since he heard the mellow sound of the small waves.

She nodded and gave Dante—who had found a shady spot under a palm tree and was contemplating the sea from a distance—an encouraging push. He trotted shyly but stopped just as his little paws touched the first ripples of water. I was about to persuade Togo to do the same when his dark shadow rushed right past us, all sixty pounds of muscle and stamina leaping on the beach sand and straight into the water. He came out to bounce on the shallow waves, effectively drenching Dante—who was a little spooked at first, but then perked up and started wagging his tail. A couple of barks and a whole lot of splashing later, he joined Togo in the water. And then it was playtime, with both dogs bouncing happily on the waves, running back to us as if thanking us, then going right back in.

"He never goes in the water!" Nina exclaimed. I could tell she was enjoying our little outing. She'd had a tough week, too. More than once, I'd caught the light from her laptop seeping in through the slit under my bedroom door, hours after we had said our good nights. That morning, with nothing but our dogs and the ocean and each other as company, we let our shoulders soak in the sun rays and dipped our feet in the fresh seawater. We filled the space between us with more silence than words, because there was already enough transparency between us to know what the other was thinking. And that morning, we had secretly agreed to seize a moment of hard-earned bliss.

When Togo leaped out of the water and rolled on the sandy beach, covering his entire body with a thick paste of sand, Nina turned to face me, one finger pointing at my chest. "You are helping me clean the car." She chuckled.

I had given up my car the previous week, when the quote to fix everything wrong with it was more expensive than buying another second-hand vehicle. I sold it to the same mechanic who told me it was already en las últimas, *on its last breath*, which was his way of saying it was a matter of days until it dumped me in the middle of the expressway.

It was a twenty-minute walk from Nina's apartment to the Lamballe office, and Linda had made clear that I could work from home on days with no meetings, so letting my transportation go seemed the logical thing to do. What little money I received for the junked car went to my savings account, together with the rent deposit that I fought long and hard to get back from the landlord. Not wanting to burden Nina, I had looked for a new place to live, but she wouldn't hear of it. She insisted I put it off, at least for a few months. She had—she pointed out—*an apartment large enough to accommodate us and our two dogs*, and *haven't you learned anything?*, and *focus on saving enough money to keep your ass in Miami if you lose your job at Lamballe.*

The last warning made me cringe with worry, but deep inside, I knew she was right. The only concession I won was that I would pay her a small rent—less than a third of what I was paying at the previous apartment—to cover my room and utilities. She initially rejected the idea, but when my first Lamballe paycheck came in, I proudly Zelle'd the money over with the note "October Rent" and—other than a scowl and a *you didn't have to do that*—she accepted it. She knew it was my way of saying thank you for being the first one to give me a chance to live my dream.

Far away—past Togo and Dante's splash zone, past the orange kayaks floating on the water—the silhouette of speedboats and small yachts sliced through the surface of the ocean. Some of them were close enough to make out the forms of people dancing away, others were fleeting silver bullets on a race to the open sea. My heart—fickle as it was, and no doubt jealous that lately all my attention had gone to work and getting my life back together—decided to flash me with images of that summer morning months earlier, vivid thoughts of Esteban crowding out all the events that came before and after him. I closed my eyes and let those memories fill me in; I felt the intensity of his gaze, the way that morning the waves gently pushed my body against his, that burning desire I felt to learn everything about him and to reveal everything about me. I relived all the sensations until I was left wondering whether our story was really over, and I felt the irresistible urge to pull out my cell phone and text him.

My eyes followed the vessels until they became smudges in the distance, and I understood my time with Esteban had been as fleeting as those speeding boats.

Maybe in another time, under other circumstances, that thought alone would've been enough to sink me. But not that day. Not after feeling the relief that comes with the first gasp of air after staying underwater for too long.

After I signed with Lamballe, I realized I didn't know when I would be going back to Bogotá. I felt like I had won some immigration lottery and had been given a second chance. Despite the relief, I was consumed by a sudden, bitter nostalgia about my country. Quite similar to the emotions I felt when I first decided to move to Miami. Had I given up on my country for good? Would I ever return? Would I still be considered Colombian, even if, years from now, I become a U.S. citizen and pledge my allegiance to a different flag?

I thought the answer was evading me, but eventually I realized it had been with me the entire time. I could respect and love and be grateful to live in this new country, and I could still be loyal to the culture that raised me, to the blood in my veins.

I didn't have to be *in* Colombia to *be* Colombian. Because Colombia would always be a part of me. And if my face giving it away isn't enough, then it's the itch in my feet every time I hear salsa music, the spark of joy when I recognize my accent on someone new, or the way my mind unconsciously searches for the voices, the screech of bus brakes, and the *vallenato* coming from the neighbor's kitchen when I wake up.

That morning at the beach, I felt Dad was close, nodding with approval somewhere. I felt that by fulfilling his dream, I was carrying on with his legacy.

"Are you thinking about him?" Nina asked. She had been staring at me for a few minutes, had noticed how my gaze was lost somewhere in the sea.

I nodded because somehow, in our silent conversation, she knew I was thinking about Dad.

The man sitting with his son rose from his folding chair and made his way over to us. He was holding a small Styrofoam cup with tiny plastic cups on top. We accepted his invitation to try his coffee, thanked him, and then watched him move to the next family.

I gingerly took a sip of the black liquid. It was strong, sweet, Cuban coffee. It was amazing. After I drank the rest, I was keenly aware of its effect on every nerve on my body, the heightened sharpness of my senses. I took a deep breath. The air was filled with the scent of sea salt and coffee beans, my two halves that had finally met right in the center.

I looked up to the sky, to the cloudless spot where I was sure Dad was looking back at me, smiling proudly. I stayed in that position until I felt his presence enveloping me, certain as the sea breeze brushing my skin. Then I closed my eyes and sent him a message only he could hear.

Remember our dream? We finally made it.

One Month Later

I like to be the first to arrive at the office every morning, walking in to activate the automatic blinds and let the sunlight in. It gives me a head start before the meetings take over the day, and I can drink my coffee in absolute silence. As a new employee, I'd been afraid I'd be relegated to a gray cubicle with high walls, far from any window. But Lamballe doesn't believe in cubicles. An open floor plan with pink and gold everything sprawls before me. The twentieth floor is framed by floor-to-ceiling windows overlooking the water. There is a seating area with an oil diffuser that fills the area with orange blossom notes. When they gave me a tour of the office, they showed me how to use the fancy coffee machine in the break room. Now it is my daily ritual to beat everyone to it.

When Linda arrives, my coffee mug is already empty, and I have cleared my inbox. It might sound dorky, but I'm relieved to see her. I never thought I could get along with a manager, yet here we are. Wearing relaxed jeans and an oversized white shirt, she sits at the desk next to mine, and we go over the due dates and the meetings we have for the day. There's a one-hour meeting scheduled with the commercial team in the afternoon, and I'm not dreading it. Right after it, I'll work on the job description for our new intern. Linda wants me to craft it because the intern will report to me. She says I'm ready, and she wants our team to grow. I'm still trying to come to terms with all her faith in me, but I know I'll get there.

The only meeting I haven't prepared for is the ten a.m. meeting in a few minutes. Linda sent the invite late last night, and the subject line reads "Review Marketing Plans." I'm about to ask her what the meeting is about when she gets on a call. So, other than the meeting being held at the large conference room, I'm in the dark.

I run to the bathroom before the meeting starts and bump into Linda there.

"This one should be pretty straightforward," she says when I ask what the meeting is about. "The agency was briefed weeks ago, and today they'll be presenting their media proposal. Just stay sharp and ask all the questions you have. Piece of cake for us. I'll see you in a few minutes."

I retouch my lip color using a new shade of bronze Laura from the education team got me yesterday. She said it complemented my skin tone. I apply two coats, then stare at my reflection in the mirror. She was right. The color pops against my skin—trigueña con pecas. I walk out of the restroom and find Linda in the hallway waiting for me, laptop in hand.

"Ready?" she asks.

"Let's do this." I smile.

She takes a few quick steps and suddenly stops, turning briskly towards me. "You know, I just realized that if you had gone to work at WorldMedia, you'd be presenting these media plans to me. Isn't that funny?"

"Oh," I reply.

Oh.

My gut twists into a tight knot. My feet decide to quit taking orders and anchor firmly to the floor. I haven't talked to Esteban since that day at Café del Mar. Haven't had the courage to reach out to him again—even though I see his face every night when I close my eyes. I was aware of his new position and knew that someday our paths might cross, but how could I know? He could've switched companies in the past month—which I know well enough is not an issue for him. Or he could've been reassigned to another account. Or perhaps our relationship would be limited to two-hour Zoom meetings once a month, his face trapped in a digital rectangle on my computer screen.

Unable to move, I watch Linda reach the glass double doors and stop when she notices I'm not trailing behind her.

"What's wrong?" she mouths when she sees I'm petrified in the middle of the hallway.

But I'm out of time to double-think anything. WorldMedia is already here, and it's a minute past the hour. My pulse quickens as I mouth a halfhearted *nothing* to Linda and force my feet to move forward.

I pause before walking in. Linda's voice—the same kind voice that gave me a chance to stay and live my dream—greets the WorldMedia team and introduces me as their new Category brand manager.

When Linda says Sofia Rodriguez, I have no other option but to join them.

I try to make eye contact with everyone, but who am I kidding? The second my eyes lock with his, I can't look away. He's here in my office. And we're about to have a *work meeting*.

For the first time, his face isn't a mirage that pops up at random moments of the day. After so many weeks wondering what bumping into him would feel like, I can't take my eyes off him—the lips I kissed for hours, the eyebrows I traced with my fingers so many times, the muscles I once held on to while I straddled him against the bed. He's also staring back at me, his expression unreadable.

"Hi, Sofia," he says.

I should've known he wasn't the type to pretend we were not acquainted.

"Hi, Esteban."

Linda is also not the type to wait to ask questions later. "You guys know each other?" She asks in her peppy voice.

I don't know what to say.

"We met a few months ago," Esteban fills the silence.

We met a few months ago? Is that how he summarizes what happened between us? I force a polite smile as every pair of eyes in the room lands on us, then find the chair farthest from him and take a seat, determined not to let him, Linda, or my colleagues know how mortified I am. He introduces himself as our new senior account manager, followed by the team that'll manage our account—three WorldMedia employees reporting to him.

After all those weeks of competing against him for the same job, silently admiring his career, and wishing I had his luck, I can't believe we're working together. We are finally on the same playfield.

For the duration of the meeting, I try to prioritize the media plans over the images of him that are popping into my head.

Not just images. *Memories. Sensations.*

My fingers tingle when I remember how I used them to hold on to him, to stroke and pull his body closer. Even my stomach dips a few times. I catch him stealing glances when he thinks I'm looking at my laptop.

Halfway through the presentation, a chat message from Laura pops up in the lower corner of my laptop. *Omg, the new media manager is hot.*

I close the chat before anyone sees it.

For the past month, I've been focused on me, convinced that I need to get my act together before replying to his texts. Waiting for the right moment to start fresh, not having to conceal anything, or needing to ask any favors. I've been ready for a week now, and still I haven't mustered the courage to reach out to him.

Until this moment.

It's Esteban's turn to talk, and it's the first time I've seen him in work-mode—Relaxed shoulders, sharp sentences, just the right amount of hand gestures, the works. In less than five minutes, he's got the entire table nodding and is pausing to take questions. That's when Linda asks about audience size, given our high-end and very niche target. The blank look on Esteban's face is priceless. He gives two different answers, but there's a piece of information he doesn't have, and he knows it. His gaze turns to me, and he rambles another half-ass explanation.

Is this even possible? Corporate ladder climber extraordinaire Esteban doesn't know the answer and is nervous about it?

"I think we should fine-tune the audience we are working with," I offer. "I can put together some parameters we might've missed on the brief and share them with Esteban's team later today. How does that sound?"

"That'll be excellent, Sofia, thank you," Linda says.

Esteban seems relieved to have been given a way out. "You can send them over to me, Sofia. I'll check they're considered before we share this deck with everyone."

Is it just me, or is his gaze pausing on me longer than on anyone else?

After another grueling hour of marketing and fantasizing, we all stand up and walk the WorldMedia team to the door. Esteban hangs back, as if waiting for his colleagues to jump on the elevator and disappear.

I stay behind, too, until it's just the two of us in the lobby.

"I've wondered what happened to you all this time." I try to read the emotions in his eyes—is it admiration? Nostalgia? Desire? "It's good to see you here, Sofia. Congratulations."

"Thank you," I reply, trying to read him as much as he is trying to read me, "You know, I never thought I'd get to work with you."

"You're my client now." A hint of a smile appears, and I must bite my lip to keep myself from smiling back.

"Wasn't this your plan from the very beginning?" I laugh, and he laughs back. Now that we are alone in the hallway, with all this delicious energy flowing between us, I let my guard down.

"Thanks for saving my ass back there," he says.

"Anytime." I lower my head a little. I still get shy about receiving compliments on my work. "Don't get too used to it, though."

He steps forward, then says in the smooth voice I've craved for nights, "So I take it you are staying in Miami, permanently?"

"I don't know if it's permanent, but I am here now."

My gaze instinctively lowers—it is hard to keep eye contact with someone who can easily make me forget my reasoning and inhibitions. His fingers gently catch my jaw and bring my face level with his, our mouths so close that if anyone sees us, I'd find it impossible to convince the office that we are only friends.

"I've thought about this for a long time. You have stuff going on in your life, like the rest of us. I would love to try this again. No secrets.

Let's just be upfront with one another, see where it takes us." Then his voice turns playful for an instant. "And I don't want to see you running off again."

He moves even closer. And it's as if the wall I built during that tragic date at the restaurant comes crashing down.

"I've missed you," he whispers into my lips.

"I've missed you, too."

"What do you say, corazón? Do you want to have dinner with me tonight?"

Acknowledgments

When I had the idea to write a book back in January 2020, I had no idea what I was getting myself into. To give you a hint of how clueless I was, one of my 2020 resolutions was to *publish a book* which I had not even started writing.

I would like to thank the people who took part in this process, and I would like to do it in the order in which they joined my writing journey.

My friend Anamaria was the first person I told about wanting to write a novel. She didn't think it was a bizarre idea; instead, she encouraged me to follow my dreams. Thank you, Anama, for this and many other reasons, I am immensely lucky to have you in my life.

Christian, my partner in life, who believes in my potential more than I do, thank you for making life so easy that I can take time off to work on projects such as this one.

To my writing coach since 2020, Julie Tyler, and the members of Storybold's Author Exchange, especially Ellen Ellzey and Céline Leboeuf. Your input shaped Sofia's story in so many ways. Thank you for your encouragement, patience, and for being the tribe I needed at just the right moment.

The writing community is truly the best community. I was fortunate to connect with amazing early readers and critique partners Carol Ervin, Lisa Carnochan, Claudia Armann, and Helen Marie Webster. Thank you for your time and for sharing your writing knowledge with me. To Zania Sala for your support and encouragement, and to Najla Mamou for your thoughtful insights, which helped me enhance the tone and voice of this story.

Thank you to the WFWA community that opened a world of opportunities and connections, without whom this publication would not have been possible. And thank you for organizing the 2023 Writers' Conference, where I met my publisher.

Thank you to the Rising Action Publishing team, especially to Alexandria Brown and Tina Beier, for taking a chance on me and this story, and for their relentless effort to support diverse voices. To Nat Mack for capturing the essence of Sofia's dream with the most gorgeous and colorful cover design.

Thank you to Celeste Baker, Madeleine Saade, and Danielle Bombonato who helped fact-check different elements of Sofia's story. If you find any anomalies, they are entirely on me!

I am blessed to have so many strong, independent women in my life who inspire me every day. Anita, Lika, Monique, and Kari, mis besties since high school, alguien debería escribir una novela de cada una de sus vidas. To my Hasbro siblings, Stephanie Prentice and Ursula Fernandez-Davila, how lucky am I to work alongside two of the most talented and professional women I have ever known? A mis Guachafita moms: I have said it time and time again: there is something I admire from each one of you, thank you for walking alongside me in this parenthood adventure.

To Tomi and Salo, for challenging me to be the best version of myself every day. Thank you for filling my life with laughter and stories, and for making my world brighter. You will get to read Sofia's story when you are older.

To Mami and Annie, like Sofia (and like me), you both lived in Colombia and now call Miami home. Although each immigration story is unique, there is usually a shared sense of uprootedness and longing for the life that was left behind. This book is for you.

Thank you to the readers for picking up this book and helping me make my dream of becoming a writer come true. To anyone who sees themselves in all or part of Sofia's story, please know that I have the utmost admiration for your journey. Keep speaking up and chasing your dreams.

About the Author

Grace Santamaria is a Colombian American novelist who writes contemporary and book club fiction about Latinas making bold moves and crushing life's challenges.

She holds a BBA from FIU and a Master of International Business from NOVA Southeastern University. For the past fifteen years, she has worked in different marketing roles in consumer products companies focused on the Latin American market.

Through storytelling, Grace hopes to join the new wave of Latin voices who are passionate about raising awareness regarding the lives of the Latin diaspora and women's empowerment. Grace lives in sunny Miami, Florida, with her husband, children, and overly enthusiastic golden retriever.